THE
FRONT

PART 2: ROGUE CASTES

EPISODE 2

RESCUE

RYK BROWN

The Frontiers Saga Part 2: Rogue Castes
Episode #2: Rescue

First Print Edition

CHAPTER ONE

Captain Tuplo stared at Josh as if he had lost his mind, but the young man looked serious, and in all the years Connor had known Josh, the talkative pilot had never been able to keep a straight face for long. The captain studied the faces of the four visitors in Ghatazhak-style combat armor. All of them looked stoic as well, but from what he had heard about the Ghatazhak, he expected as much.

Finally, he looked at Marcus. "You want to tell me what's going on here, Taggart?"

"You're not Connor Tuplo," Marcus said. "You're Nathan Scott."

"Nathan Scott, *Captain* Nathan Scott, captain of the Aurora. The guy from Earth."

"That's right."

"And you've known this for how long?"

"Well, as long as we've known you, I suppose."

Connor looked at Josh. "By *we*, I assume he means you as well?"

"Yes, sir," Josh replied.

"Are you kidding me?" Neli exclaimed in disbelief.

"Oh, I don't believe this!" Dalen said with excitement. "I'm flyin' with Na-Tan!"

"There's no way that Connor Tuplo is Na-Tan," Neli insisted.

"I agree," Connor added.

"Marcus and Josh were assigned to look after you, Nathan," Jessica explained, taking another step toward him.

"Don't call me that," Connor snapped. "I'm not Nathan Scott. I told you, I'm Connor Tuplo, owner and captain of the Seiiki."

"You see?" Neli said.

"You're Nathan Scott," Jessica said, "and the ship you *think* you own is actually named the *Mirai*, and *technically* it is owned by Deliza Ta'Akar."

"Then how did I end up with it?" Connor wondered.

"It's a long, complicated story, Nathan."

"I told you..."

"I'm sorry," Jessica apologized. "I'll call you Connor for now, if it will make you feel better."

"It will make me feel better if *someone* will tell me the truth," Connor told her impatiently.

"We're tryin' to, Cap'n," Josh insisted. "You *are* Nathan Scott. Well, technically, you're a copy of yourself."

"What?"

"Josh!" Jessica chided. "Maybe you should let me do the talking?"

"Sorry."

"Oh, this is great!" Dalen exclaimed.

"A copy?" Connor said doubtfully. "Of myself? Like a clone, or something?"

"Yes."

Connor didn't know what to think at this point. "Let's just assume for a moment that I believe you... which I don't. How is it that I don't *know* who I really am? Does it have something to do with the crash?"

"The crash is just a story they planted in your head," Jessica replied. "Look, I'll explain everything to you, I promise. But not here. This place is within the Jung's single-jump range. We need to get someplace further away, someplace safe."

"That's what I've been saying," Neli agreed.

"Shut up, Neli," Marcus scolded.

"I'd love to go with you, lady," Connor said, "but I've barely got enough propellant left for one cycle, so, unless you're offering to pay me, or at least fill up my tanks, I'm afraid we're staying put."

"Come with us, and we will give you all the propellant you can carry," General Telles promised.

"What do we have to do for it?" Connor asked suspiciously.

"Just come with us to Burgess and hear us out, that's all we ask," Jessica assured him.

"Burgess?" Connor said in surprise. "In the Sherma system?"

"That's the place."

Connor looked at Jessica and the general for a moment, then at Josh and Marcus.

"It'll get us off this rock, and what, like a hundred light years away from the Jung?" Marcus pointed out.

"One hundred eleven, point eight six, to be exact," General Telles corrected.

"That would take us completely out of the Pentaurus sector," Neli realized. "That would be a damn good start."

"No strings attached?" Connor asked.

"None," Jessica promised him.

"And after I hear you out, if I still don't believe you?"

"You're free to leave."

"To go anywhere we want," Connor added, just to make sure.

"Anywhere you want," Jessica confirmed. "We'll even give you a list of systems where you could pick up some runs to keep you going."

"What makes you think we can't get some here?" Connor wondered.

"The fact that you're almost out of propellant and out here in the middle of nowhere means you probably don't have the funds to pay Haven's meager port fees," General Telles said. He looked at the damaged cargo ramp. "And your ship appears to be in need of repair. Since the Jung have locked down the Pentaurus cluster, and will most likely do the same to the entire sector before long, your options appear somewhat limited."

"Something will turn up," Connor said.

"Something has," Jessica told him. "Us." She stepped even closer to Connor, standing less than a meter away. "Look at me," she said, gazing into his eyes. "Tell me you don't remember me."

Connor stared into her eyes, hoping he'd be able to recognize her. "I'm sorry," he whispered sadly.

Jessica's spirits fell. "That's okay," she said quietly. She looked up at him again. "Because I *do* remember *you.* Come with us, let us tell you what happened to you. What *really* happened to you. What have you got to lose?"

Connor continued looking at her, captivated by the genuine sincerity in her eyes.

"You can always return to this place afterward, if you so choose," General Telles added. "We can even help you repair your ship."

Connor thought for a moment, weighing his options, then quickly realizing that he had very few. "Very well," he sighed. "I'll hear you out. But *after* you fill up our propellant tanks."

"You have my word," General Telles replied. "Shall we depart?"

"Everyone, back inside," Connor ordered as he turned around and started up the ramp. "We're going to Burgess."

"We're *not* coming back here, right?" Neli asked, as she followed Marcus up the ramp.

* * *

The Seiiki's cockpit windows filled with dust as she slowly lifted off the ground, leaving the dusty old molo farm behind.

"Jump us to orbit," Captain Tuplo instructed Josh, in a very matter-of-fact tone. "I don't want to waste the propellant on a standard climb out."

"Even Haven has jump rules..."

"Just do it," the captain stated, cutting him off.

"If you're worried about Jess going back on her word..."

Captain Tuplo gave Josh a disapproving sidelong glance. "Do I have to take the controls, Josh?"

"No, sir," Josh replied as he punched in the jump parameters and started the ship forward. "Jumping to orbit."

The cockpit windows turned opaque. When they cleared two seconds later, they were filled with the blackness and stars of space to their right, and the gas giant that Haven orbited to their left.

"Use just enough propellant to get Tikka's gravity to pull us away from Haven, then jump us to outside the system so we don't have to burn as long to change course for Sherma," the captain ordered.

"I know how to do a minimum-propellant departure, Cap'n," Josh replied defensively. "Besides, they'll give us the propellant, I'm tellin' ya..."

"Forgive me if I don't take your word for it, Josh," the captain snapped.

Josh altered the Seiiki's course just enough to steer it toward the looming gas giant. "Are you mad at me, Cap'n?"

"I'm mad at somebody, that's for sure. I just haven't figured out who yet."

"How do you mean?" Josh wondered.

"*Someone* is lying to me."

"No one is lying to you, Cap'n."

Captain Tuplo looked at Josh. "The way I figure it, either *all* of you are lying, or *they* are telling the truth, and you and Marcus have been lying to me all along. Either way, I figure I have a right to be mad at *somebody*."

Josh was silent. He continued monitoring the ship's movement away from Haven and toward the gas giant, waiting for the right moment to execute the jump that would take them well outside the system, and away from its gravitational influences.

After several minutes, Josh finally spoke. "You know, we were just following orders."

"So, you *didn't* resign from the Alliance," the captain accused.

"No, we resigned, all right. We had to. Rescuing you was going against orders."

"If you resigned, then whose orders were you following?"

"Jessica's," Josh replied flatly. "In case you haven't noticed, she's not exactly someone you wanna piss off." Josh checked the navigation display again. "We'll be at our jump point in two minutes." He looked back at Captain Tuplo. "Look, Cap'n, if you wanna be mad at me, that's fine. But we're telling you the truth. You are Nathan Scott, not Connor Tuplo. And Nathan Scott would understand why we did what we did."

Captain Tuplo sighed. "That's the problem, Josh. I'm *not* Nathan Scott. Even if you're all telling the truth, and I *am* a clone, I *don't* have Nathan Scott's memories. I have mine...*Connor Tuplo's*...or at least those from the last six years. As far as I know, *that's* who I am."

"Just hear them out, Cap'n," Josh begged.

"I intend to. We need the propellant, as well as the list of potential systems to fly, assuming they keep their word."

"You really don't believe them?"

"No, I don't." He looked at Josh. "Would *you*, if *you* were me?"

"I'd at least want to listen," Josh argued, "and not just to fill my tanks, but to try to find out the truth about my past. You're always talking about bits and pieces of memories that you can't string together. Maybe it's finally time to fill in all the blanks."

"That's what worries me," Captain Tuplo admitted.

"Whattaya mean?"

"I mean, why now? Why not six years ago?" He looked at Josh. "There's more to this than all of you are letting on, isn't there?"

Josh sighed, realizing he had said too much already. "Just... Just hear them out. That's all."

* * *

Josh jumped down off the end of the Seiiki's damaged cargo ramp, onto the tarmac at the Lawrence Spaceport on Burgess. "Sorry it took us so long," he said to Jessica and the general as they approached. "Cap'n wanted to fly a low-consumption departure. I hope the controllers here aren't going to be too angry about our jumping in so low."

"I will take care of it," General Telles assured him. He looked at Captain Tuplo as he came down the ramp, also jumping down the last half meter to the surface. "We can begin your refueling immediately, if you'd like, Captain."

"Yes, please," Connor replied. He turned to look at Marcus, who was also coming down the cargo ramp, followed by Dalen and Neli. "Marcus, Dalen; you two see to the refueling."

Deliza and Loki walked up from behind the general, both of them looking as if they weren't sure they would be welcomed.

"Lok!" Josh exclaimed, rushing to give his old friend a hug.

"Josh," Loki replied, embracing him with a smile. "It's good to see you again."

"Damn good to see you. How have you been? How's Lael? She wise up and dump your sorry ass, yet?"

"Not exactly," Loki replied, sighing.

"What is it?" Josh wondered, noticing the concerned look on his old friend's face. "What's wrong?"

"Connor Tuplo, this is Loki Sheehan," General Telles announced.

"A pleasure to meet you, sir," Loki greeted.

"What the hell is going on?" Josh asked Loki again.

"Likewise," Captain Tuplo replied, shaking Loki's hand.

"Do you mind if I borrow your copilot for a few minutes?" Loki asked. "We have some catching up to do."

"Go right ahead."

"And *this* is Deliza Ta'Akar."

Connor nodded respectfully at the young woman as she stepped out from behind the general. "I suppose this is why you lured me here with promises of free propellant...so that this young woman could lay claim to my ship?"

"Oh, no," Deliza insisted. "I *gave* that ship to *you*, Nathan..."

"He doesn't like to be called Nathan," Jessica warned her.

"I'm sorry," Deliza apologized. She paused for a moment, trying to decide what to say next. "May I just call you *Captain*?"

"That would be fine."

"I promise you, I do not wish to take your ship from you," Deliza continued. "As I said, I *gave* that ship to you. I mean, legally, yes, I *am* still the owner of the Mirai. I would have gladly signed the title over to you at the time, but we feared that creating such a document trail might put you at risk. So, we decided to list the Mirai as lost in space."

"But I have the title for the Seiiki," Captain Tuplo argued. "Bought and paid for with the settlement funds from the crash."

"Yeah, well, that title was pretty much forged," Jessica explained. "We had Marcus take the Mirai someplace outside the sector and *scrub her clean*, so to speak."

"I see," the captain replied, one eyebrow raised. He studied their faces a moment. The Ghatazhak general was nearly expressionless and impossible to read. But the Ghatazhak female known as Jessica was different. Her expression was quite sincere, and she had been genuinely pleased to see him back on Haven. Although he could not read the general, he was sure that *she* believed she was speaking the truth, as did the young woman named Deliza. But with Deliza, there was something more. A fear, or guilt. He wasn't sure which. "Ta'Akar," Connor said, recognizing the name. "Any relation?"

"Yes," Deliza admitted. "My late father was Casimir Ta'Akar."

Connor pulled his head back, his eyes opening wider in surprise. "Doesn't that make you..."

"Rightful heir to the throne of Takara...yes," Deliza finished for him. "My father considered you a very close, and trusted, friend."

The word *trusted* set off alarms in Connor's head.

"As do I," Deliza added. "I only hope you can forgive me."

Now he was really alarmed. "There's more going on here than you people are letting on," Connor accused. "One of you want to tell me why I'm *really* here?"

"We need you to help us conduct a rescue operation," General Telles told him.

"From where?"

"Corinair."

Connor laughed. "You're kidding, right?" He looked at their faces; none of them were smiling. "Shit. You're not kidding. Are you nuts? The Darvano system is crawling with Jung ships, and I'm sure Corinair has got boots on the ground...lots of them!"

Jessica smiled at the captain's turn of phrase.

"You are correct," the general replied, looking at Jessica. "The Jung have occupied the surface of Corinair, which is why we need you, *and* your ship."

"Why me?" Connor wondered. "Why *my* ship?"

"We need to extract at least twenty people," the general explained. "Possibly as many as fifty."

"Why not just use one of those things?" Connor asked, pointing to the boxcar near the hangar.

"They are too large, and not terribly maneuverable. Nor are they very accurate in their jumps. We need a ship that is just big enough to fit in a small space. And it needs a highly skilled pilot. One who is adept at jumping in very close to the surface."

Connor's eyebrow went up again. "How close?"

"Less than ten meters," the general replied.

It took a moment to sink in, as Connor again couldn't tell if the general was kidding. "I'm afraid you've got the wrong guy," he finally replied.

"Your ship cannot make such a precise jump?" the general asked.

"I'm sure it could, assuming everything was in proper working order," Connor replied. "I mean you've got the wrong *guy*. I've never made a close-in jump like that. Hell, I've never even jumped in at less than *ten thousand* meters, let alone less than ten."

"I'm afraid you misunderstood me, Captain," the general said. "I was not going to ask *you* to perform the jump. My intention was to ask Mister Hayes."

"Josh?" Connor's brow furrowed. "Seriously? I mean, he's a good pilot... Okay, he's a *great* pilot, but...*ten meters*?"

"He has done it in less," Jessica assured Connor.

Connor looked at Jessica. "*Really*?"

Jessica nodded.

Connor shook off his surprise. "But you said you needed *me* and my ship. If you don't need me to pilot her, what is it you need me for?"

"Cap'n!" Dalen hollered excitedly as he came jogging around the port engine nacelle. "They've got a crew ready to start repairs on our ramp! They've got new struts, new braces...the works! They even want to replace the port shield generator for us! With a brand new unit!"

"Actually, we were planning on replacing all three of your shield generators," General Telles corrected. "It is important that your ship be in top condition for the mission."

“I haven’t even agreed to the mission, yet,” Connor argued.

“Nevertheless, we would still like to proceed with the repairs,” the general insisted. “It is the least we can do, considering the sacrifices you have made for us all, in the past.”

“Right,” Connor shrugged. He took in a deep breath and sighed. “All right. Sure. Why not. Repair whatever you like, as long as I can still turn you down.”

Dalen jumped for joy, then turned around and headed forward again, disappearing from view.

Connor looked over at Josh and Loki in the distance. His young pilot was usually quite animated, but now he appeared subdued. “You still haven’t told me *why* you need *me* on this mission of yours,” Connor reminded the general.

General Telles looked at Jessica. “Perhaps you should explain it to him?”

Jessica nodded. “Walk and talk?” she asked Connor. She noticed his confusion. “Please, Captain. Take a walk with me, while I explain further.”

* * *

Dumar studied the digital map of the Ranni Enterprises Research and Development Lab. “It is an impressive facility,” he admitted. “I can see why Deliza did not want to move the project off-world. The cost would have been astronomical, and I doubt it would have been any more secure.”

“It was a difficult decision for her,” Doran assured him, “as it was going against her promise to Jessica. But she felt it was for the best. Had she spent the bulk of her resources to relocate the project, we would still be years from completion. And had her business dealings gone sour, we might not have been able to afford to continue the process to its end stage."

"And you are at the end stage now?" Dumar asked.

Doctor Sato sighed, unsure of how to respond. "We expected to go through one more cloning cycle, to be honest. Perhaps even two...just to be sure. This version still has only eighty percent of the genetic adjustments needed to ensure a successful restoration of Captain Scott's memories and personality."

"There is also the issue that we would be transferring a consciousness that came from a genetically different host."

"But he is the same, he is a clone, is he not?"

"The word is often misunderstood," Doctor Megel explained. "The person we all know as Nathan Scott does not currently exist. At least not as a *whole* person. His body exists, yes. In fact, the body that knows itself as Connor Tuplo is an *exact* replica of the *body* of Nathan Scott, based on the DNA sample taken from him just before his death. *That* body is what most people understand a *clone* to be. We, on the other hand, refer to such exact copies as *replicas*, which is precisely what they are. Physical copies that do not carry the essence of the original. In other words, the original version's consciousness, or what some people refer to as a *soul*."

"But this *Connor Tuplo*, he *looks* like Nathan?" Dumar wondered.

"Yes, he looks like Nathan Scott," Doctor Sato replied. "He even *acts* like Nathan Scott, or at least, very similar. But he is *not* Nathan Scott. Not in the true sense."

"We believe that the personality, the emotions,

and the memories are what makes up the human soul," Doctor Megel explained. "Personality influences emotions, emotions influence memories, memories influence personality...they are all closely intertwined. To be complete, all three must be working together. Besides his physical appearance, Connor Tuplo has Nathan Scott's personality, *and* his emotions, but not his memories."

"And why not?" Dumar asked, trying to follow along.

"Centuries ago, the entire population of Nifelm were simple clones. We were grown to adulthood and awakened, but without the memories of those who had come before us. The personality and the emotions were both largely genetic, with some influence due to life experiences. We were essentially *starting over* with each cloning cycle. It wasn't until we discovered a method to transfer our memories from one body to the next that we were able to achieve something akin to immortality."

"Was *that* your goal all along?" Dumar wondered.

"For the original research colony that started more than one thousand years ago, yes. But after the bio-digital plague ravaged the core, it became a means of survival. But, because we had not yet discovered the means of transferring our memories from replica to replica, our progress was greatly hindered. We were only able to continue based on the notes of our predecessors, without the experience, wisdom, and instinct that they had developed."

"And how did you achieve this?"

"As I explained, the personality and emotions of a human being are largely genetic, but are shaped by their life experiences, which, of course, are stored as memories. It was a matter of transferring memories from replica to replica. The issue to overcome was the fact that each person's brain cells were unique. Far more so than anyone imagined. We had to find a way to make them uniform, from person to person, as well as to make them fit a structure compatible with the technology used for the transfer," Doctor Megel explained. "*That* is why we have been recloning him. In order to get his body into a genetic state that will give him the best chance of having fully restored memories. To become Nathan Scott once again, and not a mere replica."

Dumar sighed. "If you knew this to be a problem, why did you even go through with the process to begin with?"

"That is a question you should be asking Jessica," Doctor Sato said.

"I believe I already know the answer," Dumar replied.

"Honestly, we did not think the original restoration process would go as poorly as it did," Doctor Megel said. "We could not have anticipated the problems the Corinairan nanites would cause. That is part of the reason we kept the project here, on Corinair, where nanite expertise was more readily available."

Dumar thought for a moment. "I do not believe it will be too difficult to get into your lab," he explained, changing the subject. "However, getting out the clone and all your equipment, which I assume is a rather sizable amount, will be problematic."

"How are we going to even get a ship large enough down to the surface?" Doran wondered.

"Yes. The moment any ship jumps into the system, the Jung will be all over it," Dumar agreed. "That is why the ship must jump in low, and into concealment."

Doran's eyebrow shot up. "I'm assuming you have such a place in mind?"

"The Crystal Caverns," Dumar said. "They are not far from here. Perhaps half a day's journey. They are quite large, and the opening is equally massive."

"I have been to those caverns," Doran said. "They are not as big as you might think."

"They are big enough," Dumar insisted. "But that still doesn't solve the problem of getting the clone, and all the equipment out of the city."

"Maybe we don't have to," Doctor Sato suggested.

* * *

"I know this is probably difficult for you," Jessica said as they walked away from the Seiiki and toward the hangar office.

"You think?" Connor replied with a hint of sarcasm.

"Tell me something, in all honesty." Jessica stopped walking and turned to look at him. "Don't I look at all familiar to you?"

"Are you supposed to?"

Jessica sighed.

"I'm sorry," Connor said, realizing her disappointment.

"That's alright. I guess I was just hoping that a part of you would have made the connection by now," Jessica said.

"The connection?"

"You see, you still have Nathan's memories locked up inside of you. They're just blocked off, by some genetic wall, or something. Sato and Megel explained it to me at least a dozen times, but I still don't completely get it."

"You think *you* don't get it?"

Jessica smiled. "You are so much like him. Except

for the beard, of course." She sighed again. "God, I've missed you."

They continued their stroll toward the hangar in silence. When they reached the door, Connor held it open for her. "Were we close?"

"Yes," Jessica replied, "at one time, very much so."

"Wow. Now I'm *really* sorry I don't remember you."

"This is really weird," Jessica admitted as they entered the office. "Give us the room," she instructed the people inside. After they left, she sat down. "You know, I've thought about this day for seven long years, ever since you surrendered yourself to the Jung."

"No disrespect to your friend, but why would anyone do that?"

"He... You...were doing so to prevent an all-out war."

"I know," Connor said. "I mean, I know the story. I've heard people talk about it. I've heard Josh talk about it. And talk, and talk about it. But weren't you *already* in an all-out war? I mean, if the Jung haven't been able to do anything until now, doesn't that *prove* his surrender was unnecessary?"

"Or, it proves that it was," Jessica countered. "The Jung have a lot of ships, and I mean *a lot*. When I left the Sol sector, intelligence estimates put their numbers at a minimum of one hundred ships within one hundred light years of Earth. And, we strongly suspected they had ventured out deeper into the galaxy as well. For all we knew, there were hundreds more ships out there."

"But they were all FTL ships, right?" Connor surmised. "Which means it would have taken decades for the Jung to mass them into a coordinated strike on Alliance space."

"Right on both counts."

"Again, then, his surrender makes no sense. The result would have likely been the same."

"Except that millions, possibly *billions* of people—innocent people, I might add—would already be dead. Nathan knew that. He had no way of knowing if it would work, in the long *or* the short term. If he had, I'm sure the decision would have been much easier. But regardless of whether he was right or wrong, he did it for the right reasons. *You* did it for the right reasons."

"I'm still not convinced *I* did it. That *I'm* him," Connor reminded her.

Jessica thought a moment, studying him. Even through the beard, she could still see Nathan's face. The eyes, the cheeks, the chin. She had even seen a hint of that same smile that always engendered trust. "They said you might have flashes of memory."

"Who said?"

"Doctors Sato and Megel."

Connor's eyes lit up. "I remember them. They were my doctors at the hospital on Corinair. They were in charge of my recovery after the crash." A realization hit him. "Are you saying..."

"They were the doctors who cloned you."

Connor shook his head in disbelief. "I was under the impression that cloning was frowned upon on Corinair."

"Actually, they have been cloning human organs and tissue on Corinair and throughout the Pentaurus sector for centuries," Jessica explained. "Just not complete human beings. The doctors that cloned you were from Nifelm."

"Never heard of it," Connor admitted.

"Sol sector. Everyone there are clones."

"Sato and Megel from Nifelm."

"Yup."

"Then, they're..."

"Yup."

Connor sat for a moment, letting the new knowledge sink in. "So, I was cloned *by* clones?"

Jessica smiled. It was the first time he had spoken about himself as if he believed her. "Yup."

Connor noticed her smile. "Slip of the tongue. I still don't believe it."

"So, you're telling me you never have flashes of memories? Memories you don't recognize? Memories you can't make sense of?"

Connor sighed. "Yes, I have them. But they're not the kind you're thinking of. They're about my family. My parents, my sisters. At least, that's who I think they are. They could all be neighbors, or kids I went to school with, or actors I saw in a vid-play or something. Nothing about space battles and the like." Connor looked at her. "And, unfortunately, nothing about you."

"Or, they could be memories of your *real* family."

"Real as in Connor Tuplo's, or Nathan Scott's?" Connor said. "I suppose that's the real question."

"Well, at least you're willing to ask it," Jessica said comfortingly. "That's a start."

Connor sat back in his chair, thinking. "Suppose, for argument's sake, I believe you. Why now? Why not a month ago? Six months ago? Or six years ago?"

"They've been working on a way to completely restore your memories."

"They can do that?" All of sudden, Connor was curious. "I thought clones were just copies. Like empty shells that had to learn everything all over again."

"Sound familiar?" Jessica asked.

Connor frowned, not liking the comparison. He remembered waking up that day six years ago, with no memory of who he was, or what had happened. It was a terrifying feeling, one he wished he could forget.

"Sorry."

"So, the Nifelmians can transfer the memories from one clone to another. Then, why don't I have Nathan Scott's memories?"

"The Nifelmians have been genetically engineered over generations to make it possible to transfer chemically stored memories from one host to another. In this way, they have achieved a type of immortality. They just transfer their memories from clone to clone. Doctor Sato is over three hundred years old. Or, her memories are."

"That's hard to imagine," Connor said. "So, my *genetics* weren't right. If that was the case, then why try to clone me?"

"Because they thought they could overcome the problem, and at least give you *most* of your memories back," Jessica explained.

"Did anyone think to ask me? I mean, him? Nathan?"

"We did. You said yes. I mean, *he* said yes."

"So, now you're asking me. Is that it?"

"No, we *already* asked you," Jessica said. "Six years ago, when you first woke up as a clone. Your memories were tattered. They were there, but they were disconnected, full of holes. The connections kept coming and going. It was driving you mad. You begged us to fix it, but we couldn't. Finally, Doctor

Megel suggested that they wipe your memories and let you believe you were someone else. He offered you the solution, and you took it, but only on the condition that they continue their research on your full restoration. To make you Nathan Scott again."

"So, there is no Connor Tuplo, from Rakuen?"

"No, there isn't."

"And I never went to flight school?"

"Well, you did, but not on Rakuen. On Earth, at the EDF Academy in North America."

Connor leaned forward, burying his head in his hands. "This is really a lot to deal with," he admitted. "And I'm still not sure I believe any of it. Hell, I don't even know whether or not I *want* to believe it."

"Don't you want to know who you really are?" Jessica asked.

"That's just it. I don't. I don't know. As Connor Tuplo, my life is pretty mundane, but it's not a bad life. I have my own ship. I get to travel. I'm my own boss."

"You were stranded on Haven," Jessica reminded him. "You were probably a few weeks away from eating molo for breakfast, lunch, and dinner."

"Molo isn't that bad."

"Yeah, it is," Jessica insisted. "It really is."

"We would have found a way off of that rock, eventually," Connor argued. "Besides, I'm not sure being this Nathan guy is all that appealing. It sounds as if he's had a hell of a lot of responsibility resting on his shoulders. How do I know I even *want* to have his memories? They might not be all that good."

"I'm not going to lie to you," Jessica said. "I was there with you, every step of the way. And I've got a lot of really bad memories that I wish I could forget. Hell, they almost drove me over the edge. Had it not been for the Ghatazhak training, I don't know what would have become of me. But despite all that, I wouldn't give up any of it. Because those memories, the good and the bad, are what makes *me*, me. The Nifelmians are right. Personality, emotions, *and* memory. All of them make you *who you are.* Without all three of them, you *are* incomplete. And, I think deep down inside, *you* know it. You *know* there is a piece of you missing, Nathan. And until you find it, you *won't* be whole. That's why you made Sato and Megel promise to keep working on a way to unlock your memories."

Connor stared at her, trying to remember a time when he recognized her as a friend. She certainly was easy to look at. And he could see the sincerity in her eyes. As much as he wanted *not* to believe her, he couldn't. "I can't promise you anything," Connor finally said. "Not yet. But I am still willing to listen, on one condition."

"What's the condition?" Jessica wondered.

"You have to feed me first."

* * *

"So, how's he been doing?" Loki asked, as he and Josh watched the spaceport ground crew finish refueling the Seiiki.

"He's been good."

"Is he anything like the old Captain Scott?"

"Sometimes yes, sometimes no," Josh admitted.

"Does he ever have any memory flashes?"

"He talks about them here and there, but nothing significant. What's going on, Loki?"

"How's Marcus?"

"Loki, enough with the small talk," Josh insisted. "It's me. What the hell is going on? Why did they come for us now? Does it have something to do with the Jung?"

"Sort of, yeah."

Josh could see the concern on his friend's face. "Come on, Lok."

Loki looked at the ground. "It's Lael," he said, nearly losing his composure. He looked back at Josh, tears in his eyes. "And Ailsa. They're still on Corinair."

"What? Wait. Who's Ailsa?"

"Our daughter."

"Daughter? When did that happen?"

"She was born six months ago," Loki told him, barely able to hold back his tears.

"Why didn't you tell me?"

"How was I supposed to get in touch with you, Josh?"

"Through Jessica. How else?"

"It's not like I have access to a jump comm-drone," Loki said. "And the Sherma system isn't exactly on the beaten path."

"Oh, man," Josh exclaimed. "How did this happen?"

"We were on our way back from a short business trip when the Jung invaded. Josh, I *saw* the Avendahl come apart. One moment, she was on my sensors, then... We tried to rescue them. We even had a few of the Avendahl's fighters trying to cover us."

Josh looked past his friend at the heavily damaged corporate shuttle near the hangar. "Is that..." he began, pointing at the damaged shuttle.

Loki glanced back over his shoulder. "The girl who took Lael's place when she left to have Ailsa was in the back when we were hit. She didn't make it. If they would've been in the back when..."

Josh reached out and grabbed his friend, pulling him in tight and wrapping his arms around him as Loki started sobbing. "We'll get them out, buddy. You and me. We'll find a way, I promise you. We'll find a way."

* * *

Jessica pulled the vehicle through the front gate and headed up the short, dirt path that led from the main road to the main house. It had taken them only ten minutes to travel here from the Lawrence Spaceport. The drive had been somewhat relaxing for Connor. Meandering roads dotted with similar properties. Fields of crops, small groves of fruit-bearing trees, all spotted with ponds of varying sizes. Lawrence had been nothing more than a small collection of shops, restaurants, and government buildings, along with a few apartments for those few people who wanted to live in the city, itself. On Burgess, cities were for gathering and trading goods. People lived in the country, only traveling into town when they needed supplies. It was a life that Connor had often considered for himself. Simple and quiet, with nothing more to worry about than the crops you grew and traded for other goods. A wife, children, and a piece of land he could call his own.

What he couldn't understand was *why* he found the idea of such a life so appealing. According to his record, or that of Connor Tuplo, he had no exposure to such a lifestyle. Rakuen, the world on which he was supposed to have been raised, was fully industrialized, and grew no crops of its own. If he *had* grown up there, it would be unlikely that he would even know what a farm was, let alone think it was a good place for him to live out his life.

The dirt road passed through a small grove of

trees covered with blue-green leaves. Once they were through the grove, the path split out into several different roads, each leading to a separate house. They followed the center path, toward a two-story, wood-framed home, surrounded by trees and grass, as well as a few well-placed flower gardens. The air was clean and fresh, a stark contrast to the polluted air he normally found around spaceports and the congested cities.

"How many people live here?" Connor wondered as they pulled up to the main house.

"My parents and my daughter, Ania. I only stay here a few days a week. Most of the time, I live on base with the rest of the Ghatazhak." Jessica climbed down out of the vehicle. "My brothers and their families live in these other houses. They all work this farm together."

"Is this where you grew up?" Connor asked. "It's nice."

"No, we've only lived here for about six years now. We're all from Earth, born and raised, just like you."

Just like me, he thought. Connor had no memory of Earth. As far as he knew, he had never been there. Of course, he had no memory of Rakuen, either. Just bits and pieces. Images that occasionally flashed in and out of his mind. For all he knew, those images *could* have been from Earth, and not Rakuen.

"Why did you all move here?" Connor asked. "I thought Earth was supposed to be a great world. Some sort of magical paradise, with everything anyone could ever want."

Jessica looked at him, puzzled. "Is that what people out here think of Earth?"

"I don't know. That's just the impression I got from all of Josh's stories."

"Don't listen to Josh," Jessica laughed. "He compares everything to Haven. *I* left because I wanted to stay with the Ghatazhak and continue my training. My parents came because they were helping to raise Ania, and they didn't want me to be separated from her by such vast distances. My brothers came along because it just made sense to keep the entire family together. Besides, at the time, the Earth was still pretty screwed up from the Jung attacks. It still is, in a lot of ways."

"So, not so much the magical paradise that Josh made it out to be, huh?" Connor said as he followed her onto the front porch.

"Don't get me wrong, Earth *is* an amazing planet. Of all the worlds I've seen, it has the greatest variation of climates, cultures, geography... You name it, Earth's got it." Jessica stepped through the front door. "Ania!" A squeal of delight echoed from somewhere in the home, followed by the sound of tiny, bare feet running on the hardwood floors. A moment later, a little girl, wearing light blue overalls with her hair in blond pigtails, bolted through one of the nearby doors, ran across the room, and leapt into Jessica's open arms. "How have you been, kiddo?" she asked as she squeezed her tightly and kissed the side of her face repeatedly. "Have you been behaving?"

"No," little Ania squealed in delight.

"Don't believe her," Jessica's mother said as she entered the room.

"Mom, this is, uh... Connor. Connor Tuplo. Connor, this is my mother, Laura."

Laura reached out to shake Connor's hand, looking at him with a curious expression. "Have we met before?"

"No, ma'am," Connor replied as he shook her hand. "It's a pleasure to meet you."

"The pleasure's mine, Mister Tuplo. You do look familiar, though. Are you staying for dinner?"

Connor looked at Jessica.

"Yes, he's staying for dinner."

"Are you sleepin' here tonight, Jess?" Ania asked.

"Sorry, sweetie, but I've got to take Mister Tuplo back to his ship after dinner," Jessica explained. "But I'll come home for a few days soon, I promise."

"Come along Ania," Laura said. "Help me set the table."

Jessica and Connor watched them leave the room, then Connor spoke. "She doesn't call you mom?" he wondered.

"She's not my biological daughter. Her mother was a friend of mine. She and her husband were killed when the Jung glassed their world. Ania's twin sister, as well. I couldn't let her become an orphan. There were already so many of them, both from Tanna and on Earth. So, I took her in, and my parents and I have raised her ever since. I think of her as my daughter, but truth is, I'm more like a big sister. The main thing is that she's happy, and safe."

"Seems like she is."

"Come on," Jessica said, gesturing for him to follow her. She led him through the house and out into the backyard. Stretched out before them was a valley of rolling hills, bordered by mountains on the far side. The setting sun was about to dip down behind the mountains, casting an odd, orange shadow across the land. Above them, Burgess's moon, Anthon, filled a quarter of the sky, casting its own bluish glow wherever the light of Sherma did not reach. "Pretty cool, huh?"

"It's beautiful," Connor agreed. After staring at the sunset for a moment, he asked. "*Have* I met your mother before? I mean, did *he*?"

"Actually, no," Jessica said, as she sat down on the back porch steps. "Nathan never actually met my mother. He was on the news a lot, though. When they first thought the Aurora was lost, Nathan's picture was on the news because his father was running for president. A lot of people say the sympathy vote is what got his father elected."

"Here, everyone seems to think of him as *Na-Tan*," Connor commented, one eyebrow raised.

"I take it you don't?"

"A mythical savior foretold in the legends of a cult religion? Interesting bedtime stories for children, and placebos for the oppressed masses."

"Maybe," Jessica agreed. "But, you have to admit, you did save the cluster from oppression."

"*He* saved them, for all the good it did. If you ask me, saving them only weakened the entire sector, making them a soft target for the Jung."

"You'd rather have Caius still in power?"

"I don't know," Connor replied honestly. "I have no memory of him. Only what I've been told. At the very least, he would have made a more formidable opponent for the Jung."

"I disagree," Jessica replied. "We took him down with one jump ship, a band of rebels, and the Corinari. The Jung attacked with a fleet of jump ships. The old empire wouldn't have lasted any longer."

"Perhaps. Like I said, I don't remember the empire. I don't remember much of anything prior to the crash."

"What do you remember about the crash?" Jessica wondered.

"Only what I read," Connor replied. "A faulty thruster caused the transport I was flying to crash. I was the only survivor. I was in a coma for two years, and woke up not knowing who I was, or what had happened. I was offered the Seiiki as part of my settlement by the company that made the faulty thruster. I think it was the owner's personal shuttle, or something."

"*Dinner is ready!*" Jessica's mother called from inside.

"Let's eat," Jessica said, rising to her feet.

* * *

Connor followed Jessica from the vehicle to the office at the Ghatazhak hangar at the Lawrence Spaceport. It was late, and most of the Ghatazhak personnel had left for the evening. Only a small security detachment remained, along with the mechanics working on the Seiiki.

"Are they going to work all night?" Connor asked.

"If that's what it takes, sure," Jessica replied.

"You still haven't told me what you want from me and my ship," he reminded her.

"That's not my place," Jessica explained, as they entered the office.

Inside, Connor found General Telles, and the rest of the Seiiki's crew, all waiting for him. "Shouldn't you guys be out there, helping them fix the ship?"

"Are you kidding?" Dalen replied. "Those guys are so far over my head... We'd only be in the way, Cap'n. Trust me."

Connor looked at Marcus, who nodded his agreement.

"Captain," General Telles began, "I trust you were well fed?"

"Yes, thank you." Connor looked at his crew.

"Don't worry, Cap'n," Marcus assured him. "They took us into Lawrence and treated us. This city's got some fine eats, let me tell you."

"Since the mission we are proposing affects all of you, I thought it would be best if *all* your crew were present when we shared the details of how you got to be known as Connor Tuplo. Assuming, of course, that you have no objections."

Connor thought for a moment, looking at the faces of his crew.

"Come on, Cap'n," Dalen begged. Neli said nothing, still looking as undecided as Connor.

"Well, apparently, Marcus and Josh already know more than I do, so I don't suppose it will hurt for Dalen and Neli to know, as well. After all, crew is family, right Marcus?"

"Damn straight, Cap'n."

"Very well," General Telles replied. "Please," he added, gesturing for Connor to sit. "This will take some time, I'm afraid."

Connor sighed, as if facing his own execution. He took his seat, then looked at the general.

"You must all understand that everything we are about to tell you must be kept in the strictest of confidence. Your very lives, and possibly the lives of billions more, may depend on your secrecy."

"Then why even tell us?" Neli wondered.

"Because you have a right to know. Not only what we are asking you to do, but why," the general explained.

"Plus, what he said about billions of lives depending on it, probably doesn't really apply, now," Jessica added.

"It still might," General Telles disagreed.

"Oh, come on," Jessica argued. "The Jung have

already broken the cease-fire, and they have jump drives. I doubt they're going to care that Nathan is still alive. For all we know, they might not even consider a clone to be the same as the original. A lot of people don't, you know."

"Arguments aside, it would be best if none of this was repeated outside of present company," the general insisted. "Do you understand?"

Neli and Dalen both nodded.

"Very well," the general said. He looked at Jessica. "Lieutenant?"

"Seven years ago," Jessica began, "you, Captain Nathan Scott, surrendered to the Jung as a war criminal. He knew that by taking full responsibility for the KKV strike against the military base on Zhu-Anok, which resulted in collateral damage costing millions of civilian lives on the Jung homeworld, Nor-Patri, he could put a stop to the war between the Jung and the Alliance. He knew that by sacrificing himself, billions would be saved, on both sides. *That* is the kind of man Nathan Scott was, and *that* is the kind of man *you* are."

Connor stared at Jessica. "So, if the Jung found out that I...... *he*, was still alive?"

"They would not be happy," Jessica replied.

"Prior to the Jung invasion of the Pentaurus cluster, it is logical to assume that an all-out war would follow such a discovery," General Telles added. "Now, there is some debate over what their reaction might be, and if it even matters at this point."

"So *that's* why you're telling me all this now?" Connor wondered. "Because you think it's *safe* for the truth to get out? A bit of an unnecessary risk, don't you think?"

"I don't get it," Neli interrupted. "If the Jung

finding out that Nathan Scott is still alive is so risky to begin with, why did you even rescue him in the first place?"

"Because it was Nathan," Jessica replied. "And because he didn't deserve to die."

CHAPTER TWO

Jessica walked into the admiral's office located deep inside the Karuzara asteroid base in orbit high above the Earth. "Lieutenant Commander Nash, reporting as ordered," she announced, standing at attention and offering a salute.

"At ease, Lieutenant Commander," Admiral Dumar said, returning her salute. He nodded at the aide who had led her in, then quickly left the admiral's office and closed the door behind him. "Take a seat."

"Beg the admiral's pardon, but I'd like to know what we're going to do about rescuing Captain Scott."

"Take a seat, Lieutenant Commander," the admiral repeated, more firmly this time. When she did not immediately take her seat, he looked up from his data pad. Her eyes were full of anger and determination, neither expression unusual to see on the young spec-ops-trained lieutenant commander. But he also saw frustration and panic, both of which he had never witnessed in those eyes. She had been through a lot in the last two years, more specifically in the last three weeks. The rescue of Doctor Sorenson and her family, the destruction of Tanna, the loss of her friend... Had it not been for the infant Ania, who had miraculously survived the devastating attack, the lieutenant commander might have completely lost, herself. And now, the loss of one of her closest friends...her captain, who had surrendered himself to the Jung only a day ago. "I won't ask again," the admiral added, still staring at her.

Jessica begrudgingly took a seat across the desk from the admiral. "You asked to see me, sir?"

"Yes, I did," the admiral replied. "I'm reassigning you."

"You're *what*?"

Admiral Dumar looked at Jessica, one eyebrow raised in disapproval at her tone. "You are to report to Porto Santo tomorrow morning."

"Why?"

Admiral Dumar looked at her again. "Your skills are required there."

"To do what?"

The admiral leaned back in his chair, crossing his hands in his lap. "I wasn't aware that I was required to explain my decisions to you, Lieutenant Commander."

"No disrespect intended, Admiral, but in this case, I think you at least owe me an explanation."

Admiral Dumar thought for a moment. Had such a response come from any other officer under his command, he would have had them thrown into the brig for insubordination. They had been through a lot together, going all the way back to the moment on the Aurora when he had finally confirmed that his oldest friend, a man he had thought long dead, had in fact been alive, and was leading a resistance against the very leader Admiral Dumar had then served. "I suppose I do owe you that much," he admitted. "You are being assigned to the Ghatazhak training unit. You're going to help train Alliance Marines, again."

"Again, why? Telles and his bunch are far better qualified to teach them how to fight."

"But you can teach them covert operations," the admiral explained, "something that the Ghatazhak know little about."

"Oh, they know more about it than you think," Jessica argued.

"Nevertheless, those are your orders."

"Again, no disrespect intended, Admiral, but that's bullshit, and you know it."

Admiral Dumar chuckled. "You just don't know when to quit, do you, Nash?"

"We shouldn't even be wasting time talking about this," Jessica insisted.

"Then what is it we *should* be talking about?"

"About rescuing Nathan!" Jessica replied. When the admiral didn't respond, it began to make sense to her. "That's why you're reassigning me, isn't it? You're afraid I'm going to go off all half-cocked and try something on my own!"

"The thought had crossed my mind," Admiral Dumar admitted.

"Then, tell me what you're planning to do about rescuing Nathan, so you won't have to worry!"

"It's not that simple, Jess, and you know it."

"The hell it's not!" Jessica argued.

"Don't you think I *want* to rescue him?" the admiral yelled back, finally losing his patience with her. "Do you know how hard it is not to say, *fuck it*, and authorize a goddamned rescue? Knowing that the man who saved *my* world is sitting in a Jung prison right now, probably undergoing all manner of torture and interrogation, and God knows what else?"

"Then fucking do something!" Jessica demanded.

"I can't! And you damn well know it! Billions of lives, Jessica! Billions of lives are at stake here! You know it! And Nathan knew it! That's why he surrendered! To save billions of lives...ours and theirs! And I will not dishonor his noble sacrifice!"

"It's not right!" Jessica protested.

"I know it isn't!" the admiral agreed. "But it was *his* choice to make, and I have to respect it."

"*You* may have to respect it, but..."

"And *that's* exactly why you're being reassigned!" the admiral pointed out. "Goddamn it, Jessica. If you try and rescue Nathan on your own, you'll not only get yourself killed, but you'll be sacrificing everyone else you talk into helping you. And, in the end, Nathan will still die at the hands of the Jung. Then they'll *have* their Tonba-Hon-Venar, and billions *will* die. Is that what you want? The blood of *billions* on your hands, *and* Nathan's?"

Jessica looked as if she would explode. Her eyes darted about in confusion and frustration, welling up with tears, despite her attempts to suppress them. "I can't just do *nothing*," she finally whispered. "I can't."

"I know," the admiral replied in hushed tones. "That's why I'm transferring you to Porto Santo... So you can't."

* * *

Nathan stared at the ceiling, his focus on the light directly over his head. Throughout his body, pain receptors fired as a nano-war between good and evil raged within him. His hands and feet were bound by hard restraints which held him firmly against the table. Intravenous lines inserted into his femoral veins and arteries kept him alive, despite the myriad of chemicals and nanotech circulating within him. It was a horror like no other. One that simply could not be imagined. Pain without injury. Suffering without relief. Not even the lingering hope of escape through death.

Technicians routinely checked on him. Indifferent to his suffering, some even enjoying it, as if they had been blessed by the opportunity to participate. After all, he was the object of evil in their minds. The cause of all the death and destruction their world had suffered only a few weeks ago. The man who had ordered the strike on Zhu-Anok... The strike which had sent countless pieces of that moon hurtling toward Nor-Patri, killing millions.

The longer Nathan was kept alive to suffer, the happier they would be.

He had been in Jung captivity for just over a day, as best as he could determine. If by no other measure than the number of shifts of technicians that had cycled through since he was first strapped to this table. Yet, they had not asked him a single question. In fact, no one had spoken directly to him since he had set foot on the Jung homeworld. He wasn't even sure he was *on* Nor-Patri, or any world, for that matter. There had been no windows on the shuttle, and his head had been covered when he was hauled from the shuttle upon its arrival. He had no idea where he was. All he knew was pain.

The odd thing was, he was not tired, yet he was sure he had not slept. Nor was he hungry or thirsty, despite the fact that he had not been given food or water since his surrender. He didn't even need to use the toilet.

"Captain Scott," a familiar voice called from out of Nathan's line of sight. He heard slow, steady footfalls. Solid and sure, boots treading on the tile floor, approaching from the unseen doorway to his right and above.

A face came into view. Old, distinguished, thin... Bacca. Nathan tried to speak, but nothing came out, at least nothing intelligible.

"Ah, I see the meds are beginning to take their

toll on you," the old general smiled cruelly. "The ability to speak is one of the first to go. Actually, bladder control is the first to go, but you've been catheterized, so do not be concerned." The general looked down at Nathan's groin. "They weren't very neat about it, were they? No matter. I don't suppose you'll have much need for your penis from this point forward." The general looked back at Nathan. "Quite the noble sacrifice you've made, surrendering yourself to us. Stupid, but noble nonetheless. Of course, you realize the nanites your people injected will not protect you. In fact, they are the primary cause of your discomfort at the moment. Eventually, our nanites will overpower yours, and we shall have complete access to everything you know. I would urge you not to resist, but, quite honestly, you do not have the *ability* to resist...not with all the nasty stuff they are pumping into your system at the moment. But do not worry; no true harm will come to you. A lot of pain and suffering, yes, but you will not die, of that you can be sure. I cannot allow that. You see, *after* we have finished extracting information, you shall be put on trial for crimes against the empire. It will be broadcast to every corner of the empire. You'll have the best advocates available. You *shall* lose, of course. Only then will you be allowed to die, while on display, for all the people of the Jung Empire to witness. I believe your world calls that closure." The general smiled once more, then glanced up at the time. "Oh, dear, I must be going. They are pinning another medal on me, and I don't want to be late." The general disappeared from Nathan's view. "I will check in on you later," the general promised as he left the room.

Now, at least, he knew this would all eventually come to an end.

* * *

A knock sounded at Admiral Dumar's office door. He looked up from his desk and saw Commander Telles standing in the doorway, dressed in a standard Alliance officer's duty uniform, sporting the rank of lieutenant. "Lieutenant?" he said in surprise, asking more about the rank than the fact that he was not wearing his usual Ghatazhak uniform.

Commander Telles closed the door behind him without saying a word. A simple look at the admiral signaled Dumar to activate the room's sound-suppression fields to ensure they would be speaking in private.

"Why the uniform and rank change?" the admiral asked.

"Low profile," the commander replied.

"You do realize that most of my officers would recognize you, with or without your usual Ghatazhak accoutrements."

"It is not your officers from which I wish to go unnoticed."

"I see," the admiral replied. "Then, I take it you have something of importance you wish to discuss. Something that you could not discuss on secure vid-link?"

"The only truly secure discussions take place between two trusted allies, in a sealed, shielded, and swept room, Admiral."

As usual, there was no arguing with Ghatazhak logic. "If you have come to try to persuade me to rescue Captain Scott, I'm afraid Lieutenant Commander Nash has already beaten you to it."

"Asking you for permission to mount a rescue

would be a waste of our time, as we both know you could not grant such a request."

"I'm glad *someone* understands," the admiral said. "Perhaps you can explain it to Jessica, when she reports to Porto Santo tomorrow."

"I shall do my best."

"So, why did you come?"

"I believe we should insert operatives onto the Jung homeworld as soon as possible," Commander Telles announced.

Admiral Dumar leaned back in his chair, intrigued by the commander's suggestion, but said nothing.

"We know the Jung have had operatives on Earth for at least a decade, perhaps longer. And I suspect that such operatives are still among us."

"Not within the Alliance," the admiral protested.

"Doubtful, but there are likely still some of them among the general population. Of course, I cannot be certain of this, but one would be foolish to assume otherwise."

"Agreed. And who would you suggest we trust with such an assignment?" the admiral wondered.

"Several of Lieutenant Commander Bowden's men were once Jung soldiers, and have proven themselves to be loyal to the Alliance."

"What would you propose?"

"I propose we establish regular jump comm-drone service with the Jung homeworld, under the guise of keeping the lines of communication open between the Jung Empire and the Sol-Pentaurus Alliance."

"You want to routinely put a jump-enabled comm-drone into Jung space?" the admiral asked, surprised that the commander would make such a suggestion.

"It would not be difficult to create a tamper-proof drone," Commander Telles explained. "Simply program it to jump in near Nor-Patri, wait a specific period of time, then jump out again. Any attempts to capture, disable, or otherwise tamper with the drone would result in its immediate destruction. Such a drone could be used to exchange not only communications between the Jung and the Alliance, but also between the Alliance and our operatives on Nor-Patri."

"I can't say that I am completely comfortable with the idea of regularly putting a jump comm-drone into Jung space," the admiral admitted, "tamper-proof or not."

"I am sure it can be made safe," the commander insisted. "If not, then we simply send manned vessels to exchange messages."

"You realize the Jung may not allow this," the admiral said. "They will see through this ruse. They will assume we have ulterior motives. At the very least, they will suspect that the jump comm-drone is conducting surveillance."

"It is to their advantage to maintain the lines of communication," the commander replied. "And, from the distance the drone would jump in at, reconnaissance would be of little value. The Jung would know this."

"And, would they not also assume that we could use this drone to communicate with *our* operatives on *their* world?"

"They would," the commander replied. "But, they might also see it as a way to possibly track and arrest such operatives, or better yet, to feed them false intelligence. Either way, they would likely agree to it, as it would give them opportunities that they might not otherwise have."

Admiral Dumar considered the commander's words. "And should the Jung agree, how would we insert these operatives?"

"The same way we inserted the team onto Kohara," the commander replied. "The conversion of three mini-subs into jump subs began during the preparation for the Kohara mission. There are still two mini-subs that are partially converted. All they need is to be outfitted with their mini-jump drives."

"So, besides putting a jump comm-drone into Jung space on a regular basis, you also want to park two jump subs in their oceans?"

"They, too, can be made tamper-proof," the commander pointed out.

"I would feel more comfortable if they were destroyed after delivery," the admiral admitted.

"You would be committing the operatives to a one-way mission. Besides, there is likely plenty of debris already in those oceans, the result of larger pieces of destroyed ships having passed through the atmosphere of Nor-Patri without burning up. It could be decades before the Jung even notice something unusual was on the bottom."

The admiral shook his head, sighing. "Still, it is a very dangerous proposition. Why would any of these men be willing to take such risks?"

"Why do any of us take such risks?" the commander asked. "Because we believe in what we do."

* * *

Jessica pulled the door open and found Vladimir standing on the other side.

"What do you want?" she demanded, turning around and heading back to her bed to continue packing.

"I came as soon as I heard," Vladimir said as he

entered Jessica's quarters, closing the door behind him. "Is it true?"

Jessica looked at him, sneering. "No, I'm packing up all my shit because I'm going on vacation."

"Maybe if we ask the admiral to..."

"Who do you think transferred me?" Jessica replied, cutting him off.

"I do not understand," Vladimir said. "Why transfer you? We are already without a captain. Now, we will be without a security chief?"

"He was afraid I'd try to rescue Nathan," Jessica said as she continued packing.

"Where are they sending you?"

"Porto Santo, so I can't do anything crazy."

"If he thinks that would stop you, he does not know you very well," Vladimir said.

Jessica looked at him. "He's right, Vlad," she admitted. She stopped packing for a moment, then sat on the edge of her bed in resignation. "It's all I can think about, ever since Nathan surrendered." She looked at him. "How I can rescue him."

"Then you have a plan?" Vladimir asked, moving toward Jessica. He sat down on the bed next to her. "You must tell me."

"That's just it," she said, her voice quivering. "I don't. I can't think of any way to rescue him, at least none that have the slightest chance of success." She looked at him, tears in her eyes. "The most I could hope for is to get to him and kill him myself, to end both our suffering."

"Well, that's a terrible plan," Vladimir said, putting his arms around her to console her.

"I know, right?" she sobbed. "I don't know what to do, Vlad."

"You have to let him go, Jess," Vladimir replied. "We both do."

"I can't," Jessica cried. "I can't."

* * *

Nathan sat quietly in the small, nondescript interrogation chamber. It was the first time in two days he had not been strapped to a table, hooked up to tubes and wires. It was also the first time in just as long that his brain had been clear enough to think straight.

He glanced at the small bubbles in the corners of the room. Four of them, each undoubtedly housing cameras and microphones, possibly even other types of sensors to monitor his physiological responses to the questioning. *But why?* He was quite sure the Jung had methods of information extraction far superior to simple questioning. Their nanites had been able to turn loyal members of the Alliance into saboteurs. Such saboteurs had cost the lives of untold numbers, including that of his trusted bodyguard and friend, Sergeant Jerome Weatherly.

The war between the Corinairan and Jung nanites had only been raging within him for two days, yet Nathan was already having problems piecing together his memories. It was a constant conflict between his desire to remember his own life, and his responsibility to forget anything that could be of value to the Jung. He did not want to lose *who* he was to the Corinairan nanites that were currently trying to destroy the very memories that defined him, yet he knew it would be a losing battle in the end. Worse yet, it was one he *had* to let happen, despite his natural instinct for self-preservation.

Instead, he tried to focus what little cognitive abilities he seemed to have at the moment on anticipating what was about to happen. Would it be one or two interrogators? Would they play the classic friend and foe roles? Would the interrogator try to trick him into revealing information? Or would they offer him something in trade, like his own life?

Name, rank, service number. He kept repeating it in his mind.

The door opened without warning, revealing an older, distinguished looking man, dressed in what appeared to be business attire for Nor-Patri. He paused to look at Nathan, then turned to close the door behind him. "You should know that this room is equipped with automated restraint fields," the man began. His English was perfect, if heavily accented. "Should you attempt to harm me, you will become immediately and painfully incapacitated."

"I am not a violent man," Nathan replied in a nearly inaudible voice. He had spoken little since his surrender, and had very limited energy with which to do so.

"An odd statement, considering the charges you face."

"Charges?" Nathan wondered.

"My name, is Finay Gorus, son of Donley."

"Are you here to interrogate me?"

"On the contrary, Captain Scott," the man replied. "I am your advocate."

"Advocate?" Nathan asked, wondering if the man was translating incorrectly between languages.

"Your legal counsel. I have been tasked to defend you."

"What are the charges?" Nathan asked again.

"You have been charged with crimes against the people of Nor-Patri. Specifically, the attempted destruction of the Jung homeworld."

Nathan laughed. "Seriously?"

"I hardly think this is something to scoff at, Captain Scott. You are accused of acting beyond your authority, intent on vengeance for the people of Tanna."

"You glassed Tanna. You tried to glass several other worlds, including Earth, and you think I committed a crime?"

"Then, you admit you were trying to destroy Nor-Patri?"

"I was trying to destroy Zhu-Anok, and I did so. The collateral damage was unfortunate, but it was not my intent."

"Given the relative proximity of Zhu-Anok to Nor-Patri, anyone with a decent knowledge of physics, especially orbital mechanics, would expect such collateral damage. As the captain of a starship, you should have such knowledge."

"And you are *my* advocate?" Nathan quipped.

"I am only trying to establish the facts," Mister Gorus insisted. "Statements such as these will be made by the state's advocate, I assure you. I also assure you that using the Jung Empire's actions against worlds that violated the terms of their occupation will not sway the opinions of the jurors. Your best course of action will be to answer all questions as truthfully, and as simply, as possible. Do not give your accusers any more information than they ask for, for they are likely to use it."

"I see," Nathan replied. "So, assuming I am found guilty of these charges, what is the punishment?"

"Death, of course. And make no mistake, Captain, you *will* be convicted. It can go no other way."

"Then why are you even here?"

"Appearances, Captain. Appearances." Mister

Gorus placed his data pad on the table and activated it. "Now, let us begin."

"Begin what?" Nathan wondered, having already resigned himself to the inevitable two days prior.

"Your defense, of course," Mister Gorus replied. "Like I said, we have to keep up appearances."

* * *

Jessica stepped through the personnel shuttle's hatch, pausing at the top of the boarding gangway. She looked out across the tarmac of the Porto Santo Air Base. The usual assortment of boxcars, combat shuttles, troop shuttles, and cargo shuttles were there, along with the last two operational Super Falcons. In the distance, beyond the buildings lining the flight operations areas, she could see the rest of the base, spreading out into the surrounding hills. Beyond that were rows of houses, several of which were occupied by her parents and the families of her brothers. Ania was also there, with Jessica's parents, who had been caring for her since her rescue from Tanna. Although Jessica had visited Porto Santo on several occasions, both for business and pleasure, this island was now her home, at least for the foreseeable future.

Jessica slung her duffel bag up over her shoulder and headed down the gangway, following the personnel who had disembarked before her. At the bottom of the ramp, she was met by a young Ghatazhak corporal.

"Lieutenant Commander Nash," the young corporal greeted as Jessica stepped onto the gray tarmac.

"Olyetto, right?" Jessica recalled.

"Yes, sir," the corporal replied. "Commander Telles sent me. I am to take you to report to him."

"Very well." Jessica handed her duffel bag to the corporal, and followed him to the nearby open-cockpit vehicle. She climbed into her seat as the corporal tossed her bag in the back and climbed into the driver's seat.

Moments later, they were speeding across the tarmac, headed for the command center on the other side of the base. As she watched the buildings slip past, she remembered the first time she had set foot on Porto Santo Island. It had been a sleepy little island, relatively isolated from most of the world. It was for that very reason that the Ghatazhak had chosen it as the site for their base of operations at the time. The locals had been reluctant at first, but over time they had come to cooperate and to work side-by-side with base personnel, and the Ghatazhak. Now, instead of a sleepy little island, it was a bustling military base. Nearly every business on the island served to support the base, its personnel, and the families of those who lived and worked either on the base or elsewhere on the island. Its population of a few thousand had grown to tens of thousands in less than a year. Now, Porto Santo's inhabitants enjoyed a quality of life equal to or better than most places on Earth.

But this wasn't where she wanted to be, and it definitely wasn't what she wanted to be doing.

They passed by a group of men in civilian attire, climbing into another vehicle on the side of the road outside one of the barracks. Jessica turned her head. For a moment, she thought she recognized several of them. She looked back, but they were already inside the vehicle and out of sight. She looked forward again, trying to remember where she had seen them before.

The vehicle pulled up in front of the base command building and came to a stop. The corporal quickly dismounted, grabbed Jessica's duffel, and headed toward the door.

"If you'll follow me, sir..."

"I know the way, Corporal," Jessica replied quickly, moving ahead of him.

"Yes, sir."

Jessica entered the command center, the corporal following close behind. Once inside, she stopped at the guard desk and presented her ID badge.

The guard scanned her ID badge, then pointed at the camera on the wall behind him. "Look straight ahead, sir."

Jessica did as instructed, waiting for the camera to scan her image. "When did this get installed?" she asked after the scan was finished.

The guard did not answer. A moment later, her ID was confirmed. "Welcome to Porto Santo Command, Lieutenant Commander," the guard said as he handed Jessica back her ID badge. He was suddenly far more cordial than before. "This is your base ID," he added, handing her a new ID badge. "Please wear it at all times when on base."

Jessica forced a smile as she clipped the new ID badge onto her uniform. "Thank you."

"Do you need directions to the commander's office?" the guard asked.

"Negative," Jessica replied, heading into the building.

The corporal followed, exchanging wary glances with guard.

"Have fun," the guard commented to the corporal as he passed.

Jessica ignored the comment as she continued

deeper into the building. A minute later, she was in the commander's outer office. "I'm Lieutenant Commander Nash," she said to the clerk. "I've got orders to report to the commander upon arrival."

"Yes, sir," the clerk replied. "The commander is expecting you," he added, gesturing toward the door to the commander's office.

Jessica moved over to the door and knocked.

"*Enter*," the commander replied from inside.

Jessica opened the door and stepped inside, leaving the corporal in the outer office. She closed the door behind her, turning to face the commander in proper military fashion. "Lieutenant Commander Jessica Nash, reporting for duty, sir."

Commander Telles rose from his seat, returned her salute, then reached out to shake her hand. "It is good to see you, Lieutenant Commander."

Jessica shook the commander's hand. "Thank you, sir."

Commander Telles's eyebrow went up when he heard her cold tone. "At ease, Lieutenant Commander."

Jessica relaxed only slightly, assuming a stance with her hands behind her back, eyes fixed on her new commanding officer.

"I am glad to have you here," the commander continued. "Despite the tentative cease-fire, the admiral insists we continue training new marines."

"Understandable," Jessica replied. "But why me? Surely your people can train recruits better than I can."

"Perhaps, but we have also been tasked to train more officers for the Earth Security Force. That is where you come in. You understand Earth social structures far better than the Ghatazhak. Your training in covert operations was geared toward societies that are Earth-like. Your skills will be useful to those recruits."

Jessica said nothing.

"Something on your mind, Lieutenant Commander?" Commander Telles wondered.

Jessica paused a moment before replying. "Permission to speak freely, sir?"

"Do I have a choice?"

Again, Jessica did not reply.

"Permission granted," the commander added.

"Bullshit."

A smirk came across the commander's face. "Care to be more specific?"

"I'm not here because you need me to train security officers. I'm here because the admiral doesn't trust me. I'm here because this is an island. An island where no one gets off without your authorization." She looked directly at the commander. "I'm here because the admiral is afraid I'm going to try to find a way to rescue Nathan. I'm *here* so that I can be contained...controlled."

"And I thought you were here because your family is here, and because after all you have done, after all you have been through, that you perhaps deserved a break. Apparently, I was wrong."

"Don't give me that shit," Jessica replied impatiently.

"Permission to speak freely does have its limits, Lieutenant Commander," the commander warned as he sat back down.

"You know damned well Dumar sent me here so you could keep an eye on me."

"Admiral Dumar reassigned you to my command because I asked him to do so. *Not*, because *he*...or

I, wanted to keep an *eye* on you." For a moment, Commander Telles looked as if he wanted to burst out laughing. "Both the admiral and myself know that you could not possibly mount any type of rescue on your own. Surely, despite your considerable over-confidence in your own abilities, you are aware of this fact, as well."

Once again, Jessica did not respond. However, her expression communicated exactly what the commander expected.

"Care for some advice, Lieutenant Commander?" the commander asked.

"Do I have a choice?"

"Take a week off. Take two. Spend time with your family, with Ania. Relax on the beach. Stop being Lieutenant Commander Nash, and try just being Jessica for a while."

"Am I supposed to stop being Nathan's friend, as well?" Jessica wondered, her voice seething with anger. "Is that what you're doing?"

Commander Telles stared at her a moment. "Our *friend* sacrificed himself so that everyone else could live...the two of us included. I am honoring his sacrifice by respecting it. I am honoring my loyalty to him by ensuring that his sacrifice is not in vain. I would suggest you stop thinking about yourself, and do the same."

"Is that an order, sir?"

"No, but I can make it one, if that would help."

More silence.

"That's what I thought," the commander added.

Jessica stiffened up again, looking straight ahead. "My orders, sir?"

"Like I said, take a week or two. Then report

to the ESF Training Command. You'll be teaching covert ops."

"Yes, sir. Is there anything else, sir?"

"Dismissed."

Jessica turned toward the door, but paused. "Care to tell me what Bowden's men are doing here?"

"Not that it's any of your business, Lieutenant Commander, but they are teaching us everything they know about the Jung."

"I see." Jessica thought for a moment. "Thank you, sir."

* * *

Commander Telles entered the briefing room and turned to the guard at the door. "Secure the room."

"Yes, sir," the guard replied, stepping out and closing the door behind him.

Commander Telles waited until he heard the tone from the control panel on the wall next to the door, indicating the room was sealed, and its sound-suppression system had been activated. He then turned his attention to the four men sitting in the room before him. They were dressed in typical Koharan clothing, were neatly groomed, and appeared physically fit, although not overtly so.

The commander turned to look at Lieutenant Commander Bowden, standing in the corner of the room next to Master Sergeant Jahal. "You trust these men?" he asked, getting straight to the point.

"I do," the lieutenant commander replied without reservation.

"With your life?"

"On many occasions. There are none I trust more."

"You will likely not see them again," the commander reminded him.

"Unfortunate, but understandable."

Master Sergeant Jahal touched his comm-set. "Understood," he replied. He looked at the commander. "Room is confirmed secure."

"Very well," the commander replied. He turned to face the four men sitting before him. "What is discussed in this room today shall not be shared with anyone, and you shall not discuss it amongst yourselves outside of a properly secured room, such as this one. Is that understood?"

All four men nodded in unison.

"The four of you have volunteered for an assignment that may, in fact, last the rest of your lives...be they long or short. You were offered this assignment because you are Jung."

"We *were* Jung, sir," one of the men interrupted.

The commander looked at him. "What is your name?"

"Masone. Reto Masone."

"You *are* Jung," the commander insisted. "All four of you were born on Jung worlds. You served on Jung ships."

"We had no choice at the time," Reto said, "but we no longer *serve* the Jung."

"I understand your change of loyalties, Mister Masone, and I applaud your decision," the commander replied. "However, I strongly recommend that you refrain from interrupting."

"Yes, sir."

Commander Telles took a breath before continuing. "I suggest you all become comfortable with the idea of being proper members of Jung society, as we plan to insert all four of you onto the Jung homeworld."

The four men looked at each other, their mouths agape.

Commander Telles looked at Lieutenant Commander Bowden. "I take it you did not tell them what they were volunteering for."

"I figured it was your place, Commander."

Commander Telles returned his attention to the four men seated before him, their mouths still hanging open. "I get the feeling you wish to say something, Mister Masone."

"You want to send us to Nor-Patri?"

"Correct."

"That's impossible."

"If it were impossible, we would not be proposing such an assignment," the commander replied.

"Even if you could get us to the surface, they will identify us the first time we walk past a data point. They'll arrest us within minutes."

"Nor-Patri is in chaos after our attack. Their data systems have been damaged, and it will take weeks, if not months, for their data point network to be fully operational once again. That should give you enough time to locate suitable targets to impersonate. Once you have found and eliminated those targets, you will remove their data chips and implant them in yourselves. From that point on, you should be able to walk freely on Nor-Patri without fear of discovery."

"You want us to kill innocent people?" another man asked.

"Regrettably, yes," the commander replied. "But it is the only way."

"And what is it you wish us to do on Nor-Patri?" Reto wondered.

"Intelligence gathering, nothing more."

"Isn't Nor-Patri sixty-five light years away? How do you expect us to communicate with you over such distances?"

"Sixty-three point eight, actually," the commander corrected. "And we are working on that."

"Just gather information, nothing else? No sabotage? No seeding of dissent?"

"Just observe and report," the commander promised.

"But the data points will notice our lack of nanites," Reto added. "That will raise suspicion..."

"You will be injected with special versions of the Jung nanites," the commander explained. "They can be read by the Jung data points, but their ability to replicate and take control of your bodies has been deactivated. Furthermore, you will be able to turn off their connections to your senses at will, so you can control what information your nanites gather and share with the data points."

"And if we become ill, or injured, they will inject us with fresh nanites."

"Your altered nanites will still protect you from illness and injury, to an extent. You will be given additional doses of the altered versions to be used as needed. With any luck, you will not need to be treated."

"And if we are not that lucky?" Reto asked.

"Then your mission will be over, and you will be free to live out your lives as you see fit."

"We denounced Jung society years ago," Reto said. "I, for one, do not wish to spend the rest of my days among them. Is there no chance of return?"

"Chance? Perhaps," the commander replied. "I do not wish to give you any false hopes. Truthfully, at this time, there is no plan in place for retrieval. However, the device that gets you *on* to Nor-Patri, could *theoretically* get you back *off* the surface as well."

"And what is this device?" Reto asked.

"The same one that delivered Lieutenant Commander Nash and her team to Kohara," Commander Telles replied as the display table behind him lit up. He stepped aside, revealing a rotating holographic image of a small submarine. "We call it a 'jump sub'. It is a Terran submarine, originally designed to transfer up to six persons, or cargo, between deep-sea complexes and the surface. Fitted with jump drives, they can deliver two occupants into a large body of water on a world as far as two light years away. We will use a jump cargo shuttle modified to carry the jump sub to its launch point, placing it on the proper course and speed. The sub will jump to Nor-Patri, coming out of its jump under the surface of one of the planet's oceans. After that, it is only a matter of driving the sub to the shore, leaving it at the bottom, and swimming the rest of the way in."

"And this sub can, *theoretically*, get us back?" Reto did not sound convinced.

"Their jump drives will have enough energy stored to complete two straight-line, fixed-length jumps of two light years each. Theoretically, you could return to the sub, drive her toward the surface at the proper angle, and jump from under the surface to a point two light years away, in space. The challenge would be in coordinating your retrieval. Since communications between you and Alliance Command would most likely be one way, even if you got word out that you needed retrieval, you would have no way of being certain that your request was received. If it was not, then you would die in space."

Reto exchanged looks of concern with his

comrades, then looked back at the commander. “And why would we do this?”

“For the same reason that you denounced the Jung,” Lieutenant Commander Bowden said. “For the same reason you suffered the agony of nanite cleansing. And, for the same reason you fought alongside me on Kohara for all those years. Because you believe that Jung dominance must come to an end.”

Reto looked at Lieutenant Commander Bowden, the man who had been his leader in the Koharan underground. The man who had believed them when they had denounced the Jung and asked for his help. He took a deep breath, then looked at Commander Telles. “How long do we have to prepare?”

“Three days.”

“Why so soon?”

“I would have you go now, but we need time to train you.”

“And you think three days will be enough?”

“We cannot afford to take any longer,” the commander explained. “If the data point network becomes operational before your arrival, your chances of success drop dramatically.”

Reto sighed. “Then perhaps we should get started, sir.”

A smile crept onto the commander’s face.

* * *

Jessica walked quietly into the small room her father had added onto their modest home for baby Ania. Her parents had jumped at the chance to adopt the orphaned child, not only for the infant’s sake, but for the sake of their daughter. It had torn Jessica apart to see her friend die, just when Synda had finally found happiness. Knowing that her friend's only surviving child, Ania, would grow up surrounded by people who cared for her, was almost enough to keep Jessica going.

Almost.

But the loss of Nathan was too much for her. Everyone was telling her to move on, to respect Nathan's sacrifice for the unselfish act that it was. He had singlehandedly brought an end to the war, saving billions of lives in a single moment. But it was unfair. The Jung had brought their destruction upon themselves. Not one of the worlds they had conquered had posed a threat to them. Not one. The one world that had come the closest was Earth, itself, and only because they had learned of the presence of the Jung and did not wish to become enslaved, as well. What right did the Jung Empire have to demand Nathan's surrender as recompense for the Alliance's retaliatory attack on their homeworld?

No, she could not accept it.

Jessica stood there for the longest time, watching baby Ania asleep in her crib. Every fiber in her being told her to hold the child close to her heart, and protect it with her life. But she still had work to do, despite the admiral's attempt to isolate her on Porto Santo Island. She would find a way to take action, or to rally others to take action on their own. Nathan would have done no less for her.

Jessica turned and headed back out of the room and into the living room. She moved over to the table and picked up the remote, activating the view screen on the wall. Using the remote, she scrolled through selections on the screen, finally finding the contact she was looking for. The screen beeped several times as the comm-system attempted to make a connection. In short order, her call was answered.

"*NAU Capital Exchange. How may I direct your call?*" the voice inquired.

"This is Lieutenant Commander Jessica Nash, of the Sol-Pentaurus Alliance. I wish to speak to President Scott."

"*One moment, Lieutenant Commander.*"

A moment later, another voice came on the line. "*Lieutenant Commander Nash, your identification code, please,*" a male voice requested.

"Alpha five one seven five, tango two one seven one, foxtrot two five seven five."

"*One moment.*"

Jessica waited patiently, glancing out the window, half expecting a security squad to show up at any moment.

"*I'm sorry, sir,*" the voice finally continued. "*The president is not able to take your call.*"

"Unable, or unwilling," Jessica mumbled.

"*Sir?*"

"How about his aide, Miranda Thornton?"

"*She is also unavailable at the moment. Would you like her to return your call when she is free?*" the man inquired politely.

"Yes, please," Jessica replied, knowing full well that a return call was unlikely.

"*I will pass the message on to her, sir. Is there anything else I can do for you, sir?*"

"Negative," Jessica replied, disconnecting the call. Jessica sighed. She would call again tomorrow, and the next day, and every day thereafter, until someone responded, or until the commander ordered her to stop calling. Even then, she would most likely continue.

After all, Nathan would have done the same for her.

* * *

It was the first time he had been allowed to wear his uniform since his surrender. It had been cleaned and neatly pressed, and it looked as crisp as if it had come directly from the Aurora's laundry.

Nathan wondered why the Jung had chosen to have him in uniform for his appearance. His question had been answered the moment he saw the dress uniforms of the Jung officers as he was led into the courtroom. Black, with red and gold piping, adorned with all manner of medals and embroidery. Even with the gold trim, his dress grays paled in comparison. The Jung were masters of propaganda, a fact the Alliance had learned from the Koharans.

Nathan was led down the center aisle of the grand courtroom. It was a massive, circular room, with rows of seats filled with spectators who surrounded the center arena, stretching upward so that every seat had a clear view of the proceedings. In the middle of the room, twelve men in robes sat evenly spaced around the perimeter. On the next inward level, there were several desks and chairs, at which sat various legal teams. Finally, in the center, at the lowest point in the room, was what Nathan thought of as 'the pit'. It was here that the guards led him.

Nathan stepped down into the pit. The guards stepped back, and a restraining field shimmered to life. After a few seconds, the field stabilized and the shimmering stopped. Nathan looked at the hatred in the eyes of those in attendance. He hoped the shield worked both ways.

A man in uniform stood at one of the desks and stepped out toward Nathan. He turned to face each of the men in robes—men who Nathan perceived to be judges—as he spoke. A few seconds after the man began to speak, a voice began speaking to Nathan in near-perfect English. He looked around, wondering where the translation was coming from, but saw no one he could recognize as speaking. Either it was being piped into the pit from a translator located outside of the courtroom, or it was being translated by a computer. Either way, the words were ominous.

"*The Empire charges Captain Nathan Scott, formerly of the Earth Defense Force, and currently of the Sol-Pentaurus Alliance, with attempted genocide.*"

The room exploded with cheers. The show had begun.

CHAPTER THREE

Reto stepped up to the access tube in the floor, put one foot forward, and stepped off, falling down into the smooth, narrow tunnel. The artificial gravity of the specially outfitted boxcar, that was now on course for the Jung homeworld, pulled Reto downward into the access tube. As he passed through the lower section of the tube, the effects of the boxcar's artificial gravity lessened, and his brief acceleration ceased, leaving him coasting downward at a comfortable pace.

Moments later, Reto found himself entering the docking bay, feet first. He passed through the small bay, and his feet touched the top of the jump sub's black hull. Now in a weightless environment, he easily maneuvered himself, passing through the jump sub's narrow topside hatch and down into the tiny ship.

The inside of the jump sub was cramped, with barely enough space for two men, in addition to the equipment they required to get from the small, jump-enabled submarine to the shore once they reached their destination. Reto entered feet first, turning so that his feet pointed forward as he lowered into the ship. He pulled himself into the pilot's seat, then reached back and released the seat latch, allowing the back of the seat to spring back upright, making room for the passenger.

Reto tapped the side of his comm-set. "I'm in." Moments later, Armin descended into the seat behind him. He reached up and activated the hatch control, and the inner hatch slid closed, sealing with a slight hiss of compressed air. A clanging sound followed as the outer hatch did the same. Armin glanced at the pressure display on the side wall to his left. "Hatches are closed and locked. Internal pressure is good. You're clear to retract the docking bay."

"*Copy, clear to retract,*" the voice replied over their comm-sets.

They heard another clang. Reto looked through the tiny porthole directly over his head and watched as the docking collar rose away from them, retracting back toward the underside of the modified boxcar.

"*Last jump in ten seconds,*" the voice announced over their comm-sets.

"All systems show ready," Reto reported, after quickly scanning his control console. The rebuilt jump sub's control console was much the same as it had been during its time as a transfer sub in Earth's oceans. The only notable difference was the jump drive control interface, which was nothing more than a small touch screen mounted along the top edge of the console. Controlled by a computer in the aft compartment, the interface was a status display, and a button that read 'Jump'. It was simple enough to operate; the hard part would be trusting the technology to jump them from the outer edges of the Jung home system, across two full light years of space, and place them a few hundred meters under the surface of one of Nor-Patri's many oceans. Everything had to be exact. Their course, their speed...and the empty space between them and their destination. Anything bigger than a human head would cause the jump fields to fail, and allow the object to slam into them. They would not survive such an impact.

Of course, if it did happen, neither of them would ever know it. Death would be instantaneous. No one would know what had happened to them, as their ship would likely be vaporized by the combination of the kinetic energy of the impact and the sudden destabilization of the jump fields. There would be guesses as to their final fate, but no physical evidence.

If that were not enough reason for any man to refuse the journey, the oceans of Nor-Patri, while numerous, were nowhere near as large as the oceans of Earth, requiring an even greater degree of accuracy. From such a distance, a single thousandth of a degree could cause their tiny ship to slam into solid ground, resulting in a noticeable impact event on the Jung homeworld...one that would be difficult to explain, as there would be little to no proof of their ship's existence.

Reto tried not to think of the myriad of ways that their lives could come to an end in the next sixty seconds.

Sixty seconds. He had never understood the Terran system of measuring time. Sixty seconds in a minute. Sixty minutes in an hour. But then, for some strange reason, twenty-four hours in a day. Even Kohara had a similar system for measuring the passing of time. The Jung method, being base ten, was so much easier.

"*Jump complete,*" the voice reported. "*Releasing docking clamps.*"

As their ship was released and began to separate from the boxcar, Reto briefly thought about the other jump sub being delivered from the opposite side of the Jung system in a few hours. The two men in that ship, just like Armin sitting behind him, had been his friends for the last fifteen years. In Reto's mind, the hardest part about this mission was the fact that he would likely never see his friends again.

"*Course and speed are right on target,*" the controller from the boxcar stated. "*Out of short-range secure comms in twenty seconds. Good luck, gentlemen.*"

"Thanks," Reto replied. A bright flash of blue-white light lit up the small portholes on the jump sub, briefly filling the interior with its ghostly glow. Reto looked outside after the flash subsided. As expected, the boxcar that had jumped them deep into Jung space and placed them on what they hoped was a perfect intercept trajectory, was now gone. Reto sighed. "There's no turning back now, Armin." He looked warily at the jump button. His mind was filled with trepidation. Pushing the button could mean an instantaneous death. However, not pushing the button meant slow, lingering death, in the bitter cold of space.

"Let's do it," Armin urged him from the back seat.

"Activating the jump sequencer," Reto announced as he pressed the button. "Jumping in five...... four......three......two......one......"

Both men closed their eyes tightly as the jump flash filled the cramped interior of the jump sub. They were thrown forward against their restraints, the straps digging into their shoulders and waists as the jump sub suddenly transitioned from the void of deep space to the oceans of Nor-Patri. They had been traveling at only a few meters per second when they had jumped...practically a standstill by comparison. But it had been more than enough. It was an abrupt arrival to say the least, but at least they had made it...alive.

The resistance of the water brought them to a

stop, and the tension on their restraints eased. Reto glanced at the console. "Three hundred thirty-seven meters." He activated the sub's propulsion and navigation systems, as well as its terrain and obstacle avoidance sensors. The ship began to move forward. "Propulsion and navigation are online. Time to debarkation point; four hours and twenty-seven minutes, Terran time."

"Guess that's the last time we'll be using the Terran clock," Armin commented.

Reto smiled. They had done what most would not believe possible, and had survived. However, there were still many more ways for them to die, both under the water, and once they made it to dry land.

Their mission had only just begun.

* * *

Jessica stood in the nursery, staring at baby Ania asleep in her crib. As she watched the infant breathe, she heard a creak from the door behind her. She turned slightly to see who was entering. Her eyes widened, and her mouth fell open, as she saw Nathan entering the room. "I thought you were in a Jung prison cell," she whispered in shock.

"They let me out for good behavior," Nathan replied in hushed tones, as he quietly closed the door behind him.

"What?"

"I'm kidding, Jess." Nathan walked over to stand next to her. "I broke out. Killed the guard with my bare hands, just like you would have."

"What?" Jessica repeated, still in complete disbelief.

"I'm kidding again, Jess. This is a dream. I'm not really here. *You're* not really here." Nathan looked around the room, a puzzled look on his face. "To be honest, I'm not even sure where *here* is. What is this place? It looks like a twelve year-old girl's bedroom."

Jessica also looked around, realizing for the first time that she was not in the nursery her father had added onto their Porto Santo home for baby Ania. "Wait a minute. This is my room. I mean, it *was* my room, when I was *twelve*."

"Interesting," Nathan commented as he looked around. "I wonder what you looked like at that age. Did you already have... You know..." Nathan cupped his hands in front of his chest, as if holding a pair of breasts.

"Watch it, or I'll wake up and *you'll* be back in a Jung prison cell." Jessica looked at Ania again. "Besides, there's a child present."

"How is she doing?" Nathan asked, embarrassed that he had not yet asked.

"She's fine," Jessica replied. "She's lucky. She's so young, she'll probably never remember anything, not even her real parents."

"But you'll tell her, right?"

"Of course, I'll tell her," Jessica replied. "When she's older. She should know the truth...especially about the Jung."

"Are you sure about that?" Nathan wondered.

"My parents never hid anything from us when we were growing up, and I'm not going to hide anything from Ania, either."

Nathan looked down at the sleeping baby girl. "It seems a shame to burden an innocent child with such horrific truths."

"The galaxy is full of horrific truths, Nathan," Jessica replied. "You should know that better than anyone." Jessica looked back down at Ania. "I don't want her to grow up with any delusions that everything is fair and just. It will be too painful when she finds out that the universe isn't fair."

"Just don't make her too jaded," Nathan warned.

"I just don't want her to have any false hopes."

"Hope is what gives us strength, Jess," Nathan explained. "It's what gets us out of bed each morning. It's what keeps us alive."

Jessica looked at Nathan. "Is that *really* what you believe?"

"Yes," Nathan replied without hesitation. "Yes, it is."

"Even though you're sitting in a prison cell, facing certain execution?"

"Yes."

Jessica sighed. "How can you possibly have any hope left, Nathan?"

"My hope is not for my own survival, Jess. It's for the survival of my world. For you, little Ania...all of you. That's why I surrendered to the Jung. To give you all a chance."

"You were tricked," Jessica insisted.

"I wasn't tricked, Jess." Nathan argued. "I knew Bacca was setting me up to save his own reputation. I saw it for what it was; an opportunity. And I seized it. It's as simple as that."

"It isn't fair," Jessica said, looking back down at Ania. "You don't deserve to die."

"No one deserves to die, Jess. But it *is* the one inescapable truth in life...that we must *all* die. I simply chose to die now, in order to save others. And I'm okay with that."

Jessica looked at Nathan. "Well, I'm not. And I never will be."

"You need to let me go, Jessica. You need to get

on with your own life. If not for your own sake, then for Ania's."

"I can't," Jessica whispered. "I won't. I will find a way to save you, Nathan."

"Jess, I'm locked up in what is definitely the most secure facility on the entire Jung homeworld, sixty-something light years from Earth. Anyone who tries to rescue me will not only die in the attempt, but they will likely trigger exactly what I was trying to prevent...an all-out war between the Jung and the Alliance."

Jessica turned away, unable to look at him. Nathan put his fingers under her chin, forcing her to look him in the eyes.

"Be happy, Jess. I am."

"But..."

"Let me go... It's the only way."

Nathan faded away, disappearing in front of her. Jessica's eyes welled up with tears. "I can't," she whispered, still looking where he had been standing a moment ago. "I can't."

* * *

After parting company with Armin, it had taken Reto three days to make his way from the shore into the nearest city on Nor-Patri's main, largest continent. The size and proximity of the Jung's once largest moon, Zhu-Anok, had such a dramatic effect on the planet's tides that no cities were ever built along the planet's ocean shores. Not even on those of her largest lakes. The only exceptions were two floating cities located in the middle latitudes.

Of course, the tides were no more, just as Zhu-Anok was no more. All that was left of the massive, gray ball that had always loomed over one third of Nor-Patri's sky was a ring of debris that was slowly making its way around the Jung homeworld. In the daytime, it was nothing more than a faint shadow that sliced across an otherwise brilliant, topaz sky. But at night, it was visible. A collection of rock, dust, and building debris that twinkled like the distant stars. Some large, some small.

On this night, like many others, the sky was decorated by streaks of light as debris blown too close to Nor-Patri burned up while passing through its atmosphere. Most of the pieces large enough to reach the ground had already done so, often times with devastating consequences. That which had not yet found its way to low orbit was in the process of being cleaned up by what remained of the Jung home fleet.

Reto had never been on the Jung homeworld. Like most others in service of the Jung, he had been born and raised on one of the empire's many worlds. However, having served for more than a decade before deserting and joining the Koharan resistance, he knew as much about the customs of Nor-Patri as any native. On every world the Jung conquered, they forced the locals to adhere to Jung customs and to speak the Jung language. Those who served with distinction were allowed to reside on Nor-Patri upon completion of their service. It was the dream of every loyal member of the Jung warrior caste; to someday live on the Jung homeworld.

For Reto, it seemed more a punishment than a reward. This world reeked of all that he had come to despise over the decades. He had little enthusiasm for the empire as a lad, and even less after a decade of forced service. He had always found it odd that an empire that considered itself so superior to every other form of government out there, could only achieve greatness by forcing its own people to serve. A truly great empire would not need to require service. It would instead, *inspire* such service.

Reto sat on the side of the road, watching people go about their daily lives. The city of Oretza, itself, seemed grimy and unkempt, although Reto suspected that it was not always so. The people here wore nice clothing, although most appeared to not have washed their attire in several days. Like most cities on Nor-Patri, Oretza was just now starting to get its basic infrastructure back on line. The debris from the breakup of Zhu-Anok had caused so much destruction, it would be decades before the Jung homeworld would return to normal, if ever. They could rebuild, yes. But no one really knew what the long-term effect would be on the planet's ecosystem, now that the mighty Zhu-Anok was no longer dragging Nor-Patri's waters up and down her shores.

Reto watched as broadcast drones drifted overhead, their massive holographic displays streaming images from all over the planet. And, of course, every hour, like clockwork, it showed images of the first day of the trial of the war criminal, Nathan Scott. It gave the people a target for their anger. Blame was a powerful tool. It absolved the masses of their sins of indifference, but more importantly, it brought them together, using hatred to seal those bonds.

Put roofs over their heads, clothes on their backs, and food in their bellies, and they'll believe anything you tell them. Reto was disgusted by these ignorant masses. If they should be angry at anyone, it should be at their leaders for allowing such a catastrophe to happen in the first place. All civilization had spawned from Earth more than a thousand years ago. To think that the cradle of humanity would simply roll over and allow itself to be conquered by one of her errant children was ludicrous, naive, and altogether arrogant.

Or was it Reto who was fooling himself? Was he making himself believe that these people were as much to blame as the Jung leaders, or the Sol-Pentaurus Alliance? He was, after all, about to kill one of them for his own purposes. *A shopkeeper, a teacher, a laborer? Would the man whose life he took this day have a family? Would anyone miss him?*

Reto put the thoughts out of his mind. He had a job to do. He continued looking, until he spotted a man sitting on the other side of the plaza. The man looked forlorn, as if all had been taken from him. Reto moved toward him, pushing his way through the line of people waiting for their daily rations of food and water. When he reached the downtrodden man, he sat down on the ground next to him, acting as if he was too tired to stand a moment longer.

Reto sighed as he sat down, acting relieved for a bit of rest. He looked at the people standing in line in the street, shaking his head. "Is it always like this?" Reto asked the forlorn man.

"As far as I know, yes," the man replied.

"I am Jorbar," Reto said.

"Coln," the man replied halfheartedly.

"Why do you sit here?" Reto wondered. "Shouldn't you be in line?"

"What's the point?" Coln replied.

"You don't wish to eat? To drink?"

Coln looked at Reto. "I have nothing to live for. I lost everything."

"We all lost something, or someone," Reto replied, feigning support.

"My wife, my children, my business. They are all gone," the man sobbed. "I wish Zhu-Anok would strike me down this day, to end my suffering."

Reto tried to hide his smile. Coln did not know it at the moment, but his wish to die was about to be granted. Only it would not be Zhu-Anok that would strike him down.

* * *

Commander Telles stood on the observation tower's upper deck, his eyes fixed on the urban combat training before him. Below, Lieutenant Commander Nash was putting her first group of Alliance Marines Spec-Ops through their daily training regimen. The commander watched as she barked out orders to stop the simulation, then stepped out onto the training area to reposition the trainees, pointing out their failures to adhere to the basic techniques she was attempting to ingrain in them.

Master Sergeant Jahal stepped up onto the deck and approached his commander. As he reached the rail, he looked down at the lieutenant commander, as well. "I see her demeanor has yet to change."

"Indeed," the commander agreed.

"Perhaps it is for the best. She needs the release."

"But for how long?"

Master Sergeant Jahal sighed.

"In short order, this pattern of behavior may become permanent."

"Yelling at trainees is part of the job," the master sergeant reminded him.

"When appropriate, yes," the commander agreed, "but she barks at them incessantly, and in doing so, fails to provide positive reinforcement when they perform correctly."

"It has only been a week," the master sergeant said optimistically.

"A very long week," the commander added. "I fear she may require special handling."

Master Sergeant Jahal cast a sidelong glance at his old friend. "Are you proposing what I *think* you're proposing?"

"She is headed for a complete crash. She has been ever since she returned from Kohara, and Captain Scott's surrender has only made things worse."

"She is not qualified," the master sergeant said.

"No, she is not," the commander agreed, "at least, not by traditional standards." Commander Telles finally took his eyes off of the events below, and turned to look at his trusted subordinate. "But times have changed, Elam. The house that founded the Ghatazhak is no more, and the man whom you and I were programmed to protect is facing certain execution." Telles looked back out across the base, beyond the training compound below him. "Our numbers have dwindled to the lowest in history, and now we have been relegated to teach others to be a mere shadow of what we are."

"You owe her nothing, Lucius," the master sergeant reminded him, "and without refresh, our programming is no longer binding. I, for one, no longer feel its pull."

"Does that mean our word is no longer binding?"

Elam nodded his concession.

"He would want us to keep her safe."

The master sergeant laughed. "Training her in the ways of the Ghatazhak is hardly keeping her safe. If anything, it is putting her in harm's way."

"She is headed that way regardless," the commander said. "She always has been. It is in her very nature. If that *is* what she is meant to do, then at least we will be giving her a chance to survive that which the future holds for her."

"And at the same time, we would be opening up options for the Ghatazhak," the master sergeant realized.

"If one does not adapt to change, and embrace the opportunities that change presents, one surely withers and dies."

Again, the master sergeant sighed. "You would be changing the very face of the Ghatazhak. Creating a completely new set of logistics for us to deal with."

"She is only one female," the commander replied. "And she may not even agree to commit to the training. Even if she does, she may not complete it."

"Oh, she'll complete it," the master sergeant said. "She is too stubborn to do otherwise." Elam thought for a moment. "You tried to train her before, did you not? If I remember correctly, it did not go as hoped."

"I only tried to introduce her to the basic tenants of self-control," the commander explained. "She was receptive to the training, for a short time. Unfortunately, the Jung attacked Tanna, after which she was no longer receptive."

"And what makes you think that she will be more receptive now?" the master sergeant wondered. "If anything, she is more distressed."

"All the more reason she should commit to the training. It is the only way for her to save herself. Besides, I will make her an offer that she cannot refuse."

"And what might that offer be?" the master sergeant wondered. "Or, is it better that I do not know?"

"For now, yes," the commander replied, as he

turned his attention back to Jessica and her trainees below. "But you shall know soon enough."

* * *

"How is he today?" Mister Sosna asked Miri as she entered the president's office to lay out his daily briefings.

"Same, I'm afraid," she replied, as she placed the data pads on his desk, and arranged them in order of priority. "He's still on autopilot."

"Do you think he will ever be the same?"

"He's lost his eldest son, his wife, and may lose his only remaining son...what do you think?" she snapped. Miri paused, regaining her composure. "I apologize. It has been a difficult week." She looked at the president's chief bodyguard. "He will survive this. We all will. It will not be pleasant. But we will survive. We have no other choice."

"Of course." Mister Sosna paused, listening to the message in his earpiece. "He will be here shortly."

Miri moved away from her father's desk, standing off to the side as she always did when he first arrived in the morning. Mister Sosna went to the side door of the president's office and held it open, another message alerting him that the president was in the outer corridor.

President Scott entered the office without speaking a word. He had said little more than what the position required of him during the last week, ever since his youngest son, Nathan, had surrendered himself to the Jung.

The president took his seat and picked up the first data pad, skimming the contents on its display, but not really reading it. He repeated the process with each subsequent data pad, until he had reached the last one. After the final scan, he placed it on his desk and sighed. "I just read them all, and remember nothing."

Miri looked at Mister Sosna who, taking the hint, left the room and closed the door behind him.

President Scott looked at his youngest daughter. "What am I to do, Miri?"

"You will do what you always do," she replied calmly. "The right thing."

"Even if the right thing is to leave my son in the hands of our enemy? Even if the right thing is to let him die? Is that what a father does?"

"It is what a president does, if need be," Miri replied.

"Even if it destroys him inside?" the president asked, looking at his daughter.

Miri stepped closer, putting her hand on his shoulder, just as the intercom beeped.

"*Mister President, incoming message from Admiral Dumar,*" the voice on the intercom announced.

"Put him on," the president replied, pressing the intercom button.

The view screen on the wall directly in front of the president's desk came to life, and the image of Admiral Dumar appeared. The admiral was sitting in his office on the Karuzara asteroid base, high in orbit over Earth. The admiral was never an animated man, but on this morning, his face looked more solemn than usual.

"Admiral Dumar," the president greeted curtly, not wanting to engage in conversation.

"*Mister President. I am happy to report that the Jung have decided to take advantage of our offer to maintain constant diplomatic communications via scheduled, secure, jump comm-drone message relays.*"

"Then I take it you have received your first message from them?"

"*Two messages, actually. The first, acceptance of our terms of communication...*" Admiral Dumar paused, seeming hesitant to continue.

"And the second message?" the president inquired, sensing the admiral's reluctance.

"*The second message was word that Captain Scott has been charged with attempted genocide against the Jung people. The trial is to begin in a few days.*"

"And the punishment for such an offense?"

"*We know little of the Jung legal system,*" the admiral admitted. "*However, I suspect the penalty is most severe.*"

"Thank you, Admiral," the president replied. "Please keep me posted if you receive any new information."

"*Of course, Mister President.*"

President Scott picked up the remote and ended the call, turning the view screen off. Miri watched him nervously, unsure of what to say. "Father?"

He looked up at her, his eyes welling up. "Please, leave me to my grief."

Miri wanted to say something to ease her father's pain, but could not find the words. "I'll be outside if you need me," she finally replied. She kissed him on the forehead, then left the office.

* * *

Jessica sat on the back porch of her parents' home on Porto Santo Island, watching the sun sink into the ocean while she nursed a cold beer. It had become part of her evening routine, after a long day of yelling at spec-ops trainees. Get home, leave another message with the president's office that would go unanswered, then numb herself with alcohol in the hopes that she might not be visited by Nathan in her dreams. It never seemed to work, though. Nathan came to her every night, and he always told her the same thing...to let go. And she always refused.

What troubled her most, this night, was that she was beginning to think her dreams were right.

"Got one for me?" a familiar male voice called from the kitchen door.

Jessica reached down to the bucket of ice sitting on the patio next to her, pulled out a bottle of beer, and held it up for him, without looking back at her older brother.

"That's all the greeting I get?" Robert asked.

"It hasn't been that long, Robert," Jessica replied, taking another sip from her bottle.

"Forty-one, forty-two days?" Robert opened his bottle and took a long drink. "Ahh. We don't have this on board the Tanna, that's for sure." He looked at the bottle, not recognizing the label. "Where do you get this?"

"It's brewed locally," Jessica replied as she continued to watch the sunset. The big, orange sun was halfway into the ocean.

"I didn't know they brewed beer on Porto Santo."

"The island is full of scrub marines now. It was only a matter of time." Jessica took a deep breath, letting it out slowly. "You know, when I was little, I used to wake up early and sneak out before sunrise. I'd walk down the street to the beach, and watch the sun slowly rise up out of the water. I always thought that if the waves wouldn't make so much noise, I might be able to hear the water boiling around the sun as it rose up out of the ocean. It was magical."

"Everything is magical when you're young."

Jessica took another drink of her beer. "You come to tell me to let go as well?"

"Nope. I learned long ago that it was a waste of time trying to tell *you* what to do, Jess."

"So, Telles or Dumar didn't send you?"

"We're getting resupplied," Robert told her. "We'll be in orbit for a few days, then we're going back to Tau Ceti to have some additional plasma turrets installed."

"So, you haven't heard how I've been beatin' up trainees?"

"Oh, I've heard all right. I just wasn't planning on bringing it up." Robert took another sip of beer. "But, since you brought it up..."

"Relax, they can take it," Jessica assured him, also taking another swig off her bottle. "If they can't, they don't belong in spec-ops."

"I expect you would know."

Jessica finally turned to look at her brother.

"I just mean, I imagine you ran afoul of a few instructors during your time in the academy."

"I was a perfect cadet," she said defensively.

"Right."

They sat in silence for several minutes, downing another round as they watched the sun disappear completely into the ocean. After a few more minutes of sitting in the darkness, Jessica finally spoke.

"I'm thinking about resigning," she said in hushed tones.

Robert said nothing.

Jessica turned and looked at him again. "Aren't you going to ask why?"

"I figured you'd tell me if you wanted me to know, whether I asked or not."

Jessica sat silently in the darkness for a few more

minutes before speaking again. "I've lost the desire. My heart's just not in it, anymore."

Robert could tell by his little sister's tone that she was upset by that fact. "It's nothing to be ashamed of, Jess. You did more for the people of Earth...hell, for people from all over the galaxy, than most people do in a lifetime of service. I doubt anyone would speak ill of you if you quit." Robert downed the last of his beer. "Especially since you'd kick their ass if they did."

Jessica said nothing, only sighed.

Robert rose from his seat, placing the empty bottle on the patio rail. "Just do us both a favor, Jess. Think about it for a while. All things change with time. This one may, as well."

She looked at him again. "I don't think so, Robert."

Robert reached down and pulled the last bottle out of the ice bucket, opened it, and handed it to his sister. "Give it another week...for me."

Jessica sighed again as her brother went back into the house, then started to work on the last bottle for the night.

* * *

It had been nearly two weeks since Nathan had been formally charged in the Jung courts. Two weeks of poor sleep, lousy food, and endless interrogations by, not only Jung intelligence, but also the prosecution. It seemed odd to him that today was the first time he had seen his own advocate since his first appearance in the Jung Hall of Justice.

Mister Gorus sat quietly across the table from Nathan, studying the documents on his data pad. His face was expressionless, his only tell being the occasional rubbing of his chin, although Nathan had no idea *what* it was telling of.

"So," Nathan finally began, "am I screwed?"

Mister Gorus looked puzzled. "Screwed?"

"Screwed...as in 'big trouble, with no way out.'"

"I see. Then yes, you are indeed *screwed.*" Mister Gorus set his data pad down. "Of course, you have been since the moment you surrendered."

Nathan sighed. "I don't get it. Your own people, time and again, have taken the position that they were just following orders, expecting to receive absolution because of it. Yet *I* am not to be given that same dispensation?"

"Are you saying that one of your superiors *ordered* you to fire on Nor-Patri?" Mister Gorus inquired, his demeanor remaining calm.

"My orders were to do whatever was necessary to show the Jung leadership that the Alliance could quite easily attack them right where they live."

"To what end?"

"In the hopes that the Jung people would insist on the withdrawal of Jung forces from the Sol sector. You see, human history is replete with examples of civilian populations that supported the use of military force to ensure their national interests, when such actions took place on foreign lands, but failed to support those actions when they resulted in attacks on their *own* lands."

"I'm afraid your plan backfired," Mister Gorus said. "If anything, it made those castes who do not support expansion, especially when it involves the use of military force, mute for fear of retaliation by the other castes. Your attack galvanized the castes, as well as the general population thereof. *Everyone* on Nor-Patri wishes to see the Earth destroyed. It is actually quite surprising that they are willing to settle for your public execution alone. Were it not for the influence of the anti-expansionist castes, every ship in the fleet would be on its way to Earth this very moment."

"Which would result in the immediate destruction of Nor-Patri, as well as many other Jung-occupied worlds in the Jung sector," Nathan reminded him.

"Such statements will not gain you sympathy among the arbiters," Mister Gorus warned. "They do not care for ultimatums."

"Odd, since your people seem so fond of issuing them, as well as carrying out the penalty when those ultimatums are ignored," Nathan added thoughtfully.

"I ask again," Mister Gorus said, remaining calm, and ignoring Nathan's statements. "Did any of your superiors order you to launch a kinetic energy weapon against Nor-Patri?"

"No, they did not," Nathan replied. "But I did not launch the weapon against Nor-Patri. I launched it against Zhu-Anok."

"Were you not required to study basic physics at the EDF Academy?"

"Of course."

"Then, you were aware that, given the proximity, a strike of such magnitude against Zhu-Anok represented a significant threat to Nor-Patri as well, were you not?"

"Yes, I was aware of the risk. However, the trajectory of the weapon *should* have sent the debris field *away* from Nor-Patri, not toward it. It was the detonation of the reactors deep inside Zhu-Anok that sent debris on a collision course with your world, not the impact of our kinetic kill vehicle."

"You were not aware that there were reactors within Zhu-Anok? Where did you think the power that ran the facility was coming from?"

"Of course I knew there had to be a power source on that moon. But I had no way of knowing the amount of energy contained within, nor the pattern of release when our weapon struck."

"Yet, you still gave the order to launch the weapon."

"Yes, I did," Nathan admitted, realizing that the statement would be the final nail in his coffin.

Mister Gorus leaned back in his chair a moment, thinking. "My best advice, Captain Scott, is to stand tall and take full responsibility for your actions."

"You want me to admit that I'm guilty?"

"Yes, I do."

"I brought no more destruction upon your world, than your people did upon mine. *Definitely* not as much as your people brought upon Tanna."

"Irrelevant."

"How is that irrelevant?" Nathan demanded in exasperation.

"It is the Jung way. The strong take from the weak. The fact that we offer the weak an opportunity to live, under Jung rule is, in itself, an act of mercy. We are not responsible if the population of a world chooses death over life under Jung rule. It is their choice."

Nathan shook his head. "That is the most twisted logic I have ever heard."

"Perhaps, from your perspective, it is. But not from ours."

"And you agree with this philosophy?"

"What I, or any other person believes is also irrelevant," Mister Gorus dismissed.

"Governments are supposed to be representative of the wishes of the people they govern," Nathan said.

Mister Gorus placed his hands together on the

table. "Over the centuries, the Jung came to realize that *the people*, of which you speak, only cared about two things. Survival, and sustenance. As long as those two basic needs are met, they are willing to accept that many atrocities are necessary to ensure the ongoing provision of those two basic necessities."

"History is also replete with examples of empires with similar philosophies, all of which fell either under their own weight, or at the hands of a disenfranchised population."

"Earth history, perhaps," Mister Gorus responded.

"*Human* history, Mister Gorus." Nathan looked the old advocate squarely in the eyes. "Someday, the Jung Empire will fall."

"Perhaps," Mister Gorus admitted. "However, I doubt that either of us will be around to witness its demise."

* * *

Jessica followed the Ghatazhak corporal down the dimly lit corridor. "I'm not familiar with this building," she said. "What did you say it was called?"

"I didn't, sir," the corporal replied. Like every other Ghatazhak she had ever dealt with, the man revealed only what was required of him.

Jessica glanced at the signs on the doors on either side of the corridor. They showed only numbers. She also noticed that the doors were not the usual composite construction. They all had sealing frames, like the ones in the interrogation rooms over in the base detention center. She remembered similar door frames back at the fleet academy where she had trained. They had been used to seal off soundproof rooms, where covert methodologies had been taught to spec-ops cadets. While it was not surprising that such facilities existed here on Porto Santo, she was curious why she had been brought into such a building.

"Where are we going?" Jessica asked.

"The commander requested that I bring you to see him," the corporal replied.

"You already told me that," Jessica said.

"I'm sorry, sir. That is all that I am authorized to tell you."

Jessica rolled her eyes.

The Ghatazhak corporal finally stopped, opening up one of the doors and taking up a guard position outside of it. "Sir," the corporal said, nodding toward the open door.

Her left eyebrow went up as she looked at the corporal and entered the room. As soon as she stepped inside, the corporal reached in and pulled the door closed behind her, locking it.

Sitting on the edge of the conference table in front of her was Commander Telles, his usual, unreadable expression adorning his face. He said nothing, waiting until he received confirmation over his comm-set that the room had been sealed and their conversation would be truly private. "Lieutenant Commander," he finally acknowledged, nodding.

"You wanted to see me, sir?"

Commander Telles could tell how difficult it was for her to use the word. These days, it seemed that everything about wearing the uniform was difficult for her. And he was not the only one who had noticed it. His right-hand man, Master Sergeant Jahal had commented on her struggles as well. "Yes."

"In a secure room?"

"It seemed appropriate," the commander replied, "considering the topics we have to discuss."

"Why is it I don't like the sound of that," Jessica commented dryly.

"Please, sit," the commander insisted, pointing to a nearby chair.

Jessica looked at him for a moment.

"Please, Jessica."

The commander was not one to use first names, which made Jessica even more suspicious. Finally, she grabbed the chair and pulled it over, taking a seat. "What's this about?"

"Your demeanor as of late has been, shall we say, less enthusiastic than we had hoped."

"*Enthusiastic*?" Jessica almost laughed. "You're asking a bit much, don't you think?"

"No, I don't," the commander replied.

Jessica looked the commander square in the eyes. "I do my job," she said coldly.

"Yes," the commander agreed. "But your heart is not in your work."

"My heart? I didn't ask for this assignment, you know."

"I am aware of that fact. Nevertheless, something must change."

"Why? If I'm doing my job..."

"If you continue in this fashion, your anger will eventually be your undoing," the commander said.

Jessica stared at him. "You don't know *anything* about *my* anger," she scowled.

"Your response proves my point. If you do not take steps to resolve the conflicts within you..."

Jessica stood suddenly. "My only *conflict* is with this damned alliance. What kind of an alliance lets its founder rot in an enemy prison?"

"Jess..."

"Nathan saved us all. Corinair, Takara, Earth...

the core worlds. If it wasn't for Nathan, the Jung would control this entire sector, and you'd still be killing innocent people in the name of Caius Ta'Akar!"

"No one is disputing this," the commander reminded her.

"But no one is lifting a finger to save him, are they! Not the Alliance, not you, not even his own father," she added, throwing up her arms, turning away and kicking her chair over.

"This is exactly the kind of behavior that concerns me."

"What the hell do you want me to do?" she cried out. "It's all I can do to put this damned uniform on each morning! If it wasn't for Ania..."

"Exactly," the commander said. "For Ania. For that little girl, I want you to face your own shortcomings. I want you to overcome them. To become better than you ever thought you could be."

Jessica shook her head, confused. "What are you talking about?" she asked, tears welling up in her eyes.

"You have so much potential, Jessica," the commander said. "More than any non-Ghatazhak I have ever seen. If you could only get some control over your emotions—develop your mental, as well as your physical abilities—you could be so much more."

"How?"

"Train with us. Become one of us."

"One of you?" Jessica shook her head again. "You want me to become a Ghatazhak?"

"It is the only way you will reach your true potential."

"But..."

"I know. There are no women in the Ghatazhak.

Times change, and the Ghatazhak must change with them."

"I was going to say you're all the same size, and I'm not."

"Yes, there is that, as well. Regardless, I believe that becoming a Ghatazhak is the only way. But it will require you to resign from the Alliance."

"Why? You're part of the Alliance."

"We don't plan to remain a part of it. A year at the most. Once we have trained enough marines, we will go our separate ways."

"Where will you go?"

"We will find a world back in the Takaran sector. A world where we can continue to train, continue to prepare."

"Prepare for what?" Jessica wondered.

"The need for the Ghatazhak will arise from time to time. Conflict is the nature of humanity. When such conflicts arise, and grow beyond the capabilities of most men—and women—we will be ready. But *we* will decide who is deserving of our sacrifices, instead of being *told* to whom we must remain loyal."

Jessica was still confused. "I still don't understand why I have to resign from the Alliance. At least not right away. You said a year, right?"

"You are a good soldier," the commander said. "Despite your unpredictability, your lack of self-discipline... Despite all of these things, you still follow orders. *That* is why I need you to resign."

"I'm not following your logic, here, Telles."

"If you are a Ghatazhak, you will be sworn to follow *my* orders, even if they violate those of the Alliance."

Jessica cocked her head to one side, examining

the commander. "What's really going on, here, Telles?"

The commander looked at her, long and hard. "Resign your commission, and swear your allegiance to the Ghatazhak, here and now."

"Not unless you tell me why."

"I cannot, unless you join us." Telles kept his eyes locked on hers. "You must trust me, Jessica."

She continued staring at the commander. Finally, she reached up to her collar, removed her rank insignias, and placed them on the table. "It's just a gesture, you know. I'm sure there's some paperwork to fill out, or something."

"Will you join us?" the commander asked in all seriousness.

"Sure. Why not?" Jessica replied casually.

"Do you swear on your honor, that you will follow my orders, without question, and that you will serve the Ghatazhak with your very life?"

"Jeez..." she said, rolling her eyes. "Fine, I swear it. Go get a bible, if you like."

"Very well. You are now a Ghatazhak."

"Just like that?" she joked. "No paperwork?"

"We can deal with the formalities later," he replied. "Everything discussed from this point forward is not to be discussed with anyone else without my express permission. Is that understood?"

"Of course," Jessica replied.

"Very well." Commander Telles took a breath and sighed. "The Alliance has established daily jump comm-drone relays with the Jung homeworld," the commander began.

"Are you kidding?" Jessica said, surprised. "I hope it's got fail-safes."

"Multiple. It is impossible for them to take the

drone intact. Its self-destruct device is designed to activate if it is unable to return to this system within a certain amount of time from departure. It cannot be disarmed. Not even by the Alliance."

"I sure hope you're right."

"I am."

"But that's not what you wanted to talk to me about, is it?" she surmised.

"The Alliance received its first transmission two days ago," the commander continued. "Captain Scott has been charged with attempted genocide against the Jung people."

Jessica did not respond, only continued staring at the commander, waiting for him to continue.

"According to Lieutenant Commander Bowden, the trial is just a formality. If he has been charged, he will be convicted...and executed."

"How did you learn about this?"

"Captain Scott's sister, Miranda. The president's aide. She informed me yesterday."

"Why did she tell you?" Jessica wondered.

"She asked me to tell you personally, although I suspect there was additional intent, which she did not disclose."

Jessica was trying to add everything up, but she wasn't coming up with an answer. "Why are you telling me this?" she wondered. "You know how I feel about Nathan. You know how this will affect me."

"I am telling you this for the same reason that I asked you to resign your commission and join the Ghatazhak. I need a few people that I can trust."

"Trust for what?" Jessica asked.

"I plan to rescue Nathan Scott."

CHAPTER FOUR

Although Jessica had made the gesture of removing her rank insignias a few days ago and sworn her loyalty to the Ghatazhak, as expected, there were more procedures involved. It would take several days before her resignation would become official. In the meantime, Commander Telles had suggested that she stand down as a spec-ops instructor. She had offered to finish out the class, but the commander had other plans.

As far as the Alliance knew, she was still on Porto Santo. She had been smuggled off the island on one of the shuttles that hopped between the island and various parts of Europe several times per day. It only took a fake ID, a simple disguise, and a port security guard who had been sworn to secrecy.

Now Jessica found herself walking casually down the main boulevard of central Interlaken, dressed in typical attire for the Swiss city, attempting to blend in as much as possible. It had been months since she had done anything resembling covert ops, not since her time on Kohara in the Tau Ceti system. It had been what she originally trained for...what she had dreamed of doing from the moment she entered the academy.

Jessica could speak several languages, including German and French, so blending in was easy. In addition, there were so many people from nations all over the world working on the restoration of nearby Grindelwald, that English had become the norm, even in this remote mountain location.

After several minutes of walking, she found the cafe in question. Being mid-afternoon, the establishment was not crowded, making it easy for Jessica to spot Deliza. She made her way to the corner of the cafe, where Deliza was sitting in a corner booth, drinking tea and studying a data pad. Jessica glanced around, then approached her. "Deliza?"

Deliza looked up from her data pad, startled by the sound of someone calling her name. Other than Yanni and a few of his friends, no one in Interlaken knew her. "Yes?" she replied, her brow furrowed suspiciously. "Do I know you?"

Jessica sat down across the booth from her, removing her sunglasses.

"Jessica?"

"Surprise," Jessica whispered.

"I didn't recognize you. Did you color your hair?"

"Wig," Jessica replied, keeping her voice low.

"What are you doing here?"

Jessica signaled Deliza to keep her voice down.

"Sorry," Deliza said quietly, doing as instructed. "What are you doing here? What's going on?"

"Can't a girl just pop in on an old friend?"

"Well, certainly, but how did you even know where to find me?"

"I'm in intelligence, remember?"

"But I thought you were transferred to Porto Santo?"

"I was," Jessica confirmed. "But I'm not staying there."

"Where are you going?" Deliza asked.

"I'm resigning from the Alliance."

Deliza's eyes widened. "What? Why?"

"It's complicated."

Deliza was reeling from the news. "Of all people, I never thought *you* would resign."

"I wish I could tell you why, but I can't."

Deliza cocked her head, studying Jessica's face a moment. "You didn't track me down to tell me you're resigning."

"No. I didn't," Jessica admitted. "I have a favor to ask of you. A big one."

"How big?"

"*Really* big. *Huge*, in fact. But I can't tell you why."

"What's the favor?"

Jessica looked around, checking that no one was eavesdropping on their conversation. "I need to use the Mirai."

"Why?" Deliza's eyes widened again, the revelation hitting her. "This is about Na..."

Jessica cut her off with a gesture and a stern look, before Deliza could finish saying his name. She looked around again, double-checking that no one was watching them. "Yes," she confirmed in a whisper. "But you can tell no one, not even Yanni."

"He will figure it out sooner or later," Deliza warned, in a hushed tone.

"Probably. When he does, you can tell him. Just make sure he tells no one. And I mean *no one*. You shouldn't even talk about it yourselves. You never know when someone might be listening."

Deliza looked concerned. She too glanced around the cafe, as if checking to see if anyone was spying on their conversation.

"Relax. It's too soon for anyone to have caught on to our plan."

"Our? Who else is involved?" Deliza wondered.

"It's really better that you know as little as possible, Deliza. Trust me on this."

"I do. Just tell me what you want me to do," Deliza replied.

* * *

"Where the hell are we?" Josh wondered as he and Loki followed the Ghatazhak corporal down the dimly lit corridor. "Hey, Corporal. I thought you were taking us to see Commander Telles."

"I am, sir," the corporal replied.

"Isn't his office in the command building?" Loki asked.

"Yes, it is, sir."

Josh looked at Loki. "Then, why aren't we going there?"

"This is where I was told to take you, sir," the corporal replied evenly. The corporal stopped, opened the door to his right, then stood to one side, gesturing for them to enter. "Sirs."

Josh looked at Loki again, before entering the doorway with Loki close behind. The room was dark, illuminated only by the scant light from the corridor. Once they were inside, the corporal closed the door behind them. They heard the door latch lock, and they were left in the darkness.

"This can't be good," Loki mumbled.

They both heard a muffled voice from the far side of the room, as if over a comm-set.

"Is somebody in here?" Josh asked.

The lights came on, revealing Jessica sitting at the back of the room.

"Jessica!" Josh said in shock. "What the hell?"

"Sorry about that, boys," she apologized, "but I had to secure the room before anyone said anything."

"What's going on?" Loki asked, looking suspicious.

"No one can know that we met," she instructed.

"Okay," Josh replied cautiously.

"I take it we're not here to lecture your spec-ops

trainees about deep space reconnaissance?" Loki surmised.

"Not exactly, no."

"Then why *are* we here, Jess?" Loki asked.

Jessica took a deep breath, letting it out slowly. "Before I can tell you, you must both give me your word that, regardless of your decision, you will not speak of this to anyone. Not even amongst yourselves, in private."

"What's going on?" Josh wondered.

"Swear to me, on your honor."

"That's going to be kind of hard, seeing as how I don't really have any," Josh joked.

"I'm not kidding, Josh," Jessica warned him. "This is life and death shit here. Yours, if it comes to that."

"Jesus, Jess," Josh exclaimed. "I was joking. Of course, I promise not to say anything."

Jessica looked at Loki.

"Me, too."

"Are you both sure?" she asked. "What I'm about to tell you could change your future, for better or worse. It could even put your lives in danger."

This time, Loki looked at Josh.

"Not like it would be the first time," Josh commented. "What's up?"

"You're sure you want to know?" she asked again.

"Hell, yes," Josh replied without hesitation.

Jessica looked at Loki again. "Loki?"

"Yes, I'm sure."

"Very well," Jessica said. "We need your help."

"Who's we?" Loki wondered.

"Better you don't know at this point."

"What do you need us to do?" Josh asked.

"I need you both to resign your commissions," Jessica explained.

Both Josh and Loki looked surprised.

"Uh, you *do* know how hard I worked to get my commission, right?" Josh said.

"Yes, I know," she replied. "Believe me, it's not something I take lightly. And the only reason I *am* asking the two of you, is because you are the only two pilots I can trust."

"Why do you need us to quit the Alliance?" Loki asked.

"So that you can take a new job, as Deliza's private flight crew," Jessica explained.

"Flying the Mirai?" Josh said skeptically. "Hardly a step up," he added under his breath.

"Doesn't she already have a flight crew?" Loki pointed out.

"Captain Navarro will soon be requesting their return, due to his own shortage of qualified pilots," Jessica explained.

"Why the hell do you want us to fly the Mirai?"

"That's not the only reason you want us to resign our commissions, is it?" Loki suspected.

"No, it's not," Jessica confirmed. "I need you to resign, because I'll be asking you to do something that will go against orders."

"Oh, shit," Loki mumbled, a chill washing over his body.

"What?" Josh wondered, noticing his friend's sudden change in disposition. He looked at Jessica. "What? What are you going to ask us...to......" Josh felt the same ominous chill down his spine. He looked back at Loki. "She's not wearing any rank insignia," he realized. He turned to Jessica. "You've already resigned, haven't you?"

"Three days ago. I'm just waiting for the request to get processed," Jessica replied.

"We're in," Josh announced enthusiastically.

"I haven't even told you what I need you to do."

"You want us to help rescue Nathan, right?" Josh asked.

"Yup." She looked at Loki. "I know Josh always volunteers you both before you get a chance to say anything about it, so..."

"I'm in," Loki added without hesitation.

"You're sure?"

"Quite," Loki replied. "In fact, it's the only thing I've ever been sure about."

Jessica smiled. "The Mirai has a minimum flight crew of three," she said. "Two pilots, and a crew chief. Any idea where we can find a crew chief who's crazy enough to take on this mission?"

This time, it was Josh who smiled. "I know just the guy."

* * *

"I do not mean to belittle his sacrifice," Commander Golan said, "but there is no denying that it was a mistake to allow himself to be drawn into a situation from which there was no escape."

Captain Navarro looked away from his executive officer, his gaze drifting across his ready room aboard the Avendahl, finally landing on the ship's schematics on the opposite wall. After a few moments, a sigh escaped him. "I suppose you are correct," he admitted, looking back at his second in command. "Have you considered, however, that he may have anticipated the likely course of events, and allowed them to happen so he would be in a *position* to save his world?"

"No one could have anticipated such events," Commander Golan argued.

"Most men, no. On that we agree," Captain Navarro replied. "But, you must admit, Captain Scott was not *most men.*"

"Is," the commander corrected. "He is not dead, yet."

"According to this," Captain Navarro said, holding up the data pad containing the latest communications from the Sol sector, "he soon will be." He sighed again. "A great waste. He was an exceptional young man, and I believe he would have gone on to accomplish great things."

Commander Golan's eyes narrowed. "You don't buy into the whole *Na-Tan* thing, do you?"

"Of course not," the captain said dismissively. "Educated men such as us do not put stock in legends. Still, the events of the last two years do give one pause."

"I don't believe I'm hearing this."

Captain Navarro chuckled. "Do not be concerned, my friend. I am not about to start preaching from the Legend of Origins just yet. However, when you take the legend of Na-Tan exactly as it reads, and ignore the various broad interpretations that are out there, its accuracy is somewhat...unsettling."

"Except for one thing," the commander pointed out. "According to legend, Na-Tan cannot die."

"As you said, Commander, he is not dead, yet," the captain reminded him.

Commander Golan smiled. "Even *Na-Tan* cannot escape a Jung prison...*on* the Jung homeworld."

The door buzzer sounded. Captain Navarro pressed a button to open the door, revealing his communications officer, Ensign Permon.

"I have a message for you, Captain," the ensign reported as he entered the captain's ready room.

"From?"

"I do not know," the ensign replied sheepishly. "It is encrypted."

"Even the headers?" Commander Golan wondered, sounding surprised.

"Yes, sir," the ensign nodded. "The recipient's name was the only part that was not encrypted."

Captain Navarro took the data pad being offered by the ensign. "Thank you, Ensign. That will be all."

Ensign Permon nodded, turned smartly, and exited the ready room, the door closing automatically behind him.

Captain Navarro activated the data pad's display and placed his palm on the screen. A moment later, the decrypted message appeared on the screen. "Interesting," the captain muttered as he read.

"What is it?" Commander Golan wondered.

"It seems that young Miss Ta'Akar wishes to return the Mirai's crew to us."

"Then you will get your prized yacht back," the commander jested loftily.

Captain Navarro raised his eyebrow at his executive officer's jab. "Not the Mirai," he corrected, "just her crew. And she wants me to make the request to Admiral Dumar, as if it were my idea."

"Odd. Did she say why?"

"No. She did not...which is even more odd."

"Well, we are short of crew, especially pilots," the commander commented. "Even two would be a welcome addition." He thought for a moment. "Did she say who will be flying the Mirai in their place?"

"No," the captain replied. "Nor did she say what she plans to do with it."

"I still think it was a mistake to give her that ship."

"I thought you disliked the Mirai."

"I did not dislike her, only the scant decor. Practicalities aside, a man of your position deserves better."

"It is an unusual request," the captain decided. "However, I will honor it."

"You think she is up to something?" the commander wondered.

"She is the daughter of Casimir Ta'Akar," the captain replied gravely. "I have no doubt that she is up to something."

* * *

Marcus opened his door and found Josh standing in the corridor outside his quarters. "Josh. I wasn't expecting you." Marcus stepped aside to allow Josh to enter. "I thought you and Loki were down on Porto Santo?"

"We were," Josh said as he entered Marcus's quarters. "You got a minute?"

"Sure," Marcus said, closing the door. "I was about to go chew on a sergeant's ass, but I'm sure he won't mind waiting."

"Yeah, I'm sure he won't," Josh agreed, remembering all the times that Marcus had yelled at him growing up.

"What's up?" Marcus wondered, noticing the serious expression on Josh's face as he sat. The one thing that Josh was not, was serious. Not ever. "What happened? Kaylah finally dump you for good?"

"Naw." Josh looked at Marcus. "I don't know how to say this, so I'm just going to come right out with it. I'm going to resign my commission in the Alliance."

"What? Are you stupid?" Marcus yelled, jumping

back up from his seat. "I mean, I know you're stupid. That's a given. But this? This is *really* stupid!"

"I've got my reasons..."

"Did Kaylah talk you into this? What, does she want you two to run off together, get married, and start popping out kids?"

"Marcus..."

"Josh, you finally made it! You've finally made something of yourself, kid! Don't fuck it all up now just for some girl!"

"Marcus! Would you shut up for a minute and listen?" Josh insisted.

Marcus stared at Josh a moment, then finally took his seat again. "Very well."

"Loki and I are *both* resigning."

"I'm still waiting for the reason, kid," Marcus said, holding back his anger.

"There's something we have to do," Josh explained. "And we can't do it while we're still in the Alliance."

"What is it?" Marcus asked. "What is so important that you'd throw your entire future away?"

"I can't tell you," Josh said quietly, looking down.

"What?"

Josh looked back up at Marcus. "Not unless you come with us. We need a third person to have a full crew."

"Jesus, kid. You realize what you're asking of me?" Marcus leaned back in his chair. "I'm a master chief, now. Hell, I'm *chief of the boat*. That doesn't happen to guys like me. Not ever." Marcus looked from side to side, conflicted in his decision. He looked at Josh again. "Crew for what?"

"I can't say."

"Can you say where you're going?"

Josh just shook his head.

"Can you say when you'll be back?" There was still no response. "Can you say *if* you'll be back?"

"Sorry."

"Jesus, Josh. Will I ever see you again?"

"You could come with us," Josh reminded him.

"Is it dangerous? Whatever it is you're doing?" Marcus wondered.

Josh chuckled. "Does it matter?"

"Of course, it matters," Marcus insisted. He shook his head. "What the hell is so important?"

"Like I said, I can't tell you," Josh replied. "Not unless you agree to join us."

"Without even knowing what it is?"

"Trust me, Marcus. If you knew what it was, you'd come with us," Josh promised.

Marcus looked long and hard at Josh, studying his face...his eyes. He had always been able to read Josh, ever since he was a child. He had never seen him look more determined than he did at this moment. Finally, Marcus sighed in acceptance. "All right. I'm in."

"Are you sure?" Josh asked.

"No, but I'm still in," Marcus replied. "Now, tell me what the hell is going on."

Josh smiled. "We're going to rescue Captain Scott."

Marcus rolled his eyes, and threw up his hands. "Why the hell didn't you say so to begin with, you little shit! You know damn well I would've said yes!"

Josh's smile grew broader. "I was just having some fun with you, old man."

* * *

Jessica reached her front door and peeked through the window to see who was ringing the bell. "Holy shit," she mumbled to herself as she unlocked the door and opened it wide. “Admiral,” she greeted, surprise obvious in her voice.

“Jessica,” Admiral Dumar replied. He waited a moment for her to respond. When she didn’t, he spoke again. “May I?”

“Of course,” Jessica replied, embarrassed.

“I apologize for the unannounced visit,” the admiral said as he entered her home.

“What are you doing down here? I mean, over here. I mean...on Porto Santo.”

“You mean, what am I doing *here*?” the admiral corrected.

“That too,” she said as she closed the door. Jessica pointed toward the living room. “Please.”

Admiral Dumar entered the living room, immediately spotting baby Ania playing on the floor. “Is this her?”

“Yes,” Jessica replied. She squatted down and picked up Ania to show her to the admiral. “This is Ania. Ania, this is Admiral Travon Dumar.”

“She is beautiful,” the admiral said softly. “Such expressive eyes, especially for one so young.”

“Yeah, she’s something,” Jessica agreed, setting the child back on the blanket on the floor.

“It is a wonderful thing you are doing, Jessica, taking this child into your home to raise as your own.”

“Yeah, well, my mom has been doing most of the work, along with my brothers’ wives. I’m hardly ever here, it seems.”

“I take it she is the reason you are resigning your commission?”

Jessica looked at the admiral. “Surely, you didn’t come all the way down here just to try to talk me out of it.”

"Not that I wouldn't have," the admiral began. "I had a meeting with President Scott. I thought that as long as I was on Earth, I should at least come by and see if I might change your mind. But, after seeing Ania in person, I can see that I'd be wasting my time."

"I do appreciate the thought," Jessica told him.

"You have been an invaluable officer, Jessica," the admiral said. "The Alliance will be hard-pressed to replace you."

"The Alliance?" Jessica noticed the admiral's context.

Admiral Dumar sighed. "Now that a cease-fire exists, the people of Earth are pushing for a change in leadership. Someone from Earth."

"You're kidding," Jessica said, shocked.

"I can understand their desire for a military leader more directly connected to their world. It is only natural."

Jessica closed her eyes. "Please, please tell me they are not putting Galiardi in command."

"I'm afraid I cannot."

Jessica shook her head. "You know, I wasn't entirely sure I was doing the right thing by resigning, but now I have no doubts."

"Galiardi is more than qualified," the admiral assured her.

"Maybe," Jessica admitted. "But he doesn't *care* about his people, not the way you do. To him, we're just assets."

"It is the way that generals and admirals must sometimes view things, I'm afraid."

"That's just an excuse bad generals and admirals use to make themselves feel better about the lives they throw away," Jessica insisted. "The *good* ones care. They feel the loss of every person, both ours *and* theirs."

"Perhaps."

"That's what made you a good leader, sir."

Admiral Dumar smiled. "Thank you."

The two sat in silence for several minutes, watching baby Ania chew on her toys.

"Where will you go?" Jessica wondered. "Back to Corinair?"

"Of course. I have family there. A wife, a son, and a daughter."

"What will you do?"

"We have some land in the mountains, a few hours from Aitkenna, by a lake. It is very beautiful, and very remote. My wife and I have often talked of building a resort. Nothing fancy. Just some secluded cabins along the shore. A place where people can come to get away from everyone and everything, to be alone with nature."

"Sounds nice," Jessica said. "Then, you will be retiring from military service?"

"Yes." Admiral Dumar sighed. "I believe the time is finally right." He looked at Jessica. "It has been a long time coming, you know."

"If you don't mind my asking, how old are you?"

"Not as old as you might think," the admiral chuckled. "I am one hundred and thirty-seven of your Earth years in age."

"Wow," Jessica replied, impressed. "You don't look a day over one hundred and ten."

The admiral laughed even harder. "Yes, well, I ran out of anti-aging a few months after you put a bullet between the eyes of Caius Ta'Akar. I never did thank you for that, by the way."

"My pleasure."

"And what about you?" the admiral asked. "Will you be staying on Porto Santo?"

"Actually, no. I'm joining the Ghatazhak."

"Really?" This time, it was the admiral who was surprised.

"Yup. Telles invited me."

"That sounds like an interesting opportunity. Although, I have to say, the thought of you with the skills of a Ghatazhak is a little frightening. No offense intended."

"Don't worry," Jessica assured him. "Telles intends to work on what *he* sees as 'self-control' issues."

The admiral nodded his approval. "I should like to meet you again," he said. "Perhaps in a decade, after you have completed your training. I suspect you will be most impressive." The admiral looked at baby Ania. "But what of Ania?" he wondered. "I understand the Ghatazhak do not plan to remain on Earth for much longer."

"Actually, the commander and I are going to find a suitable world on which to establish a permanent Ghatazhak base. Someplace near the Takaran sector, I suspect. Once we do, my family has agreed to come with me. We will need help building the new facilities, and my father and brothers are pretty good with tools. So, we'll all be together."

"That's a big step for them, is it not? Traveling to another part of the galaxy?"

"Yeah, it's a bit mind boggling," Jessica admitted. "Especially for my parents. But I have a good feeling about it."

"It sounds like a good plan," the admiral said. He rose from his seat. "Well, I shall not bother you further, since I can see that your future is well considered. I wish you much success and happiness, Jessica." The admiral reached out to shake her hand.

"Thank you, sir," she said as she accepted the gesture. "Maybe, someday, we can come and stay at your resort."

"We'd love to have you," the admiral said as he headed for the door.

Jessica followed him from the living room to the front door.

The admiral paused, then turned back to Jessica, looking her in the eyes. "Jessica, not rescuing Nathan was the hardest thing I have ever done," he said quietly.

Jessica stepped forward and wrapped her arms around the admiral. "Me, too," she whispered back. "Me, too."

* * *

Deliza spotted the admiral further down the corridor, and quickened her pace to catch up to him. "Admiral," she called out, hoping to slow him down.

The admiral paused, turning to look behind him. "Deliza," he greeted when he spotted her moving toward him at a brisk pace. "How are things going down in Grindelwald?"

"Well, I suppose," she replied as she reached his side, and the two of them continued down the corridor together. "To be honest, I do not really know. Half the time, Yanni is excited about their progress, and the other half, he is upset at how difficult it is to get anything accomplished."

"And the Data Ark?" the admiral wondered.

"Yanni said it should be up and running in another week. The new data cores provided by the Corinairans made a big difference."

"That is good to hear," the admiral said. He

paused at the door to his private mess. "Care to join me for lunch?" he asked, gesturing toward the door.

"I'd like that very much," she replied, nodding respectfully.

The admiral opened the door for her, allowing her to enter first, before following behind. "To be honest, I wasn't expecting you back today. I thought you would be on the surface until Yanni finished his project."

"There were a few things I needed from the black lab. Some project files to work on." Deliza noticed two place settings at the table, with the food already prepared. "Were you expecting someone?"

"I was going to have lunch with Captain Taylor," the admiral explained as he took his seat. "But her doctors wanted to run a few more tests before they released her for duty."

"I heard a rumor that Cameron was going to take command of the Aurora. Is that true?" Deliza wondered.

"Indeed, it is."

"I wonder, how does Commander Willard feel about that?"

"Commander Willard asked to be replaced," the admiral told her as he dished his first course. "He wishes to return to Corinair."

"Seems to be a lot of that going around these days," Deliza commented.

"Indeed."

"I heard another rumor," she said, looking tentatively at the admiral. "About you."

"That one is true, as well. I shall also be returning to Corinair."

"How soon?"

"A month...two at the most, I expect. As soon as my replacement can take over."

"And that would be the third rumor," Deliza commented as she took her first bite.

"And that one would be true as well."

"A lot of the old EDF regulars are not happy about that."

"I am aware," the admiral responded. "They are free to resign at any time."

"Can the Alliance afford to lose so many people at once?"

"Better now, while we have a cease-fire, and have time to train their replacements," the admiral said.

"I too am planning on returning to Corinair. I just haven't decided when to leave."

"How does Yanni feel about that?"

"He's fine with it," Deliza replied. "At least, he hasn't voiced any objections as of yet."

"The Alliance will have a hard time replacing you in the black lab," the admiral commented.

"I doubt it," she replied as she dined.

"Don't sell yourself short, Deliza. Your contributions have been considerable." The admiral paused and looked at her. "Your father would be proud."

Deliza smiled. "I do wish I could stay longer," she admitted. "The projects here are most challenging, and quite interesting. But Captain Navarro feels he is unable to serve as my proxy for business matters, and still run the Avendahl. He fears one, or both, will suffer. That is why I am returning."

"Yes," the admiral replied. "I received his request to recall the Mirai's flight crew. He, too, has lost several of his crew. It seems they have not fared their separation from Takara as well as he had hoped."

"Not too surprising," Deliza said. "Corinair and Takara are vastly different worlds."

"Indeed, they are," the admiral agreed. "Have you considered who you will hire to crew the Mirai?"

"Actually, I have," Deliza replied. "That's why I wanted to speak with you."

The admiral set down his utensils, waiting to hear her choice.

"I was hoping to offer the jobs to Josh, Loki, and Marcus."

The admiral thought for a moment.

"I hope you don't mind," she said, noticing his contemplation.

"Josh and Loki are two of our best pilots," the admiral said. "And Marcus Taggart is the Aurora's chief of the boat. Are you sure they'll want to leave?"

"Since the Falcon program is being discontinued, I was hoping they might be interested in the job. I thought it might appeal to them more than flying a shuttle for the Alliance."

"They'd more likely be put into Super Eagles," the admiral said. "Although, I cannot be sure, since that will be for my successor to decide."

"That's the other thing," Deliza said, as she took another bite. "I think one of the reasons so many non-Terrans are looking to return to their homeworlds is that, with the change of command, they fear favoritism toward Terrans amongst the better positions."

"Yes, I am aware of that as well."

"You don't believe it to be the case?"

"I did not say that," the admiral replied calmly.

"Then you *do* believe it to be the case?"

"I did not say *that*, either," the admiral pointed out. "However, I understand their concern."

Deliza returned to her meal. "I think they'll jump at the chance," she finally said. "Even Marcus."

"I suspect Marcus is more likely to be interested than Josh and Loki," the admiral commented. "He and Captain Taylor have never been on the best of terms."

"That is the impression I had, as well," Deliza agreed. "Then, I have your permission to contact them and offer them the positions?"

"You don't need my permission to offer someone under my command a job opportunity," the admiral said.

"Technically, no," she agreed, "but you are my father's oldest, and most trusted, friend. I felt obligated, out of respect, to seek your approval."

"I appreciate the thought," the admiral replied. "You have my approval." The admiral lifted his glass and held it out in front of him. "To your father."

* * *

Josh, Loki, and Marcus stood in the captain's ready room onboard the Aurora, facing the captain.

"Not exactly how I wanted to start my command," Cameron said as she rose from her seat. "Gentlemen, each of you have served this ship, and the Alliance in general, with distinction. While I didn't always agree with your methods, I cannot dispute your results. Each of you volunteered. Each of you offered your life to support a cause that benefited not only yourself, but all of humanity. For that, you should be proud." Cameron came out from behind her desk, moving first to Marcus. "Master Chief Taggart..." She paused a moment, leaning in closer. "Assuming that is your *real* name," she added under her breath.

"It is, sir," Marcus replied in a similar tone.

"No offense intended, Master Chief, but I can

honestly say that you would have been the *last* person I would have chosen as chief of the boat." Cameron reached out to shake Marcus's hand.

"None taken, sir," Marcus replied with a grin.

"So, you can understand how surprised I am to find myself so disappointed to be losing you as my COB."

"Thank you, sir."

"I trust you'll keep these two in line?" she asked.

"You bet your ass…uh…sir."

Cameron smiled. "Your request for transfer to Fleet Command on the Karuzara, for detachment-from-service processing, is hereby approved. Good luck to you, Master Chief."

"Thank you, sir," Marcus replied, offering his best military salute.

"Dismissed, Master Chief," she replied, returning his salute. She stepped to her right, moving in front of Loki. "Ensign Sheehan," she continued, as Marcus stepped back and left the compartment. "You are a pilot after my own heart. Methodical, precise, and procedural, but able to quickly adapt to changing demands. You will be sorely missed." She paused a moment. "You know, you would have made a good ship's captain, someday."

Loki looked genuinely surprised by her praise. "Thank you, Captain."

"I'm sure you'll do fine in whatever you choose to do." Cameron glanced at Josh. "Just don't let this guy get you into too much trouble."

"I'll try, sir," Loki replied, smiling.

Cameron shook Loki's hand, then stepped back. "Your request for transfer to Fleet Command on the

Karuzara, for detachment-from-service processing, is hereby approved. Good luck to you, Ensign."

"Thank you, sir," Loki replied, saluting her.

"Dismissed, Ensign," she replied, returning his salute.

Loki glanced at Josh, then stepped back, turned, and left the compartment.

"Ensign Hayes," Cameron continued as she stepped to her right, then leaned back against her desk, crossing her arms. "You know, you're about tied with Master Chief Taggart in the *least likely choice* department."

"Must've been my upbringing," Josh quipped.

"Luckily for you, your uncanny skill as a pilot has kept you and Loki alive, despite your rash decision-making, and your generally arrogant attitude."

Josh's mouth twisted to one side, unsure of how to respond.

"However, you have managed to pull off more than one impossible act, just when they were needed. The most surprising of which was passing your exams and earning your commission."

"I couldn't have done it...any of it...without Loki, sir."

"*Knowing* that is most important, Ensign. Always remember that you never fly alone. Even if you are alone in that cockpit, it takes a lot of people to get you there each time."

"Yes, sir. I'll try to remember that."

Cameron sighed. "He really liked you, Josh."

"Sir?"

"Nathan," she replied, melancholy creeping into her voice. "You two are a lot alike."

"Thank you, sir. I take that as a great compliment."

"You should," she insisted. "He saw greatness in

you. Something that took me a lot longer to notice." She paused another moment, reminiscing. After sighing again, she continued. "Just see to it that you live up to *his* expectations...understand?"

"I will, sir," Josh replied earnestly. "I promise."

Cameron stood up straight again, shaking off her remorse. "You, too, shall be sorely missed, Ensign Hayes," she said, shaking his hand. "Your request for transfer to Fleet Command on the Karuzara, for detachment-from-service processing, is hereby approved. Good luck to you."

"Thank you, sir," Josh replied. He stepped back and offered a salute.

"Dismissed, Ensign," she said, returning his salute.

Josh stepped back and turned toward the exit.

"Josh," Cameron called after him.

Josh turned back around. "Yes, sir?"

"It's a different kind of flying you'll be doing. Put the safety of your passengers and crew first... always."

"Yes, sir."

Cameron smiled. "Good luck to you, Josh. I hope our paths cross again, someday."

"I hope so too, Captain," he said, with his usual impish grin.

Cameron watched as Josh turned and exited the compartment. With Naralena having resigned the day before Cameron had taken command of the Aurora, Josh and the others were the last of those who had joined the Aurora's crew after their escape from Haven nearly two years ago.

She had once been part of a group of four. Four close friends. Comrades who had served together, struggled together, fought side by side. They had managed to accomplish great things...together. Now, only she and Vladimir were left. It would never be the same again, but it was what it was, and there was nothing she could do to bring them all back.

* * *

Armin stood with thousands of others on Nor-Patri, watching the trial of Nathan Scott on one of the dozens of video monitors that had been erected around the exterior of the judicial complex. He had traveled to the capital to witness the historic trial in person, but like everyone else, found himself stuck watching from outside.

In concert with those around him, Armin grumbled about how he could have watched from the comfort of his own home, had he known better. And about how the powers that be could have used a larger arena for the trial. After all, the trial itself was nothing more than an exhibition. The citizens of the empire were well aware of this, for the Jung leadership castes had long been masters of propaganda. It was unfortunate, to say the least, that this strategy remained so effective. So dumbed-down were the masses that they would believe any half-truth that their leaders spewed, as long as it agreed with their own sentiments.

Better a reassuring lie, than a worrying truth. Armin could remember his father's words as if they had been spoken only yesterday. From time to time, he wondered how his father was doing. Armin had not seen him since he was drafted more than a decade ago. He had heard rumors that their homeworld of Pora-Dubay had been hit by a fierce solar storm some years ago, yet he was never able to confirm this. He had tried, at the time, to send word to his father—a feat that required considerable effort while serving aboard a Jung battleship. Unfortunately, he had never received a reply, which meant that either his message was never sent, or that the reply never made it back to him... Or worse.

Armin had chosen to believe that the reply had never found him. Such was the nature of the Jung interstellar communications network. Slow and unreliable for the masses, and only marginally better for the military. It was for this reason that ships' captains and planetary governors were given so much leeway in day-to-day decisions and policy making. Without such authority, nothing would ever get done. The downside of this system was that so many captains and governors became dictators. This had been the reason Armin and the others jumped ship and escaped to Kohara less than a year after Armin's failed attempt to contact his father.

Someday, Armin would try to contact his father again, hopefully in person. Not just to learn of his fate, but also to let his only blood relative know that he was still alive and well, all things considered.

For now, however, he would have to be content living as Osa Moren, the identity he had taken from the hapless soul who had been unlucky enough to meet with Armin shortly after his arrival on Nor-Patri. Armin wondered if the others of his group felt as guilty as he had, for taking the life of an innocent man. He had no doubts that Reto had none. The man was as ruthless as they came. Armin both envied and despised Reto for that quality. He constantly reminded himself that Osa's sacrifice served a greater purpose, one that would benefit all of humanity. But that was the same rhetoric constantly used by the Jung propaganda machine to justify its actions, up to and including what the Jung referred to as the *cleansing* of an entire world.

Armin had always known such cleansings were horrific acts of incomparable violence. But he, too, had dismissed them as necessary, just as his leaders had instructed. It wasn't until he had witnessed the effect such a cleansing had on the people of that world, first hand, that he had realized what it truly was... An act of complete barbarism.

It was for this reason Armin had volunteered for this mission. He knew full well that he would likely be stranded on Nor-Patri for the rest of his days, and that was only if he was lucky enough to *not* be caught and executed as a deserter, a spy, and a traitor to the empire.

At least he had a specific mission. The others had simply been assigned to monitor events and communicate them out into the cosmos for collection by Alliance recon jump drones.

Armin reached into his pocket and pulled out his personal communications unit, holding it up in the air to record events, like half of the attendees. Only he was focusing his unit's unique sensors to detect something else: Corinairan nanites. More specifically, the movements, locations, and times of the host carrying those unique nanites. He only hoped the Jung had not yet managed to flush them from the young captain's body.

* * *

Loki let out a long, low whistle as he, Josh, and Marcus had their first serious look at the exterior of the Mirai. "I can't believe this is going to be *our* ship," he mumbled.

Josh cast a cockeyed, sidelong glance at his

friend. "It's not gonna be *our* ship, Lok. It belongs to princess perfect, remember?"

"You know what I mean."

"Technically, it belongs to Captain Suvan Navarro," a voice corrected them from behind.

All three of them turned at once to find a middle-aged sergeant sporting the uniform of the Avendahl in her new, independent state.

"You must be our replacements," the sergeant surmised, with a disapproving raise of one eyebrow. He looked the three of them over. His sour expression remained unchanged. "Sergeant Mikel Isan of the Avendahl, chief steward of the Mirai. If you have completed your gawking, I have been instructed by Lieutenant Chandler to give you a thorough tour of the Mirai."

"Who's Lieutenant Chandler?" Josh wondered aloud.

This time, it was Loki who gave Josh a dirty look.

"Lieutenant Chandler is the Mirai's commanding officer, and chief pilot. He is the one who will be training the two of you how to fly," the sergeant added, looking even more annoyed than before.

"We already know how to *fly,* Sergeant," Josh snapped back. "We just need your lieutenant to review your SOPs with us, after which we'll drop you and yours off on the Avendahl and be on our merry way."

Marcus and Loki both stood silently, waiting for the Takaran sergeant to respond in kind to Josh's declaration.

The sergeant did not. "After our initial walk-around inspection, we will enter via the aft cargo ramp, working our way forward, *slowly,* as I point out the location of all primary and emergency systems," the sergeant continued. "We will work our way forward, combing through *each* and *every* accessible compartment, until we reach the cockpit. *Then,* and *only* then, will the lieutenant review the Mirai's standard operating procedures with you."

"And how long will all this take?" Josh asked, looking skeptical.

"Several hours, at least," the sergeant replied, unwavering.

"I thought we were going for a training hop today," Loki said.

"Once we have completed the tour, and the lieutenant has reviewed the ship's operating procedures...yes."

"It'll be dinner time by then," Josh protested.

"We have a fully stocked galley," the sergeant assured them. "I will be more than happy to provide you with *snacks*, should your *youthful* metabolism require them in order to complete the day's tasks."

Josh knew an insult when he heard it, and he had detected several over the last few minutes. "Listen, Sergeant..."

"That would be appreciated," Marcus interrupted quickly.

"Gentlemen," the sergeant said, gesturing toward the stern of the ship. "Shall we begin?"

Josh scowled at the sergeant, as Loki pushed him forward.

"Pilots," Marcus said dismissively, attempting to smooth the Takaran sergeant's ruffled feathers. "A bunch of arrogant little shits, on a good day."

The sergeant looked at Marcus, his eyebrow raising once again at Marcus's sudden camaraderie. "Yes."

"Listen, Mike," Marcus continued, putting his

arm around the sergeant and leading him toward the center of the Mirai.

"Mikel," the sergeant corrected, emphasizing the proper pronunciation of his name.

"Right. I'm sure you and your crew want to get back to the Avendahl as soon as possible, and Navarro's message *did* request that you return as soon as possible. So why don't we streamline this process a bit."

"Lieutenant Chandler's instructions specifically stated..."

"Chandler's a noble, right?" Marcus interrupted. "And we all know how much nobles like to tell those of us who *know* what to do, *what* to do. So, how's about we let Itchy and Twitchy familiarize themselves with the Mirai's flight systems, while *you* give *me* the grand, detailed tour. After all, I am the one who is going to be responsible for everything aft of the cockpit, right?"

The sergeant hesitated. "That would be highly irregular. Besides, the Mirai is a complex..."

"Yeah, yeah, yeah. I'm sure she's a piece of work, she is," Marcus agreed, placating the sergeant. "But your efforts will be lost on those two, trust me. Hell, they wouldn't know a power circuit from a control line. They're pilots!"

"But how are they going to fly the Mirai, if they don't have full knowledge of all her systems?"

"They'll figure it out, trust me," Marcus insisted. "Between you and me—and I'll never admit saying this, especially not to the kid—those are two of the best pilots you'll ever find."

The sergeant looked over at Josh and Loki, who were currently inspecting the Mirai's forward docking thruster ports. "I am aware of their reputation, and of their accomplishments during their service. I have to admit, it is impressive."

"Exactly. In fact, I'd bet my ass they could fly this thing right now, without missing a beat. And if you knew how little I trust *any* pilot, you'd understand what a ringing endorsement that really is."

Sergeant Isan thought for a moment, watching Josh and Loki as they continued their inspection of the Mirai's external systems. He could tell by the two pilots' movements and the way they touched and checked each control service, thruster, and sensor, that they were no strangers to such spacecraft. Finally, he let out a long sigh. "I cannot promise that the lieutenant will agree to this, but I will do as you ask," the sergeant acquiesced. "But I warn you, *you* had better impress me with *your* understanding of this ship, or I will not sign off on any of you."

"Fair enough," Marcus agreed, leading him toward the Mirai's port engine nacelle. "Why don't we start with your mains, Mikel?"

* * *

Reto had not been told why, only that he was to scan the residential compounds of as many higher ranking members of the Jung warrior castes as possible. It was a dangerous mission, far more so than simply monitoring general events and broadcasting them covertly into space, but Reto did not mind. He had been honored when Commander Telles took him aside just before departure, and given him this special assignment.

Reto liked to believe that the purpose of his mission was to identify the locations of all the command-level officers, so that the Alliance could take them all out with precision jump weapons. But he knew no such weapons existed in the Alliance arsenal.

Reto continued to stroll down the street, looking at the various homes. Nor-Patri was unlike any world he had ever visited, and very different from both Earth and Kohara, the only other worlds he had ever spent time on. Reto had been born into a labor-caste family on Nor-Patri. Such castes had no special status in the Jung caste structure. They were given their due respect for their contributions to the empire, but not the social standing enjoyed by the leadership and warrior castes. Reto himself had once been a member of the labor movement, demanding the same opportunities as the other, more prominent, castes. Like so many others who had voiced their dissent, he had found himself drafted into service. Ironically, his efforts to move a mid-level caste into a more prominent level had, in a roundabout fashion, gotten him here. Now, he was once again fighting to change the nine hundred year-old Jung Empire. Only the change he was now hoping for would be far greater.

Reto continued down the street, focusing the scanner head hidden in his hat on each passing home, lingering on the larger dwellings. The ones owned by higher-level command officers always appeared more like compounds than typical Jung homes. Nor-Patri was a world covered with urban sprawl, so much so that the majority of its local agricultural industry took place in underground farming complexes. And those only produced one quarter of what was needed to feed the Jung homeworld. The rest was imported from nearby systems, usually spending months, if not years, in transit. It was a delicate supply chain that the Jung had once kept carefully guarded.

As the years had passed, and the empire grew unrivaled in their military might, those supply conduits had become more vulnerable. Reto had often wondered why the Alliance didn't simply cut those supply lines and starve Nor-Patri into submission, rather than destroying Zhu-Anok, an act that had inadvertently cost millions of lives, both military and civilian.

Lieutenant Commander Bowden had explained to Reto that starving the civilian population would have been interpreted the same as a direct military assault against the people of Nor-Patri. At least the collateral damage due to the attack on the Patrian moon had been accidental.

That fact was only in the minds of Alliance leaders, and not in the minds of the residents of the Jung homeworld. The Jung propaganda machine had masterfully spun that collateral damage into a planned result disguised as an accident. As usual, the masses believed every word.

Yet, Reto still overheard the voices of dissent from time to time. In the back rooms of bars where men gathered to play illegal games of chance. In *danja* circles, where the young sought to escape the ills of life through the inhalation of mind-altering smoke from the burning of various dried, Patrian plants. And in the never-ending lines where those who had lost everything waited for their daily sustenance distributions from various relief agencies. A small minority had seen it coming, and had opposed, and *still* opposed, the dreams of the expansionist castes.

It was unfortunate that such minorities would never be allowed to grow to effectual size. Every citizen of Nor-Patri knew that the isolationist castes opposed expansion. But the isolationists had not half the power of the warrior castes. And the leadership castes were only interested in maintaining their legal control over both the masses and the warrior castes, themselves. Therefore, the leadership caste had to yield to the desires of the expansionists and their supporting warrior castes.

A nearly inaudible beep sounded from Reto's pocket. He pulled out his personal data-comm unit and checked its display. The scanner head hidden in his hat had detected something unusual. A host containing Corinairan nanites.

Reto put his PDU to his ear, pretending to be taking a call. Although most of the street-level security cameras were still offline in this part of the city, those in the larger residential compounds were most likely monitored by full time security staff.

He continued walking, taking care not to change his stride or body language, continuing to speak into the receiver. He wanted to run back to his tiny, one-room apartment and send this finding into space as soon as possible, but the next transmission time was yet hours away.

He would have to wait.

CHAPTER FIVE

The four of them watched as the Mirai's crew walked down the ship's aft cargo ramp for the last time.

"Are you sure you don't need anything?" Lieutenant Chandler asked, turning back halfway down the ramp.

"We're good," Josh replied.

"Maybe I should go over the external docking procedures again," the lieutenant said nervously, looking as if he were about to head back up.

"I have studied the procedures thoroughly," Loki assured him. "We can handle it."

"It is not you that I am worried about, Ensign."

Josh said nothing, just rolled his eyes.

"Lieutenant," Jessica said, calmly intervening. "I'm sure Ensign Hayes and Ensign Sheehan appreciate all you have done for them over the past few days, as do I. But I assure you, the Mirai is in good hands." She glanced at Josh and Loki. "Besides, I'll keep them in line, I promise."

The lieutenant nodded his begrudging agreement. He looked around the interior of the Mirai's cargo hold one last time. "She is a good ship. Underutilized, to be sure, but still a good ship." He looked at Josh and Loki again. "See to it that you take good care of her, or you will have myself, and likely Captain Navarro, to answer to."

"Understood," Loki replied.

Lieutenant Chandler turned and continued down the ramp, stepping onto the Avendahl's deck and disappearing into its hangar bay.

"Jesus!" Josh exclaimed when they were finally

out of view. "I didn't think they were ever going to leave."

Loki cast a disapproving look at Josh, worried that the Mirai's departing crew might still be within earshot.

"That was the longest two days of my life!" Josh continued.

"Josh!" Loki scolded.

"Quick, Marcus, raise the ramp, before Chandler remembers something he forgot to go over with us...a few dozen times."

Jessica nodded her approval. "Close her up, and let's get out of here."

"Yes, sir," Marcus replied, moving toward the ramp controls.

"You in a hurry to go home hunting?" Josh asked, surprised that she was so eager to depart.

"Yeah, Captain Navarro invited us all to dinner, remember?" Loki added.

"Which I declined," Jessica said, as the cargo ramp began to rise. "We need to get back to the Sol sector as soon as possible."

Josh looked confused, as did Loki. "So now you *don't* want to go look for a new planet for the Ghatazhak?"

"Nope, that was just a ruse," Jessica explained as the ramp sealed shut, and the inner doors closed over it. "A reason for me to come along."

"I don't follow," Josh said.

Jessica turned and headed up the forward gangway leading to the main salon. "Jump us out the opposite direction of Sol, someplace out of the Pentaurus sector, then we'll turn and head back toward Sol."

"We're going back to Earth, then?" Josh asked, as

they followed Jessica up the gangway and forward into the main salon.

"Sol *sector*," Jessica corrected. "But not the Sol *system*."

"Then where?" Josh asked.

"Need to know, Josh."

"Uh, we're going to need to know sooner or later," Loki reminded her. "We *are* the pilots, you know."

"I'll give you our final destination a hundred light years outside of the Sol sector, so you can plot a stealth-entry into our destination system."

"I thought we were all working together on this," Josh complained.

"You thought wrong," Jessica replied sternly. She turned to look at him. "You take orders from Telles, or myself in his absence...no one else. Is that understood?"

"It would be a lot easier if we just knew where..."

"Not an option," Jessica insisted, cutting Loki off. "Get your asses up to the cockpit and get us out of here. Marcus, as soon as we're off, I'm gonna need your help."

"With what?" Marcus asked.

"We have to sweep this ship for monitoring devices."

"Bugs?" Marcus asked, surprised.

"It's an interstellar jump ship, Jess," Josh argued. "How the hell..."

"Go!" Jessica ordered, pointing forward.

"Yes, sir," Josh replied, noticing the threatening look in her eyes.

* * *

Admiral Galiardi entered the conference room at the North American Union's capital complex in Winnipeg, dressed in an Earth Defense Force uniform. It took considerable effort for President Scott not to show his contempt for the admiral, since sheer political pressure had forced him to reinstate the man to his former position.

President Scott glanced over at Admiral Dumar who sat to his left, dressed in his own, more subdued version of the EDF uniform, which had been modified to serve as the uniform of the Sol-Pentaurus Alliance. If Dumar was also affected by the sight of Admiral Galiardi sporting the full EDF uniform, he did not show it. For that, President Scott envied him.

"Admiral," the president greeted him stiffly.

"Mister President," Admiral Galiardi responded. "Admiral," he added, acknowledging Admiral Dumar's presence as well. "I trust you have both had a chance to review my proposals."

"Indeed we have," President Scott assured him. He turned to Admiral Dumar. "Admiral?"

"Yes, I have reviewed them in great detail," Admiral Dumar replied. "They are...ambitious."

"The new Protector-class was on the drawing board long before the Aurora and the Celestia had even been conceived," Admiral Galiardi explained. "They were to be given faster-than-light capabilities but, at the time, the powers that be feared such ships would send the wrong message to the Jung. I believe that such ships will now send exactly the *right* message to the Jung."

"And what would that message be?" President Scott wondered, already knowing the answer.

"That the Earth is not to be taken lightly," Admiral Galiardi responded.

"I believe that message has already been delivered," Admiral Dumar reminded Admiral Galiardi politely.

"To some extent, yes. However, with the loss of

the Celestia and the Kent, we appear considerably weaker in the eyes of the Jung."

"We still have the Aurora, as well as the Jar-Benakh, and the Tanna," President Scott pointed out.

"Not to mention six jump-capable KKVs roaming about at random," Admiral Dumar added. "Considering the amount of damage we have already inflicted upon the Jung, it is highly unlikely that their commanders are 'taking the Earth lightly.'"

"Three ships and a handful of jump KKVs." Admiral Galiardi scoffed, appearing to be holding back his laughter. "No Jung admiral would consider that a significant threat, regardless of what damages we have already inflicted. I promise you both that, even now, the Jung are preparing to maneuver their ships into battle groups, and positioning them to strike...*before* we can create more ships."

"Then why bother building such massive ships?" President Scott wondered. "Such ships will undoubtedly take many years to build."

"The first ship should take approximately five years to build. Subsequent ships should only take three years each. However, we have to create the facilities to fabricate and assemble these ships. That alone will take up to two years. That is why I asked to meet with you both today. I would like to get started on the conversion of the Karuzara asteroid into Port Terra as soon possible."

"What about the destroyer proposal?" Admiral Dumar asked.

"Let the Cetians build them," Admiral Galiardi insisted. "Since the destroyer concept is based on the Jung frigate design, it will require little retooling. In addition, our fabricators will speed up the production process. Once production gets underway, the Cetians should be able to produce a dozen destroyers by the time the first Protector-class ship is launched."

President Scott sighed. "Such rapid military buildup is exactly what the Jung fear most. We will be pushing them toward renewed conflict."

"Or, make them realize that renewing the conflict is a losing proposition," Admiral Galiardi argued. "Mister President, by our estimates, the soonest the Jung could muster enough ships to guarantee victory *and* move them into position to attack, is six to eight years."

"But our KKVs..." the president began to protest.

"Are not enough," Admiral Galiardi interrupted. "The Jung Empire is vast, perhaps as many as twenty fully industrialized worlds. Even if we could take them all out at once, there would still be the battle platforms, the battleships, and countless cruisers and frigates left to deal with. It's a matter of numbers, gentlemen, and the Jung have them."

"Surely, losing a half dozen heavily populated and industrialized worlds would put a damper on their urge to fight," the president surmised.

"To the Jung, those would be acceptable losses," Admiral Galiardi argued.

President Scott sighed, looking at Admiral Dumar. "Admiral?"

"Admiral Galiardi's logic is reasonable," he admitted. "Although, much of it is based on assumptions, and those assumptions are in line with the behavior we have seen thus far. However, meeting the admiral's production timelines will require considerable effort, not only from the people of Earth, but the people from *all the* Alliance worlds.

And many of those worlds, *including* Earth, are still in the early stages of recovery."

"In a few years, we will reach a tipping point with our fabricator production. When we do, the problem will be in providing our army of fabricators with the raw materials they require. If we can ramp up our mining of the asteroid belt, we can meet those needs. Add in the technologies contained within the Data Ark that we have yet to explore... Well, let's just say the Jung won't know what hit them, should they decide to challenge us once again."

"Bold words," Admiral Dumar cautioned.

Admiral Galiardi looked reproachfully at Admiral Dumar. "Perhaps, but they are the same words I spoke to then-Senator Scott, more than a decade ago. Had those words been heeded, our situation would likely be quite different."

President Scott looked long and hard at Admiral Galiardi, remembering full well the admiral's emotionally spirited warnings so many years ago. "Thank you, Admiral Galiardi. I will present your proposals to the Alliance Council at tomorrow's meeting, and I will notify you of their decision as soon as it is made."

"Thank you, Mister President," Admiral Galiardi replied, rising from his seat. "Admiral," he added with a respectful nod toward Admiral Dumar, before turning and leaving the conference room.

President Scott waited for the door to close behind Admiral Galiardi before speaking. "You're not opposed to him gutting your asteroid?"

"It is not *my* asteroid," Admiral Dumar corrected. "It was given to the people of Earth by Casimir Ta'Akar. It is yours to do with as you please."

"How do you feel about Galiardi's plan?" the president wondered.

"As I said, it is ambitious," Admiral Dumar replied. "However, it is well considered, and it includes not only the construction of the Protector-class ships, but also the destroyers, more Cobra gunships, and more Super Eagles. The only thing I might suggest is that you include the production of jump-capable KKVs, perhaps ones with even more destructive potential. After all, the Jung will discover that we do not have as many KKVs as Captain Scott originally claimed. And, if so, the Jung will indeed consider six worlds a small price to pay for the destruction of the only entity standing in their way."

* * *

After waiting more than an hour, Jessica was finally led into Doctor Donly's office. Like most of Nifelm, it was sparsely decorated, choosing function over design. There was, however, the slightest hint of the doctor's position as chief administrator of the Nifelmian cloning facility.

"Miss Nash," the doctor greeted her, rising from her seat, then stepping out from behind her desk to offer proper greetings. She reached out with both hands, crossing them as she presented her open palms to her guest.

Jessica looked puzzled for a moment, but emulated the chief administrator's unusual handshake, crossing her own hands as she took Doctor Donly's. "Doctor Donly," Jessica greeted her respectfully. The elder woman bowed her head slightly in respect, and Jessica did the same.

"Please, call me Sora," the doctor said as she gestured for Jessica to sit.

"I apologize for the unannounced visit," Jessica said as she took her seat.

"On the contrary, I am honored to have you," the doctor said. "You are the first Terran that I have ever met. Are they all as attractive as you?"

"Uh..." Jessica stumbled, caught off guard. "No? I mean, some are more so, some are less...I guess."

"I am sorry," the doctor said, noting Jessica's discomfort. "I did not mean to make you ill at ease. It's just that I am fascinated by the diversity of your population. There are only two hundred fifty-six different human forms on Nifelm."

"Really?" Jessica was shocked. "Is that by design?"

"Not at all," the doctor explained. "Nifelm was founded by twenty-seven thousand colonists almost twelve hundred years ago, but the bio-digital plague greatly reduced our numbers."

"I thought Nifelm was a quarantined world back then?" Jessica wondered.

"In a sense, yes. But the quarantine was more political than physical. The cloning of humans was still frowned upon by the joint nations of Earth back then."

"Probably still isn't widely accepted now, either," Jessica commented.

"This is true, and it likely never will be. We accepted that fact long ago."

"Then why did your ancestors choose to clone themselves?"

"Their intent was never to conduct large-scale cloning of human beings," Sora explained. "It was to develop the ability to transfer the human consciousness from one host body to the next."

"To what end?" Jessica asked, still confused.

"It was not about an end," Sora replied, "it was

about the science. The eventual cloning was done out of desperation, as all of the survivors of the plague were left sterile." The doctor shifted uncomfortably in her chair. "But you did not come to discuss the history of Nifelm."

"No, I did not," Jessica admitted. "I seek a favor. I wish to save a life. The life of a very close friend."

"From what illness does this friend suffer?" the doctor asked. "We can easily clone failing organs and tissues."

"I'm afraid the problem is greater than that. I seek to have my friend cloned, using a small tissue sample."

"I see," Sora replied, leaning back in her chair, seeming awkward herself. "And who is this person you wish us to clone?"

"I'm not at liberty to say."

"No matter," Doctor Donly said. "The answer would be the same, regardless. I am afraid we cannot help you."

Jessica was surprised. "Doctor..." she began, hoping to change Sora's mind.

"It is not a matter of not *wanting* to help you; it is a matter of being *unable* to do so."

"I don't understand."

Doctor Donly sighed, obviously frustrated with her position. "Nifelmians have been genetically altered, through numerous cloning cycles, in order to facilitate the consciousness transfer. Without such alterations, all memories, education, training... they were all lost during the transfer process. The problem set us back centuries, as each time we were cloned, we had to relearn all that we once knew. I'm afraid your friend would be no more than an empty shell, if even that. That would be a fate *worse* than death, I'm afraid."

"Isn't there *any* way around that problem?" Jessica pleaded.

"That is precisely what the Jung were forcing us to try to solve," Sora explained. "They, too, were unwilling to accept the limitations. They wanted immediate immortality for their warrior and leadership castes. But there was none."

"Is there nothing you can do?"

"Perhaps, in time, a solution will be found, but for now, it is simply not possible for us to create a fully functional clone of a non-Nifelmian, complete with the source host's memories and personality intact."

"What if the source host, my friend, agreed to the risk?"

"The answer would still be the same. I am sorry, Miss Nash. We are not the solution to your problem." Doctor Donly studied her guest's body language in response to her flat refusal. She could see the disappointment in the young woman's eyes. "I am *truly* sorry."

"Thank you," Jessica replied quietly after a few moments. "Thank you for your time," she added as she rose.

"Would you like someone to show you out?" the doctor inquired as she stood.

"No, thank you," Jessica replied politely. "I can find my way out."

"I do hope you find a way to save your friend," Doctor Donly said, offering her crossed hands again.

"Thank you," Jessica said, shaking the doctor's hands. "Good day."

"Good day."

Jessica turned and exited the chief administrator's

office, moving quickly through the outer office and into the corridor. After a few steps back towards the building's entrance, Jessica paused, then turned around. She looked around, pretending to be confused, before continuing down the corridor. However, she was not headed for the exit, and she knew it. She was headed deeper into the facility.

* * *

Naralena was led into the same secure conference room, with no more details than Jessica had received. "Commander?" she queried, barely able to make out the silhouette of a man standing against the back wall of the dimly lit room. The sound of the door lock and the crackling of a faint voice over the man's comm-set followed, after which the man stepped forward into the light.

"My apologies for the clandestine nature of our meeting," Commander Telles said. "I assure you, it was necessary."

"I was told you needed help translating some obscure Jung dialect?"

"It seemed a logical cover story, considering your linguistic talents."

"What is this all about, Commander?" Naralena asked, a look of suspicion on her face.

"Tell me, Miss Avakian, are you planning on returning to the Pentaurus sector?"

"I was, yes. Why do you ask?"

"Might I ask why?"

"It is my home," she replied curtly.

"No other reason?"

"I wasn't aware that I needed to explain my reasons to anyone."

"You do not, of course. I assure you, I only ask out of curiosity."

"A curious Ghatazhak?"

"Please, indulge me," Commander Telles begged.

"Well, if you must know, I am leaving because I do not feel I have anything else to contribute. With the addition of the Cetians, the Alliance now has more than enough people who speak Jung, and most of the core worlds speak English as well as their native languages. Besides, I have been away from home for some time now. It is time to find a more peaceful lifestyle."

"Settle down? Start a family?"

"Perhaps." Naralena was beginning to feel uncomfortable with the commander's line of questioning. "I'm assuming there is a point to all of this?"

"What if there was still something you could contribute? Something very important. And, although I cannot tell you what it is, I *can* say that if you knew, you would want to help in any way possible."

"I would be suspicious, to say the least."

"Rightfully so," the commander agreed.

"And what would I have to do?" Naralena wondered.

"Teach me to speak fluent Jung."

Naralena's eyebrow went up. "How long do I have to accomplish this task?"

"I cannot be sure," the commander admitted. "However, I suspect that time is of the essence."

"Jung is a complex language, Commander."

"I am a fast learner, Miss Avakian."

"I see. And am I to know why you are learning Jung?"

"It would be better if you did not."

"I would need to know where you plan on using

the language. There are local nuances that could pose problems in certain situations."

Commander Telles studied her for a moment. "It would be safer, for *you,* if you did not know *that,* either."

"I'm afraid I must," Naralena insisted. "That is, if you want to be able to speak like a native."

"I see." The commander contemplated his options for a brief moment, realizing that he had none. "You are to speak of this to no one. Do you understand?"

"I do."

"Very well. I shall be going to Nor-Patri."

A smile came over Naralena's face. "You are correct, Commander."

"About what?"

"I *do* want to help."

"Then shall we get started?" the commander suggested, taking a seat.

* * *

Jessica walked up the Mirai's aft cargo ramp, looking like she wanted to kill someone.

"Uh-oh," Marcus mumbled.

"What happened?" Loki wondered, almost afraid to ask, based on the look on Jessica's face.

"They turned us down, that's what happened," Jessica replied angrily.

"Why?"

"Some bullshit about not being able to transfer the source host's memories and shit."

"What? I thought they do that all the time here," Josh said.

"They do, but only with Nifelmians," Jessica explained as she reached the top of the ramp and entered the cargo bay. "Apparently, the Nifelmians have been genetically altered to work with whatever apparatus they use to transfer their consciousness and memories from one body to the next."

"What happens if they try to clone non-Nifelmians?"

"'A fate worse than death,'" Jessica replied dryly. "At least, that's how the chief administrator put it. He'd be an empty shell."

"What are we gonna do?" Josh wondered.

"I've got half a mind to go kidnap a couple of them and force them to go with us, but I don't think that will work." Jessica plopped down on one of the cargo crates. "Besides, there were like a thousand pairs of eyes on me everywhere I went. It's kind of hard to blend in when you're the black sheep."

"The what?" Loki asked.

"There are only two hundred and fifty-six different types of clones on this world, and apparently, none of them look anything like me."

"Really?" Josh moved toward the cargo ramp, wanting to look outside. "That'd be something to see." He turned back toward Jessica. "How many of those two hundred and fifty-six are women?"

"Josh," Loki scolded.

"Are they hot?"

"Shut your yap, kid!" Marcus warned.

"Maybe there's someone else you could talk to?" Loki suggested. "Did you tell them it was Captain Scott that you wanted to rescue?"

"I couldn't take the chance," Jessica replied.

"This is probably going to sound stupid," Marcus warned, "but what's wrong with an empty shell?"

Jessica cast a disapproving look toward him.

"Seriously. Why can't we just rescue the captain, and leave an empty shell behind in his place?"

"Wouldn't the Jung figure out something was

amiss when they found a comatose clone in his cell?" Loki said.

"Just kill the clone before we go. Make it look like he killed himself."

"It's going to be hard enough to just *get* to Nathan," Jessica said, "let alone to haul a comatose clone along with us."

"I'm confused," Josh admitted.

"What else is new," Marcus quipped.

"How were you planning on pulling this off to begin with?" Josh continued, paying no attention to Marcus.

"We didn't really *have* a plan just yet. We didn't have enough information on the whole cloning process to formulate one. My job was to secure their assistance, and gather intel so that we *could* formulate a plan. All we know for sure is that we need to make the Jung believe that Nathan is dead."

"Then my idea would still work," Marcus insisted. "Get a clone of the captain, leave it in his cell on the Jung homeworld, then blow it the fuck up. The Jung will find his DNA in the rubble, right?"

"And why did his cell just suddenly blow up?" Jessica wondered.

"Like I said, a dumb idea."

"*Pardon me,*" a faint voice called from the bottom of the cargo ramp.

Josh spun around to look, as Jessica quickly rose from her seat to look down the cargo ramp.

"I am looking for a young, brown-haired..." The cloaked woman at the bottom of the ramp stopped mid-sentence, spying Jessica at the top of the ramp. "I believe it is you that I seek."

"What can I do for you?" Jessica asked cautiously.

"May I come aboard?" the cloaked woman asked meekly.

"Why?"

"I must speak with you," the woman said nervously. She looked to either side, making sure she was not being watched. "I believe I can help. May I?"

"Sure," Jessica replied.

The woman cast another furtive glance around, and then moved quickly up the ramp.

"I'm Jessica Nash," Jessica greeted, offering the traditional crossed-arm Nifelmian handshake to the young woman as she entered the cargo bay.

The woman removed the hood of her cloak, allowing it to fall to her back. She was a petite woman, with barely noticeable oriental features. "I am Michi Sato," she said, shaking Jessica's hands. "You wish to clone someone not of this world?"

"Where did you hear that?" Jessica wondered, not wanting to admit anything just yet.

"I have a friend who works in the administrator's office. It was a most unusual request."

"Why did your friend tell you?" Jessica asked.

"I was forced to work for the Jung for many years."

"Doing what?"

"Trying to devise a way to transfer their consciousness to a new host, the same way we do for Nifelmians."

"I was told it was impossible," Jessica said. "Or, at the very least, that it would take centuries to accomplish."

"You are not Jung, are you?"

"Are you kidding?" Josh blurted out.

Michi looked at him, brows furrowed at his outburst.

"No, we're not Jung," Jessica assured her. "In fact, we're from the Aurora...or at least, we *were*."

"I do not understand," Michi said, looking confused herself.

"The Aurora is the ship that liberated Nifelm *from* the Jung. I was the one firing the ship's weapons on the day you were liberated."

"I had a feeling..."

"You said you could help?" Jessica asked quickly, getting impatient.

"Perhaps we should talk somewhere more private?" Michi suggested, looking back at the open cargo bay doors and the ramp beyond.

"Close it up," Jessica instructed Marcus.

Marcus stepped over to the ramp control panel and punched the button. Two minutes later, the ramp was fully retracted, and the doors were closed.

"I am a doctor in the cloning facility. It is my job to grow the clones. To bring them to maturity, so they can receive consciousness from the source host."

"Not to be rude, but what's the point?" Jessica asked impatiently.

"Before I continue, I must know who it is you wish to clone."

"I'm sorry, but I can't tell you that," Jessica replied. "I'd be putting your life at great risk."

"My career is already at risk simply by being here, speaking to you," Michi insisted. She looked deeply into Jessica's eyes. "Besides, I believe I already know who it is you wish to clone."

Jessica glanced at Marcus.

"Don't look at me," Marcus said, "I didn't tell anyone."

"We have heard of Captain Scott's noble sacrifice.

If he is, indeed, the one you wish to save from death, I wish to help."

"I'm not saying you're right," Jessica warned, "but let's just say, for the sake of discussion, that you are. Why would you help us?"

"Because Captain Scott saved us all," Michi replied seriously.

"Then, why didn't the administrator want to help?" Jessica wondered. "He saved her life as well."

"Perhaps she suspected you to be a Jung spy?" Michi suggested. "After all, we have been lying to the Jung for decades."

"Then you *can* clone a non-Nifelmian," Jessica surmised.

"It is possible, yes," Michi admitted. "However, there is significant risk, and I cannot promise a successful outcome."

"But it *is* possible?"

"Theoretically, yes. But it may take some time."

"Unfortunately, time is something we don't have much of," Jessica replied. She looked at Michi. "How much time are you talking about?"

"It takes two years to grow a clone to maturity."

"We'd be lucky to have two weeks," Jessica said. "There's no way his trial will go on for two years."

"There may be another way," Michi told them.

* * *

"I think I have a few candidates for you," Jessica announced, as she entered Commander Telles's office on Porto Santo. "Burgess, in the Sherma system, seems like the best choice so far, but it is a bit far from the Pentaurus cluster." Jessica closed the door behind her as she continued speaking. "Then again, that might be an advantage, you never know."

Commander Telles nodded. "The room is secured," he told her.

"The Nifelmians won't help us," Jessica said, changing topics on the fly, now that she knew no one could hear them. "At least, not officially."

"I feared as much."

"The chief administrator of their primary cloning facility gave me a bunch of excuses. The bottom line is that *they* claim the process is only successful on Nifelmians. Something to do with the way their brains have been reengineered over time. That's what the Jung were trying to force them to solve."

"You said, *not officially*."

"After I got back to the Mirai, a young lady approached us. Doctor Michi Sato. She grows clones, or something. She explained it all to me. The chief administrator is sticking to her story because she's afraid, if the Jung find out the Nifelmians have been exaggerating the problem, they'll come back even stronger than before. I can't say that I blame her, really."

"So, non-Nifelmians *can* be cloned?"

"They can, but it is far more risky. Again, something about the way their brains have been reconfigured to work with the consciousness transfer system."

"Will it work on Captain Scott?" Commander Telles asked directly.

"The best odds Doctor Sato could give me were fifty-fifty," Jessica explained.

"What does that mean?"

"Fifty-fifty chance Nathan will come out not remembering anything. Perhaps not even his name."

Commander Telles sighed. "Better than his current odds."

"There's another problem, though," Jessica

continued. "It takes *two years* to grow a clone to maturity. They *can* do it faster, but they would need specialized facilities, and the odds of a successful transfer of Nathan's consciousness and personality would be even worse."

"And, their chief administrator would not likely allow the use of their facilities for our purposes," the commander surmised.

"No, she wouldn't. Although if you send me back into her office and let me loose on her, I'm pretty sure I could convince her."

Commander Telles's eyebrow shot up at the implications. "This is a covert operation. Assaulting the administrator would likely..."

"I was kidding, Lucius," Jessica said, interrupting him. "Even if we could get a clone ready more quickly, there's still the problem of getting it to Nathan's cell."

"Indeed. The odds of being discovered before we can reach Nathan are already extremely high. Dragging a comatose clone will not help matters," the commander agreed.

"There is only one way to make this work," Jessica said. "Portable Consciousness Capture Device. Doctor Sato said it was developed for use by people working in remote areas, usually in high-risk jobs. The Nifelmians normally back up their state of consciousness at regular intervals, like once a Nifelmian month, or something. Maybe less, I'm not sure. Some of them even have a replacement body in stasis, waiting for them, just in case. Worst case, they lose a month of memories. But that requires regular visits to a backup facility. They've been working on a bio-neural link that would be implanted in the base of their necks, and connected to a transceiver. The idea is to upload their consciousness the moment their heart stops beating, before brain death occurs. In the meantime, their EMS units carry the portable capture device for field use."

"And this device can be used on Captain Scott?"

"Yes, but again, because he isn't Nifelmian, there's a higher risk of memory loss, and even personality disorders. However, Doctor Sato admitted it's all speculation, based on the problems they had more than five hundred years ago. Their technology has improved greatly since then, so there's at least a *chance* that Nathan will come through it with both his personality *and* his memories *intact*."

"Odds?"

"She kept sticking to fifty-fifty," Jessica replied. "I think she's afraid of getting my hopes up."

"Too late, I see," Commander Telles commented, noting her enthusiastic expression.

"At least it's a *chance*," Jessica replied.

"How big is this device?" the commander wondered.

"From the way she described it, I'd say it's small enough to fit in a field pack," Jessica told him.

"How soon can she get us this device, and teach us how to use it?"

"She needs to convince someone else to join her. She just does the cloning. The device is all tech."

"Does she have someone in mind?"

"She didn't say," Jessica said. "But I got the impression she did."

"How do we contact her?" Telles asked.

"She gave me this comm-unit," Jessica explained, pulling a small electronic device out of her pocket and showing it to the commander. "It works much like ours. She said it would work from anywhere in their system, so I don't even have to be in orbit over Nifelm."

"You will need to return soon. We must get this device, and get trained on it as soon as possible."

Jessica looked at the commander, her eyes narrowing. "Why? What's happened?"

"We got word from one of our operatives on Nor-Patri this morning," the commander began.

"You have operatives on Nor-Patri?" Jessica was stunned.

"For several weeks now."

"How the hell do they get messages back to..."

"It is not important, Jess. Captain Scott has been convicted. His execution will take place in ten Patrian days."

Jessica sank down in her chair, her hope ripped away from her again. "How long in Earth days?" she barely managed to find the courage to ask.

"Fifteen and a half," Commander Telles replied. "Do you think you can become fluent in Jung before then?"

"Just watch me."

* * *

"You know I would go with you if I could," Yanni reminded Deliza, as they stood at the base of the Mirai's aft cargo ramp.

"You have to finish your work here," Deliza said. "I understand that. Besides, it will only be for a few weeks. And I promise, if possible, I will try to return before then, even if only for a few days."

"I still don't see why you can't hire someone to take care of your family's holdings. After all, we have twice daily comm-drones between the Sol and Pentaurus sectors."

"It is imperative that I diversify my family's

holdings, and move as much of our wealth as possible *outside* of the Pentaurus cluster. Many of our lands have already been seized by the nobles, and they will do everything within their power to get control of my father's fortune. I must invest it elsewhere...markets where the nobles have no influence."

"I know," Yanni said, looking down.

"Just work twice as fast, so we can be together that much sooner," she teased.

"Would that I could."

"You about ready, Princess?" Josh asked as he and Loki passed behind her and ascended the ramp.

Deliza rolled her eyes, annoyed by the moniker.

"You hired him," Yanni reminded her.

"I'm starting to question that decision," Deliza admitted. She kissed Yanni, then turned and headed up the ramp, turning back halfway to wave goodbye.

"Ramp coming up," Marcus announced, as Deliza reached the cargo bay.

"I hate having to lie to Yanni," Deliza said as she approached Jessica, who was standing at the front of the cargo bay.

"You'll be able to tell him the truth, eventually," Jessica promised. "For now, it's better this way."

"I do not disagree." Deliza took a deep breath and let it out. "Where to now?"

"We go to Nifelm and pick up Doctors Sato and Megel, and then take them with us back to Corinair, where you will help them acquire the equipment and materials they need to set up a cloning lab."

"We just waltz in and take a couple of Nifelmian citizens away, and no one will complain?"

"They're meeting us at a remote location, away from the biospheres."

"And no one will miss them?"

"That's all I know," Jessica insisted. "Besides, it's a planet full of clones. There are probably a few thousand of each of them running around." Jessica smiled, but Deliza just looked confused. "Why is it no one laughs at my jokes?" Jessica said, as she turned and headed up the gangway to the main salon.

"You know, cloning is highly frowned upon on Corinair," Deliza warned, ascending the gangway behind her.

"That's why we want to keep it secret. Along with other obvious reasons. Besides, it's only for a few years."

"*Everyone, prepare for liftoff,*" Loki's voice called over the ship's intercoms.

"It's not going to be easy to make this all happen so quickly, *and* keep it secret," Deliza said, as she took a seat on one of the couches.

"We already have a plan," Jessica told her, also taking her seat. "You set up a corporation...imports and exports, commodities trading, shipping, maybe buy some buildings and such. And of course, you'll have to set up an R&D lab, where your two top scientists will be developing new products to bring to market, all in secret, of course."

"That's a rather ambitious plan," Deliza commented. "I just hope we still have enough funds to make it happen."

"So do I," Jessica replied.

"*Jump to orbit, complete,*" Loki's voice reported. "*We'll be starting our jump series to Nifelm in five minutes.*"

"Well, if you'll excuse me," Jessica said, rising from her seat. "Naralena and Commander Telles are waiting for me in the guest cabin. I've been warned I have a lot of studying to do."

* * *

"You do realize how tight that is," Loki said, a skeptical expression on his face.

"It's not that tight," Josh disagreed.

"The hell it isn't."

"It's more than four times the Mirai's size," Josh pointed out.

"But it's at the end of a one-light-year jump, Josh! That cave's a pin hole, at best!"

"Can we make the jump or not?" Jessica asked.

Josh and Loki answered simultaneously, but still with opposite opinions.

"That's encouraging," Naralena commented sarcastically.

"The Mirai's jump navigation computer is precise enough to successfully make the jump," Deliza pointed out.

"The precision of this ship's jump drive is not in question," Loki explained.

"We've made jumps from further out," Josh reminded Loki.

"In a Falcon!" Marcus exclaimed.

"Those jumps weren't into caves, Josh!" Loki added. "We'll have very little room to maneuver in there. And this ship, as nice as she is, isn't *that* maneuverable."

"I say she is."

"How do you intend to stop?" Loki challenged.

"And slamming into the wall is *not* an acceptable answer," Marcus added.

"This ship's deceleration thrusters are woefully underpowered for such a maneuver," Loki continued.

"We jump in backwards," Josh suggested, off the cuff. "Problem solved."

Loki rolled his eyes. "Great, so all our control inputs will be reversed."

"No problem!"

"Jesus, kid!" Marcus scowled. "Where do you draw the line?"

"Not here, that's for sure."

"We won't be going that fast when we jump, will we?" Jessica wondered.

"No, we won't," Josh confirmed, "and Loki knows that."

"I'm right here," Loki objected.

"He's just very risk averse."

"I have to be, flying with you," Loki defended. He turned to Jessica. "Can't we just jump into the valley in *front* of the cave, and then slide inside to hide, rather than jumping directly *into* the cave?"

Jessica looked at Commander Telles. "It's not like there are any enemy ships around."

"The Nifelmians *do* have communications and survey satellites," the commander said. "If they happen to be looking at that valley when we jump in, they will detect our jump flash."

"And do what?" Jessica asked. "They don't have any military. The best they could do is to send an airship out to investigate. By that time, we'll most likely be gone. And even if we aren't, it's not like they're able to stop us."

"We are attempting to execute a *covert* extraction," the commander reminded her.

"Being *covert* won't be of much use if we slam into a wall and die," Marcus pointed out.

"Quite true." Commander Telles took out his data pad and studied the screen thoughtfully.

"What is that?" Jessica asked.

"The orbital paths of the Nifelmian satellite

networks," he explained. "I asked Ensign Sheehan to scan their orbits during your last visit to Nifelm."

"Good thinking."

Commander Telles did not respond to the compliment, but continued studying the data pad instead. "There is a small window of forty-seven seconds, during which no satellite will be in position to detect our jump flash, assuming their orbital paths have not changed since these scans were obtained." He looked at Josh and Loki. "I assume that will provide you with adequate time to jump into the valley, and move the Mirai *inside* the cave, to avoid detection."

"Piece of pie," Josh declared. Loki just glared at him.

Marcus grumbled in disapproval.

"We have to time the departure jump as well," Loki reminded him.

"Jumping out is the easy part," Josh insisted.

Commander Telles looked at Deliza.

"What?" she asked.

"It is *your* ship, your highness."

"Don't call me that." Deliza sighed. "It may be *my* ship, but it's *your* operation. Therefore, it should be *your* decision, not mine."

"Do we get a say in this?" Marcus wondered.

"You do not," Commander Telles replied. He looked at Josh and Loki. "Prepare to jump us in, gentlemen," he ordered, handing his data pad to Loki.

"Yes!" Josh said, enthusiastically.

"Lord, help us," Marcus declared, as he turned and headed down the short ladder from the Mirai's cockpit to her main deck.

Loki sighed. "Maybe you should all strap in."

"Will it make a difference?" Jessica wondered. "If we slam into a wall, I mean."

"*No one is slamming into any walls!*" Marcus shouted from the deck below.

"Even at low speed, there will be considerable turbulence due to the sudden displacement of air when we jump in," Loki explained. "It will likely be even worse, since we *are* jumping into a narrow canyon."

"Very well," Jessica replied, taking the jump seat at the engineering station behind Loki. Commander Telles folded down the jump seat behind Josh, and buckled in, as well.

"You want me to do the jump calculations, or are you going to do them?" Josh asked Loki.

"What do you think?" Loki replied, as he entered the jump parameters into the jump-nav computer.

Josh smiled as he glanced back at Jessica and Commander Telles. "Nothing to worry about, people," he announced, confidently. "Like I said, it's a piece of pie."

"Cake, Josh," Jessica corrected, as she tightened her restraints. "The expression is 'a piece of cake'."

"He knows what it is," Loki mumbled, annoyed by Josh's intentional error. "Come to two seven zero and pitch up four point two three seven degrees, relative to the system ecliptic. Reduce speed to five meters per second."

"That's practically a dead stop, Loki," Josh protested.

"That's the idea."

"You're taking all the fun out of it."

"There's no way I'm letting you jump in backwards," Loki insisted. "Five meters per second."

"Fine." Josh made the adjustments, altering the

Mirai's approach course relative to where the jump-nav computer calculated the planet would be at the time of their jump. "You got that jump ready yet?"

"Be patient," Loki insisted. "There are a lot of variables to consider for this jump."

"*We're secure back here,*" Marcus announced over the ship's intercom.

"That should do it," Loki decided.

"You double-checked it?" Jessica asked.

"Are you kidding?" Loki replied. "I quadruple-checked it. We jump in one minute." He looked at Josh. "I'm assuming you won't mind if we use the jump sequencer for this one?"

"If it will make you feel better," Josh replied.

"It will." Loki activated the Mirai's auto-jump sequencer, allowing the ship's autopilot to take control up to the moment of jump. "Jump sequencer activated. Auto-flight has the ship."

Josh placed his hands on his knees, ready to take the controls the moment the jump completed.

"Forty seconds," Loki warned. "Lift thrusters show ready, reactor is at full power. Ranging and terrain-following sensors are set to maximum sensitivity." He glanced at the jump sequencer display. "Twenty seconds," he announced over the intercom.

"*Twenty seconds.*"

Naralena swallowed hard. "They know what they're doing, right?"

"You jumped into a Koharan lake," Marcus commented. "In a frickin' mini-sub! This should be a breeze for you."

"Much bigger target," Naralena mumbled, her eyes shut tightly.

"Josh and Loki are the best pilots around," Deliza

assured them. "Just don't ever tell Josh that I said that."

"Don't worry," Marcus replied. "The boy's ego is big enough as it is."

"*Five seconds,*" Loki voiced warned over the intercom.

"Three......two......one......"

The Mirai's windows turned opaque as the jump flash washed over the ship. They shook violently, as if slapped by an unseen hand.

"Jump complete!"

"Oh, yeah!"

"Lift thrusters at forty percent!" Loki reported.

"Firing decel thrusters! Full power!" Josh announced, pushing the deceleration thruster throttles all the way forward.

"Cave entrance in ten seconds!" Loki warned.

Josh looked out the forward windows. Despite its size, the cave opening looked surprisingly small. For a brief moment, Josh wondered if the terrain maps provided by Doctor Sato were correct.

"Forward speed dropping!" Loki announced. "Two meters per second."

The mouth of the cave moved closer, as the Mirai slid low over the ground, nearly brushing the tops of trees. Josh pulled the deceleration throttles back to zero as he twisted the flight control stick to the left, causing the Mirai to yaw quickly to port.

"What the hell...!" Loki cried out in surprise, as the ship rotated around. "What are you doing?"

"Parking," Josh replied calmly.

Three seconds later, the ship had rotated one hundred and eighty degrees. The mouth of the cave swept over them, now from behind, moving away from the Mirai's bow. Josh quickly brought the main engines up a bit to further slow their descent. A quick glance at the terrain-following sensors display told him the floor of the cave was reasonably level, with no protrusions below that might damage the ship. "Drop the gear!" he ordered.

"Gear coming down," Loki replied, even before Josh finished giving the order.

Josh began to decrease the lift thrusters as the last of the Mirai's horizontal speed disappeared.

"Down and locked!" Loki announced.

Two seconds later, the Mirai's landing gear touched the cave floor.

"Contact!" Loki shouted.

Josh killed the Mirai's lift thrusters, allowing the ship to settle down gently on her main gear. He paused a moment, listening to the sound of his ship's engines as they spun down.

"Killing all engines," Loki reported. "Bringing the reactor down to one percent." Loki glanced across the console, checking all the critical systems. He wasn't yet accustomed to the Mirai's displays, and had to check everything more than once. "We're good," he finally declared.

A big grin came over Josh's face. "I told you." He turned to look back at Jessica and Commander Telles. "Piece of cake," he added with a wink.

CHAPTER SIX

"General, Lord Torret is here to see you."

General Bacca looked up from his reading pad, sharing the same surprised look as his aide. It only took a glance for his aide to turn to open the door and allow the elder statesman into the general's study.

General Bacca set his reading pad aside and immediately rose to his feet, straightening his uniform.

"Lord Torret," the general's aide announced from the doorway.

The elder statesman, and leader of the Torret family, entered the study. "General, I trust I am not intruding."

"Of course not, my lord," the general replied. He knew Lord Torret was only being polite. No man in his right mind would refuse a visit from the senior member of one of the original leadership castes of the Jung Empire. "To what do I owe the honor?"

The general was also observing formalities, adhering firmly to protocol. Truthfully, he had little regard for the isolationist caste, of which Lord Torret was a member. So overpopulated was the Jung homeworld, that it depended upon the resources of its conquered worlds in order to survive. The empire existed *because* of its conquests, beginning with its first raids on neighbors from Nor-Patri itself, long before the empire had returned to the stars. Conquest and expansion *made* the Jung Empire possible. No one could deny that fact, not even Lord Torret himself. Yet, for more than two centuries, the isolationists had fought to prevent the continued expansion of the empire, and to that end, had only recently gained a majority vote on the council. "Please," the general said, pointing to one of the two overstuffed chairs in his office.

"We have known each other for more than fifty years, my dear General," Lord Torret began as he moved to sit. "Because of this, I felt compelled to meet with you in person...to tell you myself."

"Your words carry an ominous tone, my lord. Should I be concerned?" the general asked as he sat back down.

Lord Torret sighed. "You have been a loyal servant of the Jung Empire your entire adult life, General. However, that is not always enough."

General Bacca said nothing.

"Your failure to hold the Sol system, and to defeat Captain Scott and the Aurora, is seen by many as the root cause of the catastrophe that has befallen Nor-Patri."

"Yourself included," the general surmised, no longer caring about protocol.

"One cannot deny, that *had* you defeated the Aurora and captured the Celestia, the attack on Zhu-Anok would not have taken place."

General Bacca continued to sit silently.

"While it would be against Jung law to prosecute you for your failures while in the service of the empire, some measures *must* be taken. Those officers who follow *must know*, that while victories are rewarded, so shall failures be punished." Lord Torret waited for a response, but received none. "Surely you can see the logic of this."

"And how far up the chain of command does such punishment travel?" the general wondered.

Lord Torret looked unsure.

"The generals over me, shall they too be punished,

for failing to give me the resources needed to hold the system? And those in the intelligence divisions, who insisted the jump drive project was still years from a prototype? Or the commanders of the ships who failed to destroy the Aurora when we received word of her test?"

"General..."

"Or, perhaps, the very leaders of our warrior castes, who, in their infinite wisdom, chose to invade the Sol system before adequate forces could be assembled to ensure victory?"

"I am not denying that blame exists at many levels," Lord Torret admitted. "But you know how this works. It is always one man upon whom such blame is assigned."

"I brought you the one responsible for the attack. Your own courts convicted him only a week ago," the general said. "Is that not enough?"

"For the common people of Nor-Patri, perhaps," Lord Torret conceded. "Give them someone to execute, and their anger will be forever sated. But the castes...they are an entirely different breed. We live by codes of conduct. Risks and rewards. Successes and failures. We reap the rewards of our efforts, and suffer the consequences of our failures. You know this better than most. Every officer knows this. It is written in the very oath that you, and every officer in the warrior castes, swear upon commission." Lord Torret looked at the general. "Have others not been punished in the past, for failures that could have been attributed to you as well? It is simply your time."

General Bacca glared at Lord Torret. "And what shall my punishment be?"

Lord Torret took a deep breath, preparing

himself. "You shall be stripped of all rank, and your lands shall be forfeit back to the people of Nor-Patri. Furthermore, your inclusion in the warrior caste shall be terminated, effective as of the execution of Captain Scott."

"Then I shall be left penniless...without honor."

"You shall be allowed to retain this estate," Lord Torret said. "However, I would advise you to sell it as quickly as possible, and move to less expensive accommodations, in order to ensure your continued survival. Unless, of course, you wish to join the working castes."

"And my honor?"

Lord Torret took a deep breath and sighed. "There is honor in facing one's punishment with dignity. You should take pride in the decades of service you have given the empire."

"All of which resulted in my being cast aside, in the name of political expediency," General Bacca said flatly. "Is that truly the message you wish to send to your officers?"

"They will take whatever message they choose," Lord Torret said, as he rose from his seat. "As can you. The announcement will be made by week's end."

"Why tell me now?" the general wondered, not rising from his own seat.

"As I said, we have known one another for many years. Out of respect, I felt I would give you a chance to prepare."

General Bacca glared at Lord Torret for a moment. "If you are expecting gratitude, you will be sourly disappointed."

Lord Torret sighed one last time before departing. "Fair or unfair, it is the world in which we live." The elder statesman bowed his head slightly, in one last show of respect to the general. "Good luck, General."

General Bacca said nothing as Lord Torret left his office. He had spent his entire life wanting to be in the service of the empire. He had been in command of hundreds of thousands of men, and dozens of ships. He had been the military ruler of the birthplace of humanity. Born on one of the worlds once conquered by the Jung, he had done the impossible and had climbed high enough to have his own lands on the Jung homeworld. He had been as true a Jung as any man could be. But it had all been a lie. In the end, it was not a lord of a caste who would take the blame, but an immigrant general. An outsider who dared to become one of them. And now, he was losing it all, because of *him*. Captain Nathan Scott.

General Bacca tried to take solace in the knowledge that his young adversary would be losing far more than he would, but it was of little comfort.

* * *

Jessica tightened her face mask straps and made her way down the cargo ramp to the floor of the cave in which Josh had skillfully hidden the Mirai. She turned to her right and headed toward the front of the cave, moving around the outside of the ship's port engine nacelle. Ahead of her stood Commander Telles, staring out across the snow-covered valley from the mouth of the cave, his tactical helmet under his right arm.

"How go the lessons?" the commander asked her over the mask comms as Jessica approached him from behind.

"How did you know it was me?" Jessica wondered.

"There are three women currently on board the Mirai," the commander explained. "Only one of them wears tactical boots. They make a distinctive sound when walking on the rubble of this cave floor."

"Just the boots, huh?"

"Deliza is wearing soft, rubber-soled shoes. And Naralena is at least two kilograms heavier than you."

"Impressive."

"You will learn," the commander said. "And the lessons?"

"The lessons are going well," Jessica answered, switching to the Jung language.

Commander Telles cast a sidelong glance at his new recruit. "Your accent is quite convincing," he answered in Jung.

"Thank you. It is not the first language I have studied, you know."

"I am aware, and the Jung would not use 'you know' in such fashion."

"The working castes would," Jessica defended.

Commander Telles nodded. "True, but if using the Jung language becomes necessary, it would be better for you to speak as if you were a member of the upper castes, and not a commoner."

"Of course," Jessica agreed. "Any sign of them?"

"They are three hundred meters in that direction," the commander replied, pointing slightly left, toward a thicket of trees.

Jessica strained to see, but was unable to spot them. "How can you tell?"

"A small group of birds took flight from that area moments before your arrival," the commander explained.

"You *are* good."

"Plus, I have been tracking them on my visor display," the commander admitted, holding up his helmet so she could see the two red blips on the map display inside his helmet's visor.

Jessica smiled as she continued watching the trees. A minute later, two people emerged from the edge of the forest, both of them wearing Nifelmian breathing masks. Jessica recognized Doctor Sato's petite form. She was carrying a large bag in each hand, as was the man walking behind her.

"Any idea as to his identity?" the commander inquired.

"None," Jessica replied. "She only said she needed to recruit someone with technical specialties."

"You do realize, we know little about either of them," the commander reminded her.

"I know."

"We must keep a close eye on them both, until we can determine what level of trust they can be afforded."

Jessica looked at him. "We're trusting them to grow a clone of Nathan, and to teach us to copy his consciousness into some kind of storage device. How much more will we need to trust them?"

"With the truth about the death of Nathan Scott," the commander replied. "A secret that, if revealed, could reignite a war that would cost billions of lives."

"There is that." Jessica stepped forward to greet Doctor Sato. "Glad you could make it," she said, switching back to English. "We were beginning to worry that you might have changed your mind."

"Truth be told, it had occurred to me...multiple times, in fact." Doctor Sato admitted, setting her bags down to rest. "I am leaving all that I know, after all."

"And why would that be?" Commander Telles inquired.

"Doctor Sato, this is Commander Telles, of the Ghatazhak. Commander, Doctor Michi Sato."

"A pleasure," the commander said, without moving.

"This is Doctor Turi Megel," Doctor Sato introduced her companion. "He is a specialist in the consciousness transfer technology needed to complete the cloning process."

"I'm assuming he can be trusted?" the commander asked, unconcerned with the possibility of insulting Doctor Megel.

"I have known him for many decades," Doctor Sato assured him. "I trust him completely."

The commander's eyebrow went up. "You do not appear old enough to have known him that long."

"This is my fifth body," she explained.

"I see." Commander Telles looked at Jessica.

"Yeah, it takes some getting used to," Jessica said, sensing his skepticism.

"The question still stands," the commander continued. "Why would you both leave your world so willingly?"

"The opportunity to complete our work," Doctor Sato answered. "You see, Nifelm began as a dream to extend the human lifespan, perhaps forever."

"There are many ways to extend the human lifespan, Doctor," the commander stated. "Cloning is but one of them."

"Yes, but cloning is the *only* one that can fulfill the dream of immortality. All others simply prolong life by slowing the aging process. Those that we know of, at least. Our subjugation by the Jung has made our leaders fearful of how our technology might be misused by such people."

"Technology will always have the potential to

be misused. That *alone* is insufficient reason for technologies to *not* be developed."

"I'm afraid our leaders would not agree with you, Commander."

"Then why do *you* wish to disobey them?"

"I do not *wish* to do so, but I feel obligated to do so. Your Alliance saved this world, and your Captain Scott was instrumental in our liberation. Such people *need* to be kept alive, by any means possible. If not for the betterment of humanity, then simply as a reward for his sacrifices on humanity's behalf."

"An interesting statement," the commander observed, "especially from one who *appears* so young."

"Those of us who have lived through several transfer cycles tend to become somewhat philosophical in our nature. A side effect of having so much additional time to contemplate the nature of existence."

"Another intriguing concept," the commander said. "One that I would not mind discussing further, but at a later time." He looked at Doctor Megel. "And yourself? Why are you willing to leave your world?"

"Are you kidding?" Doctor Megel replied. "There are dozens, perhaps hundreds of human-inhabited worlds out there. I have lived on this world for nearly five hundred years. I know every ridgeline, every body of water, every ice sheet. I want to see something beyond this world. I want to see them all. To do so, I fear I have no choice but to leave my world."

"And how will you maintain your immortality, once you leave your world?" the commander wondered.

"Therein lies our motivation to succeed in our assignment, does it not?"

"Good point," Jessica agreed, reaching down and

picking up one of Doctor Sato's bags. "Shall we go aboard?"

"Please," Doctor Sato said wearily. "We have been walking since sunrise."

Commander Telles stepped aside, keeping his eye on the two Nifelmians as they followed Jessica toward the back of the Mirai. He looked about the area outside the cave again, checking the visor on the helmet under his arm one last time before turning and heading back toward the cargo ramp. "Marcus, our visitors have arrived. Prepare the ship for departure. The next jump window is in twenty-seven minutes."

* * *

Admiral Dumar stared across the table at Admiral Galiardi and his staff, waiting for an answer.

"No one not of Earth will be forced to leave this asteroid under my command," Admiral Galiardi finally replied.

"Yet, you *would* prefer that they do."

"Yes, I would," Galiardi replied without reservation or pause. "As would the people of my world."

"An odd position, considering what those people, *not* of Earth, have sacrificed on *behalf* of it."

"No one is questioning the sacrifices your people have made," Galiardi pointed out. "Your intentions have been without reproach, and your efforts in the defense of Earth have been *greatly* appreciated, by *myself,* as *well* as the people of my world. But it is high time we take responsibility for our own protection, and allow your people to return to theirs." Admiral Galiardi bowed his head respectfully, "With our undying thanks, of course."

"And what of those who do not wish to leave?" Admiral Dumar pressed.

"Of course, they will be allowed to continue working, in an advisory capacity. However, I would think that they would wish to return to their friends and families back in the Pentaurus cluster."

"Most of them do," Admiral Dumar assured him. "However, some have built new lives *here*, on *your* world. Some even have started families, on *your* world."

"I promise you, Admiral Dumar, anyone wishing to remain will be taken care of, with the respect they deserve. You have my word."

"And if, in the future, they should become dissatisfied with their jobs, or for whatever reasons, wish to return to their homeworlds?"

"Then we shall see to their safe and timely return."

Admiral Dumar was unable to read Admiral Galiardi's expression. It was one of the many things he disliked about the man. "Very well," the admiral replied. "I hope I can take you at your word."

* * *

"And it will only take us two days to travel nearly one thousand light years?" Doctor Megel said, astonished.

"Actually, if we make each jump at maximum range, we can make it in a day and a half," Jessica told him.

"Incredible. And we are 'jumping' now, as we speak?"

"One jump every six minutes."

"How do you know when it occurs?" Doctor Megel wondered. "I'm told there is a brilliant flash of light."

"There is," Jessica confirmed, "but we will not see it. The windows turn opaque just before the jump occurs, and clear just after the jump has concluded. That's the only indication we get from inside."

"That's the only indication *you* get," Marcus grumbled.

Doctor Sato looked confused.

"Mister Taggart claims the jumps make his teeth hurt," Commander Telles explained.

"It ain't a claim," Marcus added. "Believe me."

"And how many jumps will it take to get there?"

"About three hundred and fifty, I think," Jessica answered.

"You poor man," Doctor Sato said, giving Marcus a sympathetic look.

"It ain't as bad on this ship, for some reason. But I can still feel it," Marcus admitted.

"Incredible," Doctor Megel repeated in awe, as he noticed the overhead windows in the main salon turning opaque.

"So, is that the device?" Jessica asked, pointing at the bag next to Doctor Megel.

"Yes, yes it is." He picked up the bag and placed it on the table in front of them. "Portable Consciousness Capture Device, or PCCD. Some people call it a 'soul catcher'."

"Interesting interpretation," Commander Telles said.

"Interpretation of what?" Jessica asked.

"Of what constitutes the human soul," the commander explained. "There are many different philosophies on this subject."

"Let's not start that conversation," Jessica suggested. "Not now, anyway." She turned back to Doctor Megel. "How does it work?"

"You place this cap onto the subject's head," he began, pulling out a small, black cap with a wire hanging off the edge. "You connect it to the device with this cable. The cap contains thousands of tiny sensors that are used to scan the subject's brain." He looked at the others. "I won't bother going into the technical details, as that level of understanding is not necessary to operate the device. After putting it on, you run the system's self-test and calibration, by pressing this button. Once completed, you begin the scan by pressing this button. The scan takes approximately five to seven minutes to complete."

"Then what?"

"Then you bring it back to us."

"The whole device?"

"Preferably, yes, but only the storage unit is required. However, the battery on the storage unit is only good for three days."

"What happens after that?" Jessica wondered.

"The image will be lost."

"How many Earth days is that?" she asked.

"Just over two," Doctor Sato added.

"Forty-nine hours, twenty-seven minutes, using Earth's time conventions," Commander Telles said.

"Seems too easy, considering what it's doing," Deliza commented.

"The device was designed to be used by first responders," Doctor Megel explained. "Prior to perfecting the implants, these devices were strategically located all over our cities. Be forewarned, they are designed to be used on a subject that is still alive."

"They *have* been used postmortem," Doctor Sato clarified. "But the time window is very short. Only two minutes, at best."

"Better the scan is completed while Captain Scott is still alive," Doctor Megel insisted. "We do not know how well it will work on someone not of our genetics."

"But it *will* work?" Jessica asked, hoping the doctors would provide some reassurance.

"I cannot promise."

"It will work," Doctor Sato insisted.

Doctor Megel glared at her in disapproval.

"What's the problem?" Jessica asked, noticing his expression.

"There is still some debate about how much of the human personality is in one's DNA, and how much is learned behavior. If it is mostly DNA, then Captain Scott would still be Captain Scott, even without the transfer of consciousness, only with slight differences. He would just be without any memory of his life prior to the capture scan. However, if the reverse is true..."

"Then he could come out as a completely different person," Commander Telles concluded.

"It *is* a possibility," Doctor Megel stated.

"A *remote* possibility," Doctor Sato insisted.

Jessica sighed, thinking for a moment. "And how long can Nathan's consciousness be stored...in this device?"

"As long as the power is not interrupted, for several years. However, the longer the human consciousness remains in storage, the lower the chances of a successful restoration. This is why, in cases of accidental death, the cloning process is accelerated."

"Why can't we just do that?" Jessica wondered. "Accelerate the process?"

"Acceleration of the cloning process has its own risks," Doctor Sato warned. "Considering that we are trying to clone a non-Nifelmian, it would be safer to take the full two years to complete the cloning process."

"How are you going to do this?" Deliza wondered. "There are no such facilities on Corinair."

"I have brought samples of the nutrient bath, and of the cloning lattice," Doctor Sato explained. "They are formulated using chemicals we believe are common throughout the galaxy, and should not be difficult to recreate on your world."

"And, I have brought the technical specifications for all the necessary equipment. The cloning chamber, the monitoring systems, the restoration matrix...all of it," Doctor Megel added.

"Based on what we have seen of the capabilities of your fabrication devices, it should not be difficult to construct our own facility on Corinair, assuming you can provide the space and the raw materials."

"And the fabricators, of course," Doctor Megel added.

"We have one in our cargo bay," Commander Telles assured them.

"Then we should be able to clone Captain Scott," Doctor Sato concluded. "Assuming that you are able to collect an adequate DNA sample, and successfully capture his consciousness."

"I am curious about one thing," Doctor Megel said. "How are you planning on getting onto the Jung homeworld *undetected*?"

"We developed a jump-capable mini-sub," Jessica explained. "We can jump from outside a system, into the ocean of the target world...undetected."

"Unfortunately, none are available," Commander Telles stated.

Jessica turned and looked at him in disbelief. "I thought we built three of them?"

"We did," the commander replied. "One was used

for your mission to Kohara, and was destroyed. The other two are otherwise occupied."

"What do you mean, *otherwise occupied*?" Jessica demanded.

"Their current use is classified," the commander replied, casting a quick sidelong glance at the two Nifelmian guests.

"Can I ask how *we* are going to get onto the Jung homeworld?" Jessica asked, having understood the commander's nonverbal message.

"We will space jump," Commander Telles told her.

Jessica shook her head. "That won't work, and you know it."

"It will if we jump from far enough away."

Jessica looked puzzled.

"Project Phantom," Deliza said.

Commander Telles closed his eyes briefly, annoyed that no one seemed concerned that they were openly discussing the details of their plan in front of two strangers.

Jessica looked at her, confused. "Project Phantom?"

"We modified the Ghatazhak space-jump rigs."

"Modified them how?" Jessica inquired.

"We made them jump-capable."

"Is this discussion necessary?" the commander wondered.

"You mean jump as in jump-drive jump?" Jessica asked, ignoring the commander.

Commander Telles sighed. "Precisely."

"And they work?"

"Initial testing has gone very well," Deliza said.

"Initial testing." Jessica was beginning to get suspicious.

"We have completed several manned test jumps," Deliza explained.

"But?" Jessica asked, sensing her trepidation.

"No jumps have been made into the atmosphere," Deliza added. "But there is no reason to suspect that it wouldn't work."

"What about the jump flash?" Jessica wondered.

"It is quite small," Commander Telles said. "And the weather on Nor-Patri has frequent electrical storms. If timed correctly, our jump flashes are likely to be seen as part of those storms."

"As if jumping a mini-sub into an ocean, from two light years out, wasn't crazy enough," Jessica mumbled to herself. "What's the range on these suits?"

"A single light year," Deliza answered.

Jessica shook her head again.

"The Mirai will put us on the proper course and speed to intercept Nor-Patri. The rest will be up to us."

"So, you two are going to fall from space, after jumping a whole light year, wearing nothing but space suits, and parachute to the surface?" Doctor Megel asked.

"Correct," Commander Telles replied, in his usual calm demeanor.

Doctor Megel looked at Jessica, then back at the commander, disbelief on his face. "You people do this kind of thing all the time?"

* * *

Nathan stared out the tiny, unbreakable window of his cell. It looked out onto a large courtyard, which had nothing more than a few small decorative bushes. At times, he would catch a glimpse of other prisoners, ones who were allowed outdoor time periodically. He often imagined what their crimes had been, to amuse himself.

The view held little interest, other than the fact it was outside of his cell. The Jung sky, or what little he could see of it from his tiny porthole, was often cloudy and overcast, especially at night. He couldn't remember ever seeing any stars since his arrival. He wondered if the entire planet had similar weather, or if it was just the region in which he was located. Probably the latter.

It had only been a week since his conviction, and already he missed his daily flight to and from the judicial complex at the center of the Jung capital city of Patrisk-Dortah. It allowed him a brief glimpse of the coastline during their short flight into the center of the city. So much of Nor-Patri was spotted with such smaller bodies of water, the majority of which were interconnected. The planet was a jumble of massive islands, separated by wide rivers and seas. They didn't seem to have the massive oceans of Earth, although their world was covered by nearly as much water, when viewed as surface area. But the seas of Nor-Patri were shallow compared to those of Earth. At least, that was his understanding. He didn't understand most of what little he was allowed to watch on their entertainment and information networks.

So now his days were spent entirely in his tiny cell, either staring outside, or staring at the display screen. On the plus side, the guards had seemed more tolerable since his conviction. Nathan postulated that they were content he would soon be executed, and they awaited the day with great expectation, as, apparently, all of Nor-Patri did.

How odd it felt, to be hated by so many. Especially

since any of them would have done the same to protect their own world. Nathan wondered if *anyone* on Nor-Patri believed his conviction to be unjust, or his sentence unduly harsh. Did *any* of the Jung citizens disagree with the views of the leadership castes? Nathan found it difficult to believe there were not at least a few who opposed the verdict. As a student of history, he could remember few events to which an entire nation's population reacted the same, let alone the population of an entire world. Did the Jung have that much control over the hearts and minds of their citizens? It did not seem possible.

But, there were no protests in his defense. No arguments against his conviction. No sympathy for his pending execution. At least, none that he had witnessed.

Nathan sighed. He had wanted to get away. Away from his family, away from politics, away from Earth. He had certainly done that. In a mere two years, he had gone from a scrub ensign fresh out of the academy, to the captain of the Aurora, and had become the savior of not only the Earth, but of all the Sol and Pentaurus sectors.

All because he had gotten drunk with his friends six years earlier, and enlisted. He remembered his mother's reaction, and his father's lack of one. His mother had offered to pull strings, to get his enlistment canceled, but he refused. He had insisted that it was his life, his decision. Had it all been worth it?

The sound of footsteps, both heavy boots and dress shoes, sounded from the corridor. Then, the buzzing of the door lock. The door swung open, revealing his advocate, Mister Gorus.

"I don't suppose you've come to tell me you've filed an appeal?" Nathan said.

"I thought you understood there would be no appeal?" Mister Gorus replied.

"It was a joke," Nathan explained.

"Of course." Mister Gorus stepped inside, and the guard closed the cell door behind him. The elder man moved to the side, taking a seat at the small table in the corner. "Surprisingly, members of the warrior caste have suggested you be allowed to take your own life using one of their blades. They argue that, despite your horrendous acts, you are a warrior and deserve a warrior's death. Personally, I believe they simply wish to possess the blade that took the life of Na-Tan."

"Oh, please, don't tell me they're calling me that here, as well?"

"Indeed, they are," Mister Gorus assured him. "At least, among the leaders of the warrior castes. I would not concern yourself. It is more of a joke, really."

"Oh, I feel so much better." Nathan sighed, his gaze returning to the tiny window to the outside. "So, why *are* you here?"

"I have managed to convince the council to allow you to send a final message home to your family, should you so choose."

Nathan looked down for a moment, thinking. He then turned to Mister Gorus. "To be honest, I'm not sure what I'd say."

"You must say something," Mister Gorus insisted. "You will undoubtedly go down in your world's version of history as a hero. Therefore, your last words will likely stand for all to see."

Nathan pondered some more. "How long do I have?"

"To submit your message? Right up until your execution, I would imagine. I see no reason for the council to decree otherwise."

"I will think about it," Nathan finally agreed.

Mister Gorus rose. "I will check back with you before your execution. If you request it, the guards will provide you with a note pad."

"I assume my message will be read by your people, before it is sent?"

"Of course."

Nathan nodded his understanding, after which Mister Gorus signaled the guard, and departed.

Nathan sighed, his gaze returning to his tiny window. *What to say?* That he might be able to share his dying thoughts with his family and friends had never occurred to him, let alone that those words might be scrutinized by future historians.

At least he had a few days more to compose them.

* * *

"It's going to take a lot of work to turn this place into a proper lab," Doctor Sato warned.

"It's the only building Captain Navarro could get on short notice with an underground basement, and a landing pad on the roof," Deliza explained. "And it has the advantage of being in an industrial area, so we are unlikely to raise any suspicion out here."

"Still, a lot of work."

"It's not that bad," Doctor Megel disagreed, walking toward the corner of the basement nearest to the freight elevator. "We just start in the corner, put in a couple walls to make just enough room to get started with the cloning process. The growing bath itself isn't that big, and that's the only part that has to be a sterile environment, right?"

"I don't know," Doctor Sato replied skeptically.

"We're not talking about an entire cloning facility with dozens of chambers, Michi. Just one."

Michi looked at Jessica. "That's why I invited him," she said. "Turi is always the optimist."

"What about all the pumps and stuff?" Deliza wondered. "Isn't there a lot of support machinery that feeds the growth chamber?"

"Yes, and ideally, they would be in a sterile environment, as well. But as long as the system is closed loop, and we put the feed ports for adding chemicals in the same sterile room as the growth chamber, we should be fine. Besides, once we get the chamber up and running, and get the clone of Captain Scott under way, we can start adding rooms. We should have a full and proper lab by the time his clone reaches maturity."

"When do we get started?" Michi asked, resigning herself to the situation.

"A work crew is scheduled to start tomorrow. We just have to draw up plans for them to follow, first," Deliza said. "Preferably ones that don't hint at what will be done in here."

"Where are we going to stay?" Michi asked.

"Aboard the Mirai, for now," Deliza replied. "At least, until we can make other arrangements."

"We need to get the fabricator and all the equipment that we brought from Earth unloaded," Commander Telles reminded them. "We only have four days before Nathan's execution, and we still have a long journey to Nor-Patri ahead of us."

* * *

After eight days of wandering about the capital, Armin was nearly out of patience. He had checked more than twenty-eight government facilities with flight decks either on top of the buildings, or in a nearby courtyard, and had scanned every one he could find. He had even scanned the ones that were obviously not detention facilities, on the off chance that Captain Scott was being held somewhere other than in one of the many holding facilities in the capital.

Patrisk-Dortah was an enormous city. It was, in fact, fifteen different cities that all ran together, sprawling over hundreds of kilometers, from the edge of the Dortahn Sea to the base of the Iridor Mountains. It was the capital of the entire Jung Empire and, thus, was constantly busy.

Luckily for Armin, the city had an extremely efficient public transportation system, most of which had managed to escape damage from the fallout from Zhu-Anok. However, on occasion, Armin had been forced to walk some distance between stations due to damaged rails and roadways, which had slowed his progress.

Unfortunately, the credit chip from the man whose identity he had assumed was running out of funds. Had it not been for the public assistance stations that had sprung up all over the city after the attacks, and the shelters that seemed to be in every neighborhood, he would have run out of funds long ago. At the rate he was spending, he calculated he would have to start looking for work soon.

Fortunately, the chaos that followed the destruction of Zhu-Anok had begun to settle. The displaced were mostly sheltered, and the hungry were being fed. In addition, the most critical infrastructures were coming back online all over the capital. Soon, the cleanup and reconstruction would begin, and work would be plentiful once again.

But, for now, Armin had a more important task

to complete. He had to discover where the Jung were holding Captain Scott, and only three days remained until the captain's public execution was to take place. All he had were the identification numbers on the side of the shuttle that had carried him to the judicial complex at the center of Patrisk-Dortah each day for trial. Always from the same general direction, that of the coast. But, he was less than a kilometer from the coastline now, and there were very few potential targets left. If the shuttle had been taking a direct path each day, then Armin would eventually detect Captain Scott's nanites. But, if the shuttle had been purposefully taking a roundabout course in order to confuse anyone who might have been tracking them, then Armin could be headed in the wrong direction altogether.

* * *

"I have an urgent message from Porto Santo operations, for Commander Telles," the Avendahl's communications officer said, from the doorway to the captain's ready room.

"Relay it to the Mirai on the surface," Captain Navarro instructed without a pause.

"Yes, sir," the officer replied.

Commander Golan watched the communications officer leave, and then shifted in his chair to look at his captain again. "You're not interested in the content of the message?"

"The message was not for me," the captain replied, his attention focused on his data pad once more.

"Even though it was marked urgent?" The commander received no response. "They are up to something."

"Of that, I have no doubt," Captain Navarro agreed.

"And you're not at all curious about what they are doing?"

"Of course, I am curious," the captain replied. "But if they wanted me to know, they would have told me."

"I'd at least peek at the message."

"It is most likely encrypted."

"Our comm officers *always* break the encryption, regardless of the recipient."

"I am aware," the captain replied. "After all, I am the one who gave them that order."

"Then why not peek?" the commander wondered. "Information *is* power."

"And too *much* information can be a curse," the captain countered. "Besides, I'm sure Commander Telles expects us to break the encryption. I doubt the unencrypted version is in plain text. Takaran, Angla, or otherwise. All we would see is a meaningless string of words and phrases, which could be interpreted in fifty different ways."

"Yeah, you're probably right," the commander resigned, looking back down at his own data pad. After a few moments, he spoke again. "I'd still peek."

* * *

Commander Telles touched the screen of the data pad several times, then carefully read the decrypted message.

"What is it?" Jessica asked.

"Two sets of planetary coordinates," the commander replied, "as well as weather forecasts for the target planet."

"I'm afraid to ask which planet," Loki said, as the commander handed the data pad back to him.

"We will depart immediately," the commander announced.

"For?" Loki cringed, awaiting the inevitable.

"The Patoray system," the commander replied. "Or just under one light year from it. I will provide a more precise arrival point once I have calculated our insertion parameters."

"Insertion?" Josh wondered. "What insertion?" Josh looked around the cargo bay. "I hope you're not planning on flying this ship to Nor-Patri. Even *I'm* not *that* crazy."

"We brought our own insertion systems," the commander replied.

"Where?" Josh wondered, looking around the cargo bay. He noticed the two long shipping crates on the port side, each of them about the size of a coffin. "Those things?"

"Personal Jump Insertion Systems," Commander Telles replied.

"I like to call them 'PJs'," Jessica commented.

"They will get us into the lower atmosphere of Nor-Patri," Commander Telles assured Josh. "All you have to do is put us on the proper course and speed. The insertion systems will do the rest."

Josh looked at Jessica. "Seriously?"

"Don't look at me," Jessica said. "It wasn't my idea."

"It's your design, I'll bet," Josh said, pointing an accusing finger at Deliza. "And you all think I'm the crazy one?" Josh exclaimed.

"If you please, gentlemen," the commander said, pointing forward. "Time is of the essence, since we may be forced to make several detours to avoid Jung patrols as we near the Patoray system."

Josh and Loki headed forward. Commander Telles turned toward Marcus. "The other crates contain the launching rig. We will need to assemble it in transit."

"No problem," Marcus assured him.

"Then, I guess I should be going," Deliza said.

"Remember your promise," Jessica said to her.

"If you do not return, I shall see to your family, and especially Ania's, well-being." Deliza stepped up and wrapped her arms around Jessica. "Good luck," she whispered, a hint of worry in her voice.

"I'll bring him back," Jessica whispered back.

Deliza pulled away from her, and looked her in the eyes. "I know that you will," she replied softly. She turned to Commander Telles. "Good luck to you, Commander," she said, offering her hand.

"Thank you, Miss Ta'Akar," the commander replied, shaking it.

Deliza smiled. "Thank you for not calling me 'princess'," she added, before turning and heading down the Mirai's cargo ramp.

"At some point, you *are* going to explain to me how to use those things, *right*?" Jessica asked, pointing at the crates containing the insertion systems.

"You are already experienced at orbital insertion jumps, are you not?"

"I am."

"And I'm assuming you have used a wing-suit before?"

"I have," Jessica replied, her eyebrow rising.

"Then you should have no problem," the commander insisted, "as the insertion devices are mostly automated."

Jessica sighed. "Why is that not making me feel any better?"

CHAPTER SEVEN

"Jump complete," Loki reported. "Scanning the area with passive."

"I can't believe we haven't run into any ships yet," Jessica exclaimed.

"The Jung have likely moved all ships near the Patoray system back to Nor-Patri in defense of their homeworld," Commander Telles said. "It will take some time for more distant ships to move into position to take up their patrol routes."

"They *will* detect our jump flashes," Loki reminded them.

"Eventually, yes," the commander agreed, "by which time our mission should be complete."

"But, *theoretically*, they *could* use old light and eventually track us all the way back to Corinair, right?" Josh postulated.

"Without jump drives, it would take them centuries to do so," the commander assured him. "Even if they *had* the resources, they would need a good reason to use them. We do not intend to give them any reasons."

"You don't think they'd want to investigate some jump flashes just outside their home system?" Loki challenged.

"The Alliance has been jumping in recon ships at regular intervals since the attack," the commander said. "Ours will be one of many flashes."

"How long are they going to be doing such recon?" Josh wondered.

"Until the Jung demand that they stop," Jessica said. "I'm sure it will come up in the cease-fire negotiations."

"Well, I'm not picking up any ships in the area, so I guess we're clear to jump in," Loki reported. He turned to look at Jessica and the commander. "You guys better head aft and get ready."

"We will require approximately ten minutes to gear up," the commander replied.

"You got it," Loki nodded.

Jessica pulled her helmet on, tightening the strap under her chin.

"Your rigging checks," Marcus announced, patting her on the shoulder.

Jessica stepped up to her insertion vehicle, climbed onto it, and lay down inside. "I can't believe I'm agreeing to this," she muttered.

Commander Telles lay down in his vehicle as well. "If all goes well, we will be on the ground before you know it."

"If all goes well," Jessica repeated as the long, half-cylindrical door swung closed over her, trapping her inside a five-meter-long, jump-enabled projectile. *You're gonna owe me big, Nathan.*

"*Sled One, secure,*" the commander's voice announced over Jessica's comm-set. "*All systems show ready.*"

Jessica glanced at the tiny display screen in front of her face. "Sled Two, secure. All systems show ready."

"*Final jump in thirty seconds,*" Loki announced.

"Hey, why do we call these things sleds?" Jessica wondered. "They're basically missiles, after all."

"*The term is less disconcerting,*" the commander replied.

"Finally, we agree on something."

"Jump complete," Loki reported. "On course for insertion. Speed is five hundred and ninety-five meters per second."

"*Why so fast?*" Jessica asked over the comms.

"Any slower and we'd have to be deep inside the Patoray system for your systems to be able to reach Nor-Patri," Loki explained. "We're only half a light year from the Jung homeworld as it is." Loki looked back down at his display. "Thirty seconds to deployment."

"How are we going to slow down?" Jessica asked.

"*After the insertion jump, a drogue chute will deploy from the tail of the sled. This will reduce our speed by twenty percent.*"

"That's still pretty fast."

"*It will be enough,*" the commander assured her. "*However, you should know that there are no inertial dampening fields in these sleds, so we will feel it when the drogue is deployed.*"

"Great."

"*Opening the cargo bay,*" Marcus announced over the comms.

"No turning back now, I guess," Jessica commented, trying to distract herself from the fact that she was about to be shot like a missile at the Jung homeworld. "You are *so* gonna owe me," she mumbled.

"*Can you repeat?*" the commander asked.

"Not important."

"*Bay is open, ramp is level,*" Marcus reported. "*Extending launch rails.*"

Jessica took several deep breaths, letting each out slowly, trying to remain calm.

"*Deployment in fifteen seconds,*" Loki added.

"*Rails extended. Ready to deploy,*" Marcus announced.

"*Deployment in three......two......one......*"

Jessica felt a small jolt as the locking clamps released. There was a crackling sound and the faint jolting of acceleration as the low-power mag rails propelled them out the back of the Mirai into space.

"*Sleds away,*" Marcus reported. "*Retracting rails.*"

"*Sleds are clearing our jump field perimeter,*" Loki reported. "*Sled speed is six hundred meters per second and holding. Course trajectory is right down the green line. Jump point in one minute. You'll be out of comm-range in thirty seconds. Good luck to both of you.*"

"Just make sure you're at the pickup point on time," Jessica said tensely.

"*We'll be there, Jess,*" Josh promised.

"*Begin radio silence,*" Commander Telles ordered.

"Killing comms," Jessica replied. "See ya on the surface." Jessica switched off her comms. Although the commander's sled was coasting just fifty meters ahead of her, she had never felt more alone. Drifting in a small metal tube, one originally constructed as a weapon, inside the Jung home system. If her jump drive failed to trigger, she would continue to coast toward the Jung homeworld, probably for hundreds of years, before its gravity well finally pulled her in and burned her up on atmospheric interface. Luckily, if that *did* happen, she'd already be dead, having suffocated several centuries prior.

She glanced at her display. *Twenty seconds left.* The Mirai had likely already jumped away, wanting to keep their risk of detection as low as possible. From the deployment point, it would take six months for the Jung to detect their jump flashes from Nor-Patri, considerably less by ships patrolling the system.

Ten seconds.

Jessica wondered what Nathan's reaction would be once they reached him and told him of their rescue plan.

Five seconds.

Most likely, he would call them crazy.

Three seconds.

He would be right.

Two seconds.

"The things I do for love," she said to herself.

One second.

Jessica closed her eyes and tightened every muscle in her body as the unseen display changed from one to zero.

The entire sled shook violently. Even though she had expected it, the violent movement nearly caused her to cry out. At the same time, the silence gave way to the roar of air rushing over the outside of the projectile.

"Oh, fuck!" Jessica swore, as the sled continued to shake. She could feel her shoulders and hips bumping into the padding around her, and immediately wished she could tighten her restraints. She opened her eyes to look at the console, verifying that she was indeed in the atmosphere of Nor-Patri, but the sled shook so much that she couldn't read anything. Instead, she tried to concentrate on the countdown display, to anticipate the opening of the drogue chute that was supposed to happen within seconds of jump completion.

There was a terrible shrieking sound, like something had torn free of the sled. The sound of the rushing air changed, and Jessica was thrust upward, toward the nose of the sled.

Or was it downward? Her shoulder restraints dug in deeply, causing extreme discomfort. "Shit!" she cried out in frustration and pain. But there was no one to hear her, and all she could do was ride it out. The next step would come in less than a minute, and despite the fact that it was the most drastic change of all, she welcomed it.

"Both sleds have jumped," Loki announced. "Can we go now?"

"*Now* we can go," Josh agreed.

"Jumping in three......two......one......"

The windows on the Mirai's cockpit turned opaque as the ship's jump fields washed over them.

"Jump complete," Loki reported. "Starting retreat jump series to staging point in thirty seconds. Come to new course. Two one four, twenty-eight down."

"Two one four, twenty-eight down," Josh acknowledged.

"That wasn't according to plan, Josh," Loki warned.

"I know," Josh replied. "I just wanted to be sure they jumped. Those things hadn't been fully tested." He looked at Loki. "Tell me you weren't thinking the same thing."

"You're right," Loki admitted. "I was."

There was another jolt. The clamps that held her in place released, just as all three sides of the cylinder split apart like a metallic flower blooming. Her ears filled with the sound of air rushing past them, as she fell away from the sled. She glanced upward, toward her toes, and spotted the sled still dangling from its drogue chute, as she accelerated away from it. Within seconds, it disappeared in the dark storm cloud that surrounded them.

Swirls of mist engulfed her, barely illuminated by the waning twilight of the Jung homeworld. Every few seconds, the mist would light up with flashes of lightning. Each time, she felt as if her heart skipped a beat, the breath stolen from her lungs. She was certain that the next flash would strike her, and her life would end.

She held her body in proper position, trying to maintain control as she continued her descent. The computerized voice counted down her altitude as she plummeted to the surface. In seconds, the automated system would deploy her drogue chute to decelerate her to safer speeds, prior to extending her arms to utilize the airfoils of her wingsuit.

The next jerk came seconds later, as her drogue chute deployed. She could feel the tethers around her legs, beating against her sides as the harness struggled to keep her in a head-down attitude. Again, her rig straps pulled hard against the tops of her shoulders, as the drogue chute decelerated her further.

The computerized voice in her helmet comms continued to call out her altitude, adding her speed every few call-outs. Jessica could barely hear the announcements over the sound of the rushing air and the thunder. Instead, she glanced at the digital displays along the top, inside edge of her visor. She was still high enough that she required her mask to breathe, but not for much longer.

Every time the lightning crackled, her eyes darted left and right, trying to catch a glimpse of

Commander Telles. But she saw nothing, only the heavy fog.

A red warning light flashed on her visor, and the computerized voice announced, "*Prepare for drogue disconnect.*" Seconds later, the pressure across the tops of her shoulders lifted, her drogue chute having detached.

Jessica spread her arms and legs, allowing the fabric between them to fill with air. Once she had spread them as far as she could, she began to pitch up. Her muscles strained against the force of the wind. She had made more than twenty jumps in wingsuits during her time at the academy, but never at such speeds, nor at such altitudes.

Seconds later, she began to feel more in control as she achieved proper flight attitude. A directional tape appeared on the upper, inside edge of her visor, adding direction of flight data as well as speed, altitude, and rate of descent. Finally, she felt as if she had some semblance of control over her situation. It was a welcome relief, but she was not down yet.

Suddenly, she was no longer in the clouds. Patrisk-Dortah appeared below and ahead of her, its lights spreading across the land as far as the eye could see. A wave of relief came over her as she spotted Commander Telles a hundred meters ahead and to her left. She followed his lead as he began a turn to the left.

The next two minutes were spent doing a series of turns to decelerate further. Finally, her speed display turned from red to green, indicating a safe chute-deployment speed.

Jessica spotted the commander's main chute trailing out of his rig, and she pulled her chute release as well. Shortly after, they were both swinging below fully deployed, dark gray canopies. She continued her descent, following the commander as he turned to parallel the coastline. It was still early, only a few minutes after the sun had set over the capital of the Jung Empire, and the risk that someone might spot them was high, but there was no other choice. Nathan's execution was scheduled for the next morning.

A minute later, she was submerged in the warm, Dortahn Sea, sinking slowly toward its murky bottom. She released her harness and wiggled out of it, allowing the weighted rig to pull itself and her chute downwards.

Jessica pulled her fins from their holding points on her thighs, and donned them. She took a moment to spin around, looking for the commander, but the light was poor, and he was nowhere to be found. She took a reading from the directional tape on the inside of her face shield, and began swimming toward the planned coordinates. Her navigation system would guide her toward the rendezvous point, and she knew that the commander had entered the water nearby.

A feeling of relief again washed over her, as she had completed the first, crucial task of the mission. She had survived insertion from half a light year away.

* * *

"Scott!" the guard called from the small window in the cell door. His voice was gruff, and his English heavily accented. To Nathan, most Jung sounded like they had a mouthful of food when they tried to speak English. "What for you to want for eating?"

Nathan looked up from his table, confused. "What?"

"Eat!" the guard repeated impatiently. "What like you?"

Nathan was confused. "I have a choice?"

"What?" The guard looked baffled by his response.

"I can choose?" Nathan repeated slowly.

"Yes! Yes! What *you* want?"

"Ah, like as my last meal?"

"Yes, yes!"

Nathan set down his pen and rose from the table. "I don't know," he said, as he moved toward the door. "I don't suppose you have dollag, do you?"

"Dollag?"

"No, I suppose not. How about some beef? You know, steak?"

"I not to know this," the guard said.

Nathan sighed. "What is your name?"

"Me? Trever. Trever Soray."

"I'll tell you what, Trever. Since I don't know what your people *have* to offer, other than the slop you've been feeding me the past month, I'll let *you* decide. What would *you* choose?"

"Me?" the guard asked, surprised.

"Yes. If this was *your* last meal, what would *you* choose?"

Trever smiled, and began describing his choices in great detail, but in Jung. It didn't matter that Nathan didn't understand a word. Just the sound of the guard's voice as he described his choice made it seem delicious.

"I'll take that, Trever," Nathan said, smiling back. "And make it a double order. One for you, and one for me. Okay?"

"Yes, yes." Trever smiled even more broadly. "Okay!" he added, before disappearing into the corridor.

* * *

The lights of the city reflected off the calm waters of the bay that ran into the side of Patrisk-Dortah. All along the waterfront, people made their way to and from the various restaurants and tourist attractions that heavily dominated the area. Despite the damage sustained by their world, the waterfront provided a much-needed escape from the difficulties that most Patrians had to cope with since the attack. It was easy to forget the problems of daily life here among the music, the calm waters, the colorful lights, and the many enticing aromas wafting from the restaurants.

People normally came from all over the Dortahn Sea to moor in the Toran Bay at the Jung capital city, even if only for a few days. Nowadays, however, their numbers were much greater, as the fallout from Zhu-Anok had damaged several of the harbors in the area. Boats that had been for recreational purposes had now become the only homes that many would know for quite some time, and there was work in the capital city, as it was to be the primary focus of the initial restorative efforts.

Raley Duntan had been lucky enough to have an employer with an eighteen-meter sailing yacht on the far side of the Dortahn Sea. The company had also been adversely affected by the attacks, but expected to be back up and running within a few months. Raley's home had been destroyed, but his employer offered to let him and his wife, Alaya, live on his yacht, in exchange for keeping it safe from desperate people who might steal or ransack the boat.

Despite having no experience on the water, Raley and his wife had accepted the offer and sailed to Toran Bay to find temporary work. Here, amongst countless other boats carrying similarly displaced families, they had found a new sense of community. Raley had secured work with a company doing demolition of some of the more heavily damaged buildings in the capital city, and Alaya had found part-time work in one of the waterfront cafeterias that served the overworked fishing fleets prowling the waters of the Dortahn Sea.

Raley stood in the cockpit, gazing out across the water. The sight of the marker lights at the tops of so many masts swaying in the water was mesmerizing. Standing outside to watch the dancing lights while drinking a bottle of ale had become a nightly ritual for him. Alaya had gone to bed hours ago, as she had to leave for work much earlier than he did. It was a far cry from the life they had known, but they were surviving...

...Until now.

So captivating was the serenity of the night that Raley did not notice the two black-helmeted heads that broke the surface of the nearby water every so often to the starboard side of their boat. Nor did he notice when the larger of the two came up silently out of the water and climbed onto the transom of his boat. By the time he felt the man's presence, it was too late.

There was a sudden, intense pain in the side of Raley's neck, followed by a warm, wet feeling on his shoulders and upper torso. He could feel a muscular arm around his neck, and a body pressing against his back. His head began to spin, and everything went dark.

Commander Telles lowered the man's lifeless corpse down to the deck without making a sound, then signaled to Jessica waiting in the water at the aft end of the boat.

Jessica climbed carefully up the boat's swim ladder, staying as quiet as possible. By the time she climbed up into the cockpit and discovered the dead body, the commander was already inside the main cabin. She quickly followed him inside, wanting to avoid being spotted by anyone in the countless nearby boats.

As she reached the bottom of the companionway, the commander was already coming out of the forward cabin, a bloody knife in his hand.

"We are in luck," he said in hushed tones. "There were both a male and female on board."

"How is that lucky?"

"We should be able to find appropriate clothing, as well as funds. We can also use their tender to get to shore without raising suspicion. This should make it much easier for us to make our way through the city."

Jessica stepped past the commander, peeking into the forward cabin. Lying on the bed was another body. A young woman, about her age, with long brown hair. For a moment, Jessica could imagine herself lying there on the blood-soaked sheets, her life unfairly taken from her. "Jesus, did you have to kill them?"

"They are the enemy," the commander said, more as a reminder than a defense.

"They're just a young couple on a boat," Jessica argued. "Couldn't we have just tied them up and gagged them?"

"And if they cried out," the commander asked, "or managed to escape soon after our departure?"

Jessica did not respond, but she also did not look pleased.

"We have a mission to perform," the commander

explained. "A Ghatazhak will do whatever is required to complete his mission, in the most efficient manner possible. If that means taking innocent lives, then so be it." The commander looked hard at Jessica. "Do you have a problem with that?"

Jessica thought for a moment. She thought about the commander's explanation, and she thought about all she had gone through. She also thought about Nathan, locked up in a prison cell, alone, facing his execution only a sunrise away. "No problem," she answered.

"Very well," the commander said. "Find some appropriate clothing and change, while I remove their ID chips and prepare them for implantation into our bodies."

Jessica looked at the young woman again. "I may be able to pass as her, but that guy was a good deal younger, and at least twenty kilograms heavier than you... And blonde."

"Most of the population monitoring systems are still down," the commander said as he moved to head back up the companionway. "Those who check the displays are overworked and understaffed. It is doubtful anyone will notice the difference."

"I hope you're right," Jessica muttered as she opened the storage locker in the forward cabin and started rummaging through the dead woman's clothing.

* * *

"Oh, my God!" Nathan exclaimed, as meat juices dribbled down his chin. "This is amazing!"

The guard smiled, nodding his head in triumph as he attacked his slab of meat as well.

"What did you say this is called?"

"*Co-rin-tah-kot.*"

“What is that? The name of the animal?” Nathan looked at the reddish-colored slab of meat on his plate. “It looks like it came from a big animal. Is it like a steer, or something?” Nathan knew the guard barely understood him, but he didn’t care. It was the first time he’d eaten with someone in over a month. Furthermore, it was the first *good* food he had eaten since his arrival on Nor-Patri.

Trever just looked at him, confused.

“Steer,” Nathan said, gesturing. “Big animal? Cow? Moo?”

“Moo?”

Nathan made a mooing sound.

“Ah! *Eerrroooo!”* the guard said, mimicking the sound the local animal made.

“So, it is beef!” Nathan declared, feeling triumphant in his breakthrough. “Or at least the Patrian equivalent.” He stabbed his slab of meat with his fork and cut off another bite. He raised it to his mouth, but Trever protested.

“No!” Trever took his own piece and slid it through the sauce on his plate, then raised it to his mouth. “Yes?”

Nathan did the same, and then placed the meat in his mouth. “Oh, yes,” he exclaimed, rolling his eyes in delight. “That *is* better!”

“Yes!” Trever laughed heartily as he cut off another piece of meat.

For a moment, as Nathan carved his next bite, the thought of stabbing Trever in the neck and trying to escape crossed his mind. But both he and the guard were locked inside the cell together. Nathan himself was in a fairly weakened state from his month of captivity, and Trever was considerably larger. Besides, Nathan rather liked the man, and he *had* procured an impressive meal for his last night among the living. He also reminded him a lot of his friend Vladimir, and their dinner was like all the meals they had shared aboard the Aurora.

"What is that?" Nathan asked, pointing at the pile of yellow, potato-like substance in a bowl in the middle of the table.

"*Ergin tota,*" Trever replied. He reached into his pocket and pulled out a small device, held it near the pile of yellow substance, and pressed a button. A spark leapt from the device, setting the pile of yellow mash aflame.

"Whoa!" Nathan exclaimed, watching the blue-green flames dancing on the food.

Trever grinned from ear to ear, babbling on about the burning yellow mash in Jung, none of which Nathan understood, but could appreciate Trever's enthusiasm nonetheless.

Nathan picked up the serving spoon and reached for the burning pile, but again Trever objected.

"We wait?" Nathan asked.

"Yes, yes. We wait."

The two of them continued attacking their respective slabs of *corintakhat*, all the while being entertained by the flickering flames. After several minutes, the color of the flames turned to amber, and the outer surface of the pile of yellow mash began to brown, becoming somewhat crusty as the flames altered the vegetable.

Finally, Trever leaned forward and blew out the flames. The pile of yellow mash was now covered with a golden brown crust that gave it the appearance of piecrust. Trever picked up the serving spoon and pushed it into the crispy outer layer, scooping up a generous portion. Much to Nathan's surprise, the yellow mash inside had turned a stark white, and had firmed up considerably. It also had streaks of pale red running through the now-firm, white mash, as if some additional substance had been swirled into the mixture without them knowing.

Trever plopped the serving onto Nathan's plate, then served himself an equal portion. "Eat!"

Nathan picked up his spoon and scooped up a small taste, making sure to include both the outer crust and the mash beneath. He brought it up to his mouth and paused, afraid that it would be too hot yet to eat. He watched as Trever shoveled a serving into his own mouth without pause, and decided to follow suit.

It was warm, but not hot. The golden-brown crust was firm, but not as crispy as it looked, and it had a flavor similar to melted, caramelized cheese, like what he remembered around the edges of the grilled sandwiches his mother used to make for him as a child. The red-tinged, white mash underneath tasted like mashed potatoes, but with a spicy kick, which Nathan decided must have come from the red stuff that seemed to swirl through it.

"What you think?" Trever asked.

"That is really delicious," Nathan said. "But where did the red stuff come from?"

Trever smiled broadly. "Magic."

They continued to eat, jumping between the two main dishes, as well as the numerous side dishes that Trever had taken the liberty of ordering. They stuffed themselves for more than an hour, before finally reaching their breaking points, although Nathan suspected that Trever could have continued eating a bit longer.

* * *

General Bacca stood looking at his relatively empty living room, after the dealer who had purchased all his precious antiques had taken the last of the furniture away. It saddened him greatly to see them go, as some had been handed down through his family for generations. Having them moved to Patrisk-Dortah had cost him more than what he earned from selling them. He could imagine the disappointed look on his late father's face, and his late mother crying.

It was necessary, he told himself. He had to survive, after all. Tomorrow morning, his name and reputation would turn from advantage to curse. He would need to sell everything in order to survive long enough to find a way off of Nor-Patri, and back to the world of his birth. He only hoped that things might be easier for him there.

"I have confirmed the sale of your private shuttle, General," his aide reported from the doorway. "They will send a flight crew out in the morning to pick it up."

"Thank you, Martile."

"Will there be anything else, sir?"

"Thank you, no," the general replied. He turned to his longtime aide, a sad look on his face. "You have been a good and loyal employee, low these many years. You have protected my house, and my assets, well while I have been away. For that, I thank you."

"No need, General. I have been well compensated for my efforts."

"As you deserved," the general said earnestly. "I trust you have secured new employment?"

Martile took in a deep breath, letting it out in a low, long sigh. "The time is not right, I believe. With so many out of work, and all. Besides, my wife has been wanting me to retire for some time, now. I am considering doing just that, as we have managed to save a tidy sum over the years."

"That is good to hear," the general said, forcing a smile. "At least something good has come from all of this. I only wish I could have added something to your retirement, as I had always planned." He offered his hand. "Good luck to you."

"And to you, General," Martile replied, shaking the general's hand.

General Bacca watched as his trusted aide turned and headed for the front door. The general moved toward his office, the only room that was still at least partially furnished. He entered the office, noticed the balcony window was open, and headed toward it. *So unlike Martile,* he thought as he closed and locked the doors.

"Rather spartan furnishings," a female voice said from behind.

General Bacca spun around, spotting a young woman with long, brown hair standing in the doorway. He instantly made a move toward his desk, but another person appeared from the shadowy corner of the dimly lit room. A man, square-jawed and muscular, with a fierce look of confidence and determination in his eyes.

"I know you," the general said, squinting his eyes to see in the dark. "From the Aurora..." He turned and looked at Jessica. "You were there, as well." He laughed. "Are you both mad? Coming to Nor-Patri?"

"Nice to see you haven't forgotten about us," Jessica said, walking toward him. "Because we sure as hell haven't forgotten about you."

"What could you possibly hope to..."

"So, it appears you've fallen out of favor," Jessica said mockingly. "Must be tough."

"A minor setback, I assure you," the general replied, standing tall in the face of the intruders. "Lieutenant Commander Nash," he said, pointing at Jessica. He turned and pointed at the commander. "And you're the Ghatazhak, Commander..."

"...Telles, quite right," the commander replied.

The general chuckled to himself again. "You both realize that your mere presence on Nor-Patri will bring the cease-fire to a grinding halt."

"Assuming anyone finds out we're here," Jessica said.

"Trust me, my dear, they will find out. And, when they do, your Alliance...your *world* will burn."

"Actually, we're no longer with the Alliance," Jessica corrected. "Well, *I'm* no longer with the Alliance. Technically, the commander never was." She looked at Commander Telles. "What was your exact function, by the way?"

"To protect Captain Scott."

The realization hit the general. "You're here to try and rescue him, aren't you?" The general laughed even harder than before. "You're fools! Both of you! You'd never get anywhere near him!"

"Not by ourselves, no," Jessica admitted. "But maybe, with the help of a prominent general..."

"Haven't you heard? I am to be stripped of all rank and privileges. I am no more able to gain access to Captain Scott than you are."

"As of tomorrow morning," Commander Telles interjected, "as I understand it."

General Bacca's eyebrow went up. "You have assets on Nor-Patri. Well connected ones, apparently."

"Not really," Jessica replied. "They're just really good at cracking your encryption algorithms, and you guys love to send all manner of communications whizzing around across the system. All they had to do was listen and decrypt."

"Regardless, what makes you think I would be willing to help you?"

"Because we would be willing to compensate you for your assistance," the commander replied.

"Turn traitor?" The general laughed yet again. "I have seen how traitors to the empire are treated. The compensation would have to be considerable, especially considering the lifestyle to which I am accustomed."

"Actually, we were thinking more of letting you live as your reward," Jessica told him.

"After tomorrow, my life here will hardly be a reward, my dear."

"We could get you off Nor-Patri," Jessica offered.

The general was suddenly interested. "How?"

"You don't really think I'm going to answer that, do you?" Jessica said.

"How is unimportant," Commander Telles said. "Trust that we can is all that is necessary."

"Obviously, you can, otherwise neither of you would be here. And, if you *are* here to rescue your captain, then you surely have a means of escape. A small jump ship, perhaps?" the general surmised. "I hope it is well hidden. Nothing happens on Nor-Patri without the Jung knowing."

"Our presence, as well as those of our previously-placed assets would indicate otherwise," Commander Telles stated.

"Hmm, I see your point," the general admitted.

"Or, you could stay here, and work for us," Jessica suggested.

"As what? Your spy? My dear child..."

"Excuse us a moment," Commander Telles

interrupted. He looked sternly at Jessica as he walked toward her.

General Bacca watched as they moved away from him to the far side of the office. The commander never took his eyes off the general. For an instant, the general considered going for the weapon kept under his desk, but the steely, confident look in the commander's eyes encouraged him to stay put.

This could be an opportunity, the general thought.

After a few moments, the commander moved away from Jessica, walking back across the office to his prior position, once again putting the general between him and Jessica.

"Come to a consensus, have we?" the general asked.

"You help us rescue Nathan, and we let you live," Jessica proposed.

"Hardly an attractive offer," the general replied, scoffing at her.

"In addition," Jessica continued, "you spy for us."

"My dear, as intriguing an offer as that might normally be, I'm afraid that my new situation will not exactly put me in a position to be of use to you."

"Unless you manage to uncover the identities of four, well-placed Alliance spies already on Nor-Patri," Jessica explained. "Would that get you back in your leaders' good graces?"

General Bacca thought for a moment, his face slightly contorted in concentration. "It might," he finally admitted, one eyebrow rising. "It just might." The general looked at the commander, then back at Jessica. "What would I have to do?"

Jessica smiled. "Like I said, help us free Captain Scott."

* * *

Admiral Dumar looked around his now-barren office. He had spent the better part of a year running, first, the Karuzara asteroid, and then the entire Earth-Pentaurus Alliance from this very room. He had made decisions that had saved millions, and he made decisions that sent thousands to their deaths. He had told himself again and again that the sacrifices, both his and those who had given their lives, had been worth it. After all, the Jung *had* been stopped. Furthermore, they had been pushed back a safe distance from Sol, and were now being held in check by the threat of ten times the devastation that they had already experienced on Nor-Patri two months earlier. Hundreds of thousands of Jung, both military and civilian, had died that day. It was a price the Jung Empire *had* to pay for imposing their will upon billions, if not trillions of others.

"Reflecting?" Mister Bryant asked from the doorway.

"You might say that," the admiral replied. He let out a sigh, then looked at his trusted right-hand man. "Was it worth it?"

"Was what worth it?" Mister Bryant asked.

"All the lives that were lost...both ours and theirs."

Mister Bryant entered the office and took a seat. "I ask myself that same question every day."

"And what do you tell yourself?" the admiral wondered.

"That only history can answer that question. *We* believe it is worth the sacrifice at the time, otherwise we would not have made the decisions we did. But those decisions are weighed against what we *hope* the outcome will be. Only *time* can tell us if we were correct."

"Was it worth sacrificing him?" the admiral asked, his voice suddenly sounding weak and unsure.

"It was his decision to make, Admiral. We both know that."

"But I put him in that position," the admiral said in horror, as if admitting it to himself for the first time.

"Captain Scott may have been young, Travon, but he was not stupid. He knew what he was walking into."

"But I left him with no good alternatives," the admiral pointed out, clearly guilt-ridden.

"*Fate* left him no good alternatives," Mister Bryant insisted. "Fate threw down the gauntlet. Nathan chose to pick it up."

Admiral Dumar sighed. "Would that I could have picked it up in his place."

"Perhaps, rather than punishing yourself, you should honor him as best you can. We should *all* honor him as best we can."

The admiral looked at his friend. "How?"

"By making the best of what he has given us... The gift of life."

Admiral Dumar nodded his agreement, forcing a smile out in the process. "Will you be attending his memorial?"

"Unfortunately, no," Mister Bryant replied. "The Glendanon departs prior to the ceremony. Most of us are departing on her, lest we have to wait two more months. Yourself?"

"I shall attend. Commander Telles has promised me passage aboard one of his boxcars, along with his remaining troops."

"I can think of no better men with which to travel," Mister Bryant said.

"I can think of one," the admiral replied.

* * *

Nathan closed his eyes, and let the sweet, fruity, gelatinous frosting melt on his tongue and drain down his throat. He normally did not have much of a sweet tooth; however, Trever's choice of desserts, just as all the other dining choices the Jung guard had made, was heavenly.

"Good, yes?" Trever asked expectantly.

"Divine, my friend," Nathan replied, his eyes still closed.

Trever smiled. "You are not bad, Scott."

"Call me Nathan," he replied, opening his eyes and stabbing another piece of the dessert with his fork.

"Nathan." Trever thought for a moment. "In Jung, is 'Nato', I think. It means...'God's gift'."

Nathan smiled. "It means the same in English." He placed the next bite in his mouth. "And in Angla, too, I believe."

"You are not afraid?" Trever wondered.

"To die?" Nathan sighed. "Sorry, yes... But afraid? No, I think not."

"You should to be," Trever warned. "Jung way is most painful."

"Okay, now I'm afraid," Nathan admitted.

Trever set down his empty dessert plate. "Why you do this thing?" he asked, looking at Nathan. "Why you kill so many Jung?"

"Why have the Jung killed so many of us?" Nathan asked.

Trever nodded. "You were doing your job, then."

"You expected a different answer?"

Trever looked confused.

"Yes, I was doing my job."

"Is difficult job."

"Yes, it is," Nathan agreed, setting down his own empty plate.

"You have woman? Child?"

"No," Nathan replied. "No wife, no child."

"That is good."

"I suppose so," Nathan agreed. "Yourself? Do you have a family?"

"*Fah-mi-lee*?" Trever replied, unfamiliar with the word.

"Woman? Child? Many child?"

"Ah! *Frantok!* Yes. I have. Woman. Child...three."

"Your child is three? Or you have three children?" Nathan wondered.

"Child...child...child," Trever explained, using his right hand to indicate several different heights.

"They were not injured, I hope." Nathan suddenly felt nervous.

"No, no, no!" Trever insisted. "They good. They home. They safe. We lucky."

So am I, Nathan thought. "I'm happy to hear that."

"You...me, we same," Trever said. "We have duty. We protect what we love."

"Yup, I guess that about sums it all up, doesn't it," Nathan said wearily.

Trever placed the dishes and utensils back onto the cart. He then leaned back and looked long and hard at Nathan. After a minute, Nathan began to feel uncomfortable.

"What is it?" Nathan asked.

Trever shook his head. "I not blame you, Nathan." Trever looked at him a bit longer. "I *respect* you." He thought a bit more, then rose from his seat. "Nato means 'strength from God', I think."

Nathan smiled. "Thanks."

Trever took the service cart and pulled it toward the door. He paused a moment, looking down at the cart, then picked up one of the meat-carving knives and placed it on the table in front of Nathan. "Jung way is *most* painful. You, Nato... You not deserve." Trever pushed the knife across the table to Nathan. "Strength."

Trever stepped back to the door and barked an order to the guard outside. Nathan moved his data pad over the carving knife Trever had left on the table, to hide it from the other guard as the door opened, and Trever pushed the cart outside. The door closed, and Nathan heard Trever arguing with the other guard over something as they walked away. Once he was satisfied they were gone, Nathan pushed his data pad aside and picked up the knife, the phrase *Jung way is most painful,* repeating in his head.

CHAPTER EIGHT

"How do I look?" Jessica asked as she adjusted her uniform.

"The trousers are a bit tight," General Bacca said with a leer, "but I'm sure the guards will not mind." He looked at Commander Telles. "You, on the other hand, are *most* convincing. You'd make a fine Jung officer."

Commander Telles ignored the comment. "This uniform is a different size. Where did it come from?"

"My younger days," the general replied. "I was a bit more robust back then."

"What about unit insignias?"

"The Jung do not advertise their division, unit, or specialty the way that Earth forces do. We prefer to keep that information *undisclosed*, unless required."

"How will we get in?" Jessica asked.

General Bacca glanced at his watch. "By now, the detention facility will be at minimal staffing for the night," he told them. "A junior officer will be in command, and most of them are easily rattled by the presence of a general."

"Even one who's about to be defrocked and publicly humiliated?" Jessica wondered, a sarcastic smirk on her face.

"Lord Torret assured me that the decision would not be made public until after your captain's execution, which means that no one, not even command-level officers, will know that I am about to fall from grace."

"And why, exactly, did this Lord Torret warn you?" Jessica asked.

"We have known each other for many years. Let's just say he owed me a favor, and leave it at that."

Jessica and Commander Telles exchanged wary glances.

"I assure you, my request to see the prisoner will meet little resistance," the general insisted, noticing their lack of confidence.

"What about this?" the commander said, placing the bag he had brought from the yacht on the table and opening it up for the general to see.

General Bacca looked into the bag, his brow furrowing as he studied the device inside. "What is it?" he asked, looking at the commander.

"A device that will allow us to copy Captain Scott's memories and consciousness," the commander replied.

General Bacca looked puzzled. "Whatever for..." His expression changed as his words trailed off and realization spread across his face. "You intend to clone him?"

"We do."

"And this device will work?"

"It should."

"It will," Jessica said confidently.

General Bacca cast a sidelong glance at Jessica, noting the personal interest in her voice. "So the Nifelmians were lying to us all these years," the general said, looking back at the commander.

"Not completely," the commander replied. "They cannot guarantee that it will work."

"And you are willing to bet your friend's life on it?" the general asked.

"There is no other viable alternative," the commander replied, "not if we wish to keep the cease-fire intact."

"If the Jung find out, they will consider it a violation of the cease-fire," the general warned.

"The only terms that have yet been agreed upon are that Captain Scott was handed over to them to stand trial for war crimes, and to accept punishment. Resurrecting the captain as a clone of the original has not been addressed. Therefore, technically, it is not a violation."

General Bacca laughed. "I assure you that the Jung will not see it that way."

"We'll take our chances," Jessica said. "So, how do we get it inside?"

General Bacca took in a deep breath and sighed as he stared at the device, pondering. "How does the device operate?" he asked.

"A cloth cap fitted with thousands of sensors is placed onto the head of the subject, connecting him to the device." Commander Telles explained.

"And how long does the process take?"

"Minutes," the commander replied.

"And how long is the device capable of storing the captain's consciousness?" the general wondered.

"That information is not pertinent to the task at hand," the commander replied sternly.

The general sighed again. "Your captain was given the same nanites that our ground troops are given prior to invasion of a new world. They are designed to protect the host from unknown pathogens, as well as from traumatic shock due to battlefield injuries."

"That explains why some of them have been so difficult to kill," Jessica quipped.

"Why were they given to him?" Commander Telles wondered.

"To prevent him from dying, of course," General

Bacca replied. "Jung interrogation tactics can be quite harsh, at times."

"Surely they were deactivated long ago?" the commander said.

"Yes, but the officer in charge of the detention facility would not likely know this."

"A bold gamble," the commander stated.

"Bold gambles make generals," the general replied dismissively. "Shall we begin?" the general suggested, pointing toward the patio door. "Unless one of you has a better idea that you would like to share."

Commander Telles looked at Jessica. "It is as good a plan as we could hope for."

"Not as satisfying as blasting our way in and out, but probably more survivable," Jessica agreed. She looked at the general. "Be warned, Bacca. One false move, and we immediately go to plan B."

"Which is?"

"Shoot our way out," Jessica replied. "Starting with you."

Commander Telles turned and headed toward the patio doors.

"After you, my dear," the general offered cordially.

"Not a chance in hell," Jessica replied in Jung, pushing the general forward so she could keep an eye on him.

"Very good," the general replied, also in Jung. "Although your accent has a slight hint of the eastern Jorsay province."

Jessica and General Bacca followed Commander Telles out the doors and across the dimly lit patio, moving quickly up the shuttle's boarding steps. The commander went forward, and the general turned to follow.

"Where do you think you're going?" Jessica demanded, putting her hand on his shoulder to stop him.

"The shuttle's controls will not recognize the commander as having authorization to operate this ship," the general explained. "I will need to grant such permissions. To do so, I must be in the cockpit."

Jessica removed her hand from the general's shoulder. "Make it quick."

The general moved forward, standing next to the commander, who had already taken the pilot's seat. He leaned forward and touched several keys on the console. "Remain still while the system scans you," he instructed the commander.

Commander Telles sat still while a scanning beam darted over him.

The console beeped and flashed a message in Jung on the screen. *Authorized: Duntan, Raley.*

"You are now authorized to operate this shuttle," the general announced. "You *do* know how to pilot such a craft?"

"I believe I can figure it out," the commander replied, as he began to familiarize himself with the shuttle's controls.

"And you, my dear?" the general asked, turning to look at Jessica behind him.

"Maybe later," she replied. "In the back."

General Bacca moved aft to the small passenger cabin.

Jessica stepped up into the cockpit, keeping one eye on the general in the back. "You good?" she asked the commander.

"This shuttle appears to be highly automated," the commander replied. "I do not anticipate difficulty."

"A simple *I'm good* would have worked," Jessica remarked, turning to join the general in the back.

"I'm assuming you already know *where* Captain Scott is being held?" General Bacca presumed as Jessica took her seat.

"We do."

"*Prepare for departure,*" the commander announced from the cockpit.

"I believe I'd prefer to return with you and the commander, and be relocated as compensation for my assistance," the general said as the shuttle began to rise off the pad. "Nothing fancy. Perhaps someplace tropical. I believe there were several small, uninhabited islands on your world."

"I'm sure something can be arranged," Jessica replied curtly, annoyed by the general's smugness.

"Maybe a boat," he continued as the shuttle began to move forward. "Something live-aboard, I think."

"Sail or motor?"

"Oh, motor, without a doubt," the general insisted. "Sailing is for romantics. I'm more the practical type, myself."

"How about you try to be the quiet type?" Jessica snapped.

* * *

Nathan sat at the small table in his cell, staring at the knife that had been left for him as a gesture of respect by the guard with whom Nathan had shared his last meal. It was a simple knife, with a ceramic blade and composite handle. Yet, sitting there on the table in front of him, it represented so much...

It represented escape. Escape from the long, torturous night of anguish that lay ahead of him. Escape from all the terrifying thoughts, and bitter disappointments, that swirled in his head. Escape from a long and painful public execution only hours away.

Nathan wondered if Trever would get in trouble for leaving the knife behind. If Nathan used it to end his own life, robbing the Jung people of the closure their leaders sought for them, Trever would likely be blamed. For all he knew, Trever might even be killed.

What about his wife? His kids?

Nathan wondered why he even cared. Trever was the enemy. A citizen of an empire that murdered millions of people on Earth, and Tanna, and likely billions more across the Sol sector and beyond. The Jung were a plague that had to be stopped.

Am I failing to stop them?

Nathan had believed that his surrender would buy the Alliance the time they needed to build a fleet that would keep the Jung in check. Perhaps even to one day bring their entire empire to its knees. But now, he wondered if he had given the Jung the same chance. After all, the Jung had greater resources, and a much larger and more capable industrial base.

But we have the jump drive.

Nathan kept telling himself that. The jump drive was their edge. *That* was what would save the Earth. *That* was what would stop the Jung. Not him. Not any *one man.*

And I saved it. I brought it back, from a thousand light years away.

It was the one thing he was proud of.

And so, he stared at the knife in front of him, trying to summon the courage to finally bring his life to a close. One last act of courage, this time, just for himself.

He suddenly realized what he wanted to say to his father.

* * *

Commander Telles climbed down the boarding steps from the shuttle in a calm, confident manner, stepping aside at the bottom and coming to attention as General Bacca emerged from the cabin door. The general wasted no time taking notice of the area surrounding the landing pad, wishing to appear as disinterested in such details as a man at his level of command would normally be.

Jessica was the next to emerge, carrying an equipment bag that she had repacked the Nifelmian device into during their flight over. She, too, appeared disinterested, although, just as the commander had done, she stealthily took notice of every detail around them as she climbed down the steps behind the general.

Commander Telles fell in place beside Jessica and behind the general, following him down the steps from the landing pad toward the guard house near the rooftop entrance.

The guard standing outside the door snapped to attention upon noticing the general's rank insignias, trying hard to hide his surprise at the unannounced visit. "General," the guard barked respectfully, his Jung curt and proper. "I am Sergeant Petray. Welcome to Detention Facility Eighteen, sir."

"Sergeant," the general replied casually. When the sergeant failed to immediately open the door for him, General Bacca paused and cast an annoyed look the sergeant's way.

"Apologies, General, but we have not received notice of your visit," the guard stated respectfully.

"I would think not," the general replied, "as my work is highly classified."

"If the general will pardon, I must speak to the

officer of the watch before I can grant entry. Again, my apologies, sir."

"No matter," General Bacca replied. "Just make it quick, Sergeant."

"Of course, General," the sergeant replied, taking note of the general's name tag. He quickly stepped into the guard house and tapped the intercom button. At the same time, he activated the scanning device in the guard house.

General Bacca did his best to appear understanding of the guard's need to follow protocol, but was nonetheless annoyed at the delay. Jessica and the commander both continued to stare straight ahead, as would be expected of them.

Moments later, the sergeant stepped out of the guard house, a nervous look on his face. "Again, my apologies, General Bacca. I have to ask about the contents of the lady's bag."

"You may ask," the general replied, "but you will receive no explanation. That, too, is classified." He looked the sergeant in the eyes. "Is there a problem... *Sergeant*?"

"No problem, General. I have been instructed to wait for Lieutenant Commander Effick, the officer of the watch. He wishes to speak with you personally, General."

"This is highly irregular," the general protested. "You *do* know who I am?"

"Of course, General. Again, I apologize. The lieutenant commander will be here momentarily."

General Bacca could see that the sergeant was already nervous enough, and decided it was best not to push the issue further. He turned to face Jessica and the commander. "Most irregular," he muttered, speaking just loud enough for the guard to overhear. "But to be expected, I suppose."

A minute later, the officer of the watch appeared from the elevator door. "General Bacca, sir," the lieutenant commander greeted politely. "I am Lieutenant Commander Effick, the officer of the watch. I apologize for the delay, sir, but we had no foreknowledge of your arrival, nor does anyone at command know anything about your visit."

"As I explained to the sergeant, I am here on highly classified business. I *could* explain the nature of my visit, but then I would have to order Mister Duntan here to kill you both."

The lieutenant commander was slightly taken aback by the general's blatant threat. At first, he thought the general was joking, but when he saw no hint of a smile on the general's face, he began to doubt himself. He looked into the eyes of the man the general had referred to as Mister Duntan as well. They were cold and calculating...definitely those of a man who found killing easy, and was likely quite skilled at it. "Of course, I understand, General. But please, you must understand that I alone am responsible for the security of this facility. There are protocols that I *must* follow. Surely you, of all people, understand that."

The young officer was not as easily rattled as the general had hoped. General Bacca sighed, looking down at the floor for a moment. He then put his hand on the lieutenant commander's shoulder, leading him away from the others as he spoke. "Lieutenant Commander—Effick, was it?"

"Yes, sir."

"What we have here is a rather sensitive situation, one that is not only highly classified, but also one that, if not handled discreetly, could cause some embarrassment to one of the lords of the leadership council."

"I see," the lieutenant commander replied.

"I was hoping to take care of this without any further complications. I promise you our visit will be brief, and uneventful."

"I would very much like to help you, General, as well as *any* lord of the council, but I'm afraid I cannot allow you, your staff, or whatever equipment the young woman is carrying, to enter without knowing for *sure* that *allowing* such unauthorized entry does not pose a risk to the security of *this* facility."

"Especially on *this* night," the general added.

"I see the general is well informed as to our prisoner roster, then?" the lieutenant commander said, catching the hint.

"Indeed, I am," the general confirmed. "In fact, the prisoner to which you allude is the subject of my visit."

The lieutenant commander looked even more concerned.

General Bacca sighed. "I suppose I have no choice but to share more with you than I should. After all, I am asking you to take considerable risk." General Bacca held up his left hand and signaled Jessica. She immediately stepped forward. "Open the bag and show the lieutenant commander the device," he instructed her.

Jessica hesitated, looking at the general.

"On my authority," the general added.

"As you wish, General," Jessica replied, also speaking in Jung. She placed the bag on the deck and opened it just enough for the lieutenant commander to peek inside.

"What is that?" the lieutenant commander wondered, speaking softly.

"Captain Scott was injected with top-secret, advanced nanites designed to keep him alive during, shall we say, *physically arduous* interrogation. Unfortunately, the officer in charge of the interrogation failed to have those nanites disabled prior to releasing Captain Scott to stand trial. As you might imagine, it would be quite disappointing if Captain Scott did not die during his *extremely public* execution in the morning. Not to mention causing embarrassment to the family of the officer who committed this error. A rather *prominent* family, I might add." The general looked at the lieutenant commander, as if asking if he understood the general's inference.

The realization swept over the lieutenant commander. "Then this device is..."

"To disable those nanites, and ensure that no such embarrassment takes place," the general confirmed.

The lieutenant commander studied what little he could see of the device through the opening. "It looks alien."

"It is based on alien technology, yes," the general admitted. "You have a good eye, Lieutenant Commander."

"Thank you, sir."

"I'm sure Lord Torret will appreciate your cooperation in this matter," the general said under his breath, "as well as your discretion."

The lieutenant commander's eyes widened. "Lord Torret? *He* asked you?"

"We go back many decades," the general explained. "A favor, for an old friend. One that I'm sure will not be forgotten."

"Of course, General, I understand," the lieutenant

commander said, suddenly eager to cooperate. "How long will you need, sir?"

General Bacca looked at Jessica for the answer.

"Fifteen minutes," she replied, "twenty, at the most."

"So long? Just to disable nanites?"

"Highly advanced, *alien* nanites," the general explained.

"The nanites are quite fast at replicating within the host," Jessica said, keeping her voice low so that the others could not hear. "We must be quite certain that they have *all* been disabled."

"I see. And this will not harm the prisoner?" the lieutenant commander inquired.

"It will render him unconscious for two, perhaps three hours," Jessica stated in a matter-of-fact tone.

"But he will be normal by the time he is to be executed?"

"Assuming we do not spend an undue amount of time discussing the issue out here on your rooftop," General Bacca added.

"Of course. Of course," the lieutenant commander agreed, signaling the guard to unlock the elevator doors. "I will show you to the prisoner myself, General. If you will all please follow me."

"Thank you, Lieutenant Commander," General Bacca replied. He turned to look at Jessica, the slightest of grins on the corner of his mouth, as he followed the lieutenant commander.

* * *

Marcus climbed up the short ladder into the Mirai's cockpit, spotting Josh sitting in the pilot's seat. "How's it goin'?"

Josh glanced back over his shoulder. "Fine."

"Where's Loki?"

"Sleeping, as you should be." Josh looked at the mission clock on the console. "You've got the watch in another hour."

"I ain't tired," Marcus grumbled. "Sucks havin' nothin' to do."

"You can always review the systems' manuals again," Josh joked. "That would make Sergeant Isan happy."

"That boy is wound too tight."

"Everyone in the military is wound too tight," Josh replied.

Marcus took a seat at the engineer's station. "You gonna miss it?"

"The military? Hell, no," Josh declared. "Everyone always yelling at me. Always having to salute someone. All that 'yes sir, no sir' crap. Not to mention all the double-shifts in the cockpit. I'm pretty sure I've got permanent indentations on my butt from that damned flight harness." Josh shifted in his seat. "How could you even ask?"

"Just wondering."

Josh sighed. "I will miss flying the Falcons, though. Even after they mucked up her slick cockpit."

"Well, if it makes you feel any better, they weren't going to keep flyin' them forever. They would've stuck you in one of them Eagles, or something."

"Yeah, that'd be *real* tough," Josh replied.

"No, you're not going to miss it at all," Marcus commented with just a hint of sarcasm.

Josh looked at him. "Fine, I'm gonna miss it. You happy?" Josh looked back out the window. "It's worth it, though."

"Assuming the plan works," Marcus added.

Josh looked at him again, this time with a serious expression on his face. "It'll work. And even if it doesn't, it's still worth it. The captain got us off Haven...showed us the galaxy. He gave us a chance to prove ourselves." Josh turned to look back out into space again. "Besides, he'd do the same for us... In a heartbeat."

"You're preachin' to the choir, boy."

Josh chuckled. "Yeah, I know." He sighed. "What about you? You gonna miss it?"

"Gettin' to boss all them young fuckers around, yell at pilots, have the captain's ear... Damn right, I'm gonna miss it!" It was Marcus's turn to sigh. "But nothin' lasts forever. And this seemed a good time to make a change... And a good *reason*, as well."

They sat in silence for several minutes, neither of them speaking.

"What do you think we'll do after we get him back?" Josh wondered.

"You mean, like, for work?"

"Yup. How are we gonna make a living?"

"I'm sure we'll find something."

"Loki will, that's for sure," Josh commented. "What with all that training of his. He's got certs in just about everything. But me? An honorable discharge and a few tall tales."

"You can fly anything around," Marcus reminded him.

"Not according to my file, I can't. I've got three certs."

"And at least a thousand hours in fighters," Marcus added, "and a lot of them in combat."

"In a fifty year-old ship, yeah."

"With jump drives," Marcus pointed out. "How many pilots back in the cluster can say that?"

Josh smiled. "Not many, I suppose. But there's

also not many jump-enabled ships in the cluster yet. At least not in the private sector."

"Why can't we just stay on this ship?" Marcus suggested.

"And taxi the princess around?" Josh laughed. "That'd be *real* exciting. What, a few flights a month, maybe?"

"Maybe she'd let us hire out? Run some charters, or freight, maybe? Split the profits three ways. Her, us, and the ship. At the very least, it'd pay for her operations and maintenance. Like you said, there ain't many jump ships in the cluster just yet."

"Maybe," Josh replied. "Still, it won't be anywhere near as exciting." His gaze returned to the stars outside. "Loki and I flew some amazing missions, you know."

"Yeah, I know." Marcus rose and patted Josh on the shoulder. "There's still a lot more of them to fly, kid. Trust me. It's a big galaxy. Now go get some sleep. I'll take over."

* * *

"Guard!" Nathan called out through the tiny window in his cell door. A few moments later, he heard heavy footsteps, followed by the sound of the door lock being deactivated.

The door swung open, and Trever appeared, a slight grin on his face. "What?" he asked, doing his best to sound annoyed for the benefit of the guards back at the central guard station.

"I was promised that I would be able to send a final message to my family," Nathan said. "I finished it." Nathan held up the data pad.

The guard looked at the data pad, then back at Nathan. "I not to see you again, Scott. My shift completed." Trever smiled again.

"Thank you," Nathan said, his face full of sincerity. "For everything."

Trever nodded respectfully, then stepped back and closed the door behind him.

Nathan stood still as the door locks activated, and the sound of Trever's boot steps faded into the distance. He heard the buzz of the gate that sealed the block off from the others, as the last person he would ever speak to headed off to deliver his final words to his father.

The last person I will ever see, or speak to, was the enemy. The thought was somehow ironic.

Nathan turned and walked across his cell to the window. The night sky was cloudy, as usual, but tonight, there were at least a few stars peeking from between swaths of dark gray clouds. They were the first stars he had seen since his arrival on Nor-Patri. They were the very stars he had once flown amongst. Stars that he had fought to protect.

All I had wanted to do was to get away, he thought. *Now all I want is to get back.*

Nathan sat down on his bunk. He wondered what time it was, and how long until his execution would begin. If he waited too long, they might discover him before he bled out. But...

I don't want to die.

It was terrible for the realization to hit him now, of all times. Since his conviction, he had been wrestling with his fate, and he thought he had come to terms with it. But now, as the moment drew nearer, it all came back.

I don't want to die.

He kept telling himself at least he was dying for a good reason, but it didn't seem to help. He thought about his father and his sisters. He thought about his deceased mother, and his older brother, who had died by his own hand. *Is there an afterlife? Will I see them there? Will I have to answer for my transgressions?*

Nathan tried to dismiss the thoughts. He had never been a spiritual person. The idea that a god, or gods, existed, or did not exist, had always been unimportant to him. He considered it a truth that was unknowable, at least in this life.

Am I about to find out?

He looked up at the surveillance camera on the wall over the door. He could imagine the guards out there at their desk, watching him, laughing at the boy captain who was about to be tortured to death.

I cannot give them the satisfaction, he decided.

Nathan pulled back the covers on his bed and lay down, facing the wall, his back to the camera. He covered himself up, as if he were about to go to sleep. Once covered, he slipped his fingers under the edge of the mattress along the wall, feeling for the knife that Trever had purposefully left behind.

He found it. Cold, smooth. He pulled it out carefully, and slowly maneuvered it into position, the tip at the center of his abdomen.

In the gut and up? Between the ribs and in?

Nathan moved the tip of the knife up to his chest, feeling with his free hand for his ribs. They were easy to find, given his undernourished state.

He felt something hard, in his shirt pocket. He reached inside to see what it was, pulling his hand out from under the blanket.

The bullet.

It was the bullet that he had fired to kill his brother. It was the only thing that the Jung had allowed him to keep when he surrendered. Nathan's eyes began to swell with tears. "Forgive me, Eli," he whispered.

With the bullet still in his hand, he pushed carefully with his fingers, finding a spot between his ribs that he presumed to be directly over his heart. He moved the tip of the knife carefully to the same spot, lining it up alongside his finger.

'*You'll never know how important you are to me.*' They were Jessica's last words to him. Odd that they would be his last thought before taking his own life.

I can do this.

Nathan closed his eyes.

One......two......

A distant sound startled him. The gate again. Boots, several of them. Different types, and even different weights. And just as many voices... One of them was familiar...

The boot steps stopped for a moment, the voices continuing in Jung. Nathan lay there, frozen, the tip of his knife against his chest, ready to dive in and take his life.

The voices ceased, and the boot steps began again. This time, there were only two pairs, but they were getting closer.

Nathan moved the knife slowly back down to its hiding place under the edge of the mattress along the wall, then pushed his covers back and sat up on the edge of his bed just as the door locks on his cell door deactivated.

The door swung open, and another guard stepped in. Nathan did not know the guard's name, but he had seen his face before, usually on night shift. The next face that appeared, he did recognize.

"Bacca," Nathan said, his voice full of contempt.

“Captain Scott,” the general replied, an arrogant smile on his face. “Happy to see me?”

“You were not on the short list of people I wanted to see before I died,” Nathan replied icily.

“You mean, before you are put through excruciating torture, and *eventually* allowed to die,” Bacca corrected. “Let’s be accurate, shall we?”

“Don’t tell me you came all the way here, at what surely must be well past your bedtime, just to rub it in.”

“On the contrary, my dear young captain, I am here to ensure that you *do*, in fact, die.”

“What?”

“You see, our nanites are quite good at keeping the human body alive,” the general explained as he paced the length of Nathan’s cell. “Especially the ones that we gave you upon your surrender. We couldn’t allow you to die during your interrogation.” The general turned to look at Nathan. “You *do* remember your interrogation, don’t you?”

“Vividly,” Nathan replied. “Thanks for the reminder.”

“You’re quite welcome. Anyway, it seems that some idiot—although a well-connected idiot—forgot to disable those nanites before turning you over for trial. And we can’t have you refusing to die for the cameras, now can we?”

“Yeah, I suppose that wouldn’t make for a very good execution, would it,” Nathan replied mockingly. “So, what are you going to do?”

“Well, we have to deactivate them, of course.”

“With what?”

The general turned to the guard, barking orders in Jung. The guard nodded, grunted acknowledgment, and disappeared back through the door.

"We have a special device," the general explained, turning toward the door. "And a special person to operate it," he added.

Nathan squinted, unsure of the general's meaning. He then noticed the light on the surveillance camera go out. Then two more pairs of boot steps in the corridor, followed by two more uniformed Jung officers entering his cell.

Nathan's eyes widened. He could feel his mouth about to fall open, but a stern look from General Bacca as he turned back around warned him against it. Nathan immediately regained control, as the guard peeked inside the room and asked the general a question in Jung. The general answered, after which the guard closed and locked the door.

General Bacca put his index finger to his lips, as Jessica and Commander Telles pulled a device out of Jessica's bag.

The commander opened the device, then removed several components, pressing them in strategic locations to break them apart and reveal an interior cavity. He pulled out another small device and activated it. "It is safe to speak, but quietly," he said in hushed tones.

Nathan allowed his eyes to open wide again, and his mouth to drop open. "What are you all doing here?"

Commander Telles immediately stepped in front of the closed cell door, effectively blocking the view of anyone attempting to peek through the tiny window from the other side.

Jessica quickly set her bag on the floor and stepped up to Nathan, throwing her arms around him.

Nathan was speechless, his mouth still agape.

He closed his eyes and embraced her, savoring the moment. "Is this really happening?" he whispered. "Are you really here?"

Jessica pulled back from him slightly, "What? You weren't expecting us?"

"I don't understand," Nathan said, still trying to fully grasp the situation. He looked at General Bacca, who was smiling with one eyebrow up. "Wait... Are you guys prisoners?"

"Of Bacca's?" Jessica scoffed. "Fat chance. If anything, he's our prisoner."

Bacca cast a disapproving glance at Jessica. "Actually, we have 'an arrangement'."

Nathan looked skeptical. "Are you crazy? You can't trust this..."

"It's a long story," Jessica interrupted, "and we don't have much time."

"You can't be here," Nathan objected. "You're jeopardizing everything." He looked at Commander Telles. "I'd expect something like this from Jessica, but not from you. Of all people, *you* should understand why I *must* die."

"I do understand," the commander replied in hushed tones. "As I also understand that you *must* live."

"You're saying that because you're programmed to protect me," Nathan insisted.

"On the contrary, Captain. I *was* programmed to protect you. But such programming requires periodic refresh, lest its effect fades. I am here of my own volition. I am here because I believe you have a much greater destiny to, yet, fulfill."

"You're not buying into the *Na-Tan* crap, are you?" Nathan wondered, shaking his head in disbelief.

"Prophecies are born of ignorance, oppression,

and discontent," the commander replied. "My belief in *your* destiny is based upon my observations of facts and events, and of *your* response to them, nothing more. I am no more likely to believe in Na-Tan than I am to believe in any of the gods of the various human religions."

Jessica pulled the Nifelmian device from her bag and set it on the table.

"This is insane," Nathan continued. "I cannot walk out of here with you. Doing so will start a much greater war. Billions will die, perhaps trillions. I cannot live with that."

"We are not asking you to do so," the commander said. "Captain, you must trust that we *have* a *plan*."

Nathan noticed the device that Jessica was setting up on the table, and the odd-looking cap to which she was connecting several cables. "What plan?" he asked. "And what the hell is that?"

"They're going to clone you," the general proclaimed in amusement.

Nathan looked at Jessica, who was now standing in front of him holding the wired, cloth cap. "He's kidding, right?" Nathan looked at Telles. "Tell me he's kidding."

"I cannot."

"We've got it all worked out," Jessica began, talking quickly. "We copy your memories and consciousness, everything that makes *you,* you. Then we take it, and a DNA sample back to the lab that Sato and Megel are setting up on Corinair. They'll clone you, and then transfer your consciousness and memories into your new body. The Jung will have their dead war criminal, and you'll still live."

"As who?" Nathan demanded. "And who the hell are Sato and Megel? Where did you get this device?"

"Sato and Megel are cloning specialists from Nifelm."

"The clone world?"

"Yes. They volunteered to help, but we had to sneak them off their world," Jessica explained.

"What? Why?"

"Another long story," Jessica replied. "It will work, Nathan. It has to."

"But where am I going to live, and who am I going to be?" Nathan demanded to know. "I can't go back to Earth. I can't *be* Nathan Scott any longer."

"We'll figure all that out later," Jessica promised him. "It's a big fucking galaxy, Nathan. Surely we can find somewhere you can live out your life, in peace. You *deserve* that much."

"Wherever it is, it'll have to be far away from the Jung, that's for sure," Nathan insisted. "How are we going to get around?"

"We have a ship already," Jessica told him. "Nathan, trust us. We've got this all worked out." Jessica looked in his eyes. "You *trust* us, don't you?"

Nathan looked at her, and then Telles. "Of course, I trust you. Both of you." He cast a disapproving look at Bacca. "You, not a bit."

"No offense taken," the general replied.

Nathan looked at Jessica again. "And I'll remember everything? I'll still be *me*?"

"Yes..." Jessica looked down, suddenly avoiding his eyes. "Probably."

"Probably?" Nathan looked at Telles for an explanation.

"The device was designed for use on Nifelmians," the commander explained. "They have been genetically altered over the centuries to facilitate the transfer of consciousness and memories along to each successive host body. There is no guarantee that it will work as intended on you."

Nathan turned to General Bacca.

"News to me, my boy."

Nathan looked at Jessica next. "What are my chances?"

"Sato and Megel are pretty sure that your consciousness and personality will be intact, but they are unsure about your memories."

Nathan noticed the worry in Jessica's eyes. "There's more, isn't there?"

"There is also risk of psychiatric disorders," Commander Telles added.

"How bad?"

"It is impossible to estimate."

"At least it's a chance," Jessica urged.

"Not much of one," Nathan muttered, contemplating the idea.

"Nathan, say the word and we'll take you with us, as you are. We'll blast our way out and be jumping to safety before you know it."

Nathan glanced at Telles, who discretely shook his head in opposition to her rash proposal. He looked back at Jessica. "You know I can't do that, Jess...as much as I'd like to."

"Such an honorable, young man," General Bacca quipped.

"Shut up," Jessica scolded him. She focused her attention back on Nathan. "Then this *is* the only way."

Nathan took a deep breath, letting it out in a long sigh.

"Time, people," the general reminded them.

"Shut up," Jessica snapped, more annoyed than before.

"The general is correct," the commander pointed out. "We must move quickly."

Jessica looked at him again. "Nathan, please."

Nathan sighed. "Promise me... If I come out a basket case, you'll take care of me."

"I promise," Jessica replied, placing her hand on Nathan's cheek.

"Very well," Nathan finally agreed. "What do I do?"

"Put this on and lie down," Jessica instructed, handing him the cap.

Nathan pulled the cap on over his head. "Like this?"

Jessica reached out and adjusted the cap on Nathan's head, making sure the marks on it were aligned according to the instructions given to her by Doctor Megel. "That's good. Now lie down and be still."

"How long will it take?" Nathan asked, as he lay down on his bed.

"The slower the scan, the better our chances of a complete copy," Jessica explained. "At least ten minutes."

"Then let's get started," Nathan told her.

* * *

Mister Bryant stepped into the admiral's office. "Your shuttle is ready, Admiral."

Admiral Dumar took one last look around his nearly barren office, then slowly rose to his feet to move out from behind his desk.

"Are you sure you don't want to stay for the memorial service?"

"That is still several days away," Admiral Dumar replied. "Besides, this is not our world. Let the Terrans honor him in their own way. We shall honor him in ours."

Mister Bryant nodded his understanding. "As you wish."

Admiral Dumar walked to the door, stopping to shake the hand of his trusted second. "We have done amazing things here. None of which I could have done without you."

"Thank you, sir. It has been my honor."

"I trust you will be returning home soon?"

"Within the month, yes."

"Good, good. I'm sure your family misses you."

"My kids, likely," Mister Bryant agreed. "My wife..."

Admiral Dumar smiled, patted his friend on the shoulder, and headed through the door.

"Attention on deck!" one of the officers in the control room outside the admiral's office barked.

Simultaneously, every person working in the Karuzara command center snapped to attention.

"CORINARI!" the officer bellowed.

"HUP! HUP! HUP!" the rest chorused in unison.

Admiral Dumar felt a tremendous surge of pride. Most of the officers and technicians in the control room had been members of Corinair's elite military, but he had not. In fact, he had been in command of the secret Takaran anti-insurgency team tasked with keeping an eye on the Corinari, lest they became too ambitious in their goals. Yet, these officers, all of them volunteers, same as he, were honoring him.

Admiral Travon Dumar raised his hand in salute, a gesture meant to show his men the admiration and respect he held for them. In unison, they returned his salute.

Dumar left the control room and entered the corridor, only to find it lined with personnel of every type. Officers, enlisted, civilian contractors, volunteers: all of them had dropped what they were doing to wish their leader a fond farewell.

Admiral Dumar had to choke back the tears as he walked down the corridor. He had never served with such people. They believed in what they were doing, with their hearts and souls. And he would likely never serve with such people again.

He continued down one corridor after another, each lined with base personnel, all of them coming to attention and saluting, making a wave-like effect as the admiral passed, until finally he stepped into the transit car, and the doors closed behind him.

As the transit car began to accelerate on its journey to one of the Karuzara asteroid's many hangar bays, one thought kept racing through Admiral Dumar's mind.

Nathan will not live to see such honors.

* * *

General Bacca paced nervously back and forth, impatiently waiting for the scan of Nathan's mind to be completed.

"You are expending energy unnecessarily," Commander Telles commented.

"You have already said as much," the general snapped. "More than once, I might add."

"Yet, your behavior does not change."

"If the lieutenant commander is at all good at his job, he will have put a request into the pipeline to at least check on the identities of the both of you," the general said. "I don't suppose you bothered to assume the identities of people within our military."

"They did not say," the commander stated.

"At this hour, it will be difficult to get anyone to respond," the general continued. "However, eventually, someone will respond."

"The identities of those within your intelligence community are so easily verified?" the commander wondered.

"Normally, no. But considering the importance of the prisoner we requested to visit..." The general shook his finger at the commander. "Trust me, someone *will* respond. And when they do, we had best be light years away, or we will be joining your captain on the execution stage." He turned to look at Jessica. "How much longer?"

"We're almost done," Jessica promised.

"You're making it awfully hard to remain calm and relaxed," Nathan said with his eyes closed, lying on his bed as his brain was scanned by the Nifelmian device.

"I am taking a *tremendous* risk on your behalf," the general reminded them.

"Oh, please," Jessica said dismissively. "You're doing this on your *own* behalf, not ours."

"The risk is there, nonetheless," the general replied. "For all of us, I should remind you."

The Nifelmian device beeped three times, and the status display changed.

"Is it done?" the general asked.

"I think so," Jessica answered, looking over the display.

Nathan opened his eyes. "Did it work?"

Jessica examined the status display once more. "It says 'scan complete', so I guess that's it."

"I don't suppose it tells you whether or not it was a good scan?"

"Megel said a good scan will take up at least eighty percent of the device's storage capacity. Yours took up ninety-three percent. Must be all that history crap you're always spouting."

Nathan took off the wired cap and handed it back to Jessica. He took a deep breath and sighed. "I guess that's it, then."

Jessica placed the cap and its cabling back into the bag, followed by the device itself. "I just have to take a DNA sample." She pulled out a small vial, opened it, and pulled out the small collector probe stored within. "Open wide."

Nathan opened his mouth to allow her to rub the collector probe against the inside of his cheeks.

"That should do it," Jessica said as she placed the collector probe back into the vial.

"Don't lose it," Nathan said. "Either one."

"Don't worry," she assured him, as she placed the vial back into the device's secret compartment.

"Then, we can depart?" the general asked, eager to leave.

"We told them he would be unconscious for a few hours, because of the procedure," Commander Telles reminded them. "You will need to lie down and remain unmoving for that time," he instructed Nathan.

"Why did you tell them that?" Nathan wondered as he rose from the bed.

Jessica looked Nathan in the eyes. "Because we cannot leave you to be tortured to death, and have it broadcast to billions." She glanced briefly to her side to ensure that the general was behind her, then mouthed *trust me* to Nathan. She turned and looked at Commander Telles. "We can't leave him to be tortured."

"This was not part of the plan," the commander warned her.

"Fuck the plan," she cursed. "I'm not going to let them make him suffer. I can't."

"Jessica," the commander said. "How are we supposed to kill him? We have no weapons."

"Neither of us needs weapons to kill," Jessica reminded him.

"It would be best if his death appeared to be a suicide," the commander told her.

"Why?" General Bacca said.

All three of them looked at the general.

"Make it look like I did it," the general added. "For revenge, or as a traitor. Whichever they choose, it is of little difference to me, as I will be far away with the both of you."

"I'm not letting you kill Nathan," Jessica argued. "I'm not going to give you the satisfaction."

"Thanks," Nathan said.

"Better that we leave now, and let Nathan accept his fate," the commander insisted. "It provides the highest probability of mission success."

"I'm not gonna argue with you about this, Telles," Jessica said stubbornly.

"No one will ever believe that General Bacca was able to kill Nathan with his bare hands," the commander warned. "Look at him. He is old and frail."

"Normally, I would take offense to that," the general said.

"Shut up," Jessica warned the general.

"He doesn't have to," Nathan interrupted.

"Doesn't have to what?" Jessica asked.

"To kill me with his bare hands," Nathan explained. "I have a knife."

"What?"

"One of the guards felt sorry for me. He left it behind after my final meal, so I could take my own life."

"There's your plan, then," the general decided. "We go about our merry way, and young Captain Scott kills himself in his cell to avoid being tortured." The general pulled out his gloves and put them on. "Shall we?"

Jessica looked at Nathan as he reached under the edge of his mattress and produced the knife.

"I......I don't know if I can do it," Nathan said quietly, looking into Jessica's eyes. "Can...you?"

"Nathan," Jessica whispered back, her eyes pleading him not to ask such a task of her. She glanced back at the commander, looking for support.

"Would you like me..." the commander began to offer.

"No," Jessica objected, holding up her hand. "I'll do it." She took a deep breath, then turned back to Nathan. "Give me the knife," she said hoarsely, her voice unsteady.

"Jess..."

"I can do it," she insisted. "For you, I can do it."

"Jess," Nathan repeated, his eyes welling up, his own voice trembling.

Jessica took the knife from him, turned it, and pointed it at his heart. She gazed into his eyes for several seconds, then kissed him gently. "I love you, Nathan."

Nathan was unable to speak, struggling to control his breathing and remain standing, in the face of what was about to happen.

Jessica tightened her grip on the knife, pushing the tip against his shirt, but no more. Her resolve was fading. Nathan could see it in her eyes. "I... I... I can't," she whispered, almost inaudible.

Nathan put both hands on her cheeks, looked in her eyes, and whispered, "I love you, too." He grabbed her shoulders and pulled her quickly into him, causing the knife to plunge deeply into his chest. An intense pain shot through him; he could even feel the tip of the blade change direction slightly on its way in, careening off his rib. His mouth dropped open, and he gasped, just as Jessica let out a tiny, startled cry of anguish.

"Oh, God. Oh, God," she repeated in horror, Nathan's ghastly expression only inches from her face.

"I love you, too," he said again, barely audible as his final breaths escaped, and his legs began to give out.

Commander Telles stood motionless, maintaining his position to prevent anyone from looking into the cell through the door window.

Jessica quickly let go of the knife, still stuck in his heart, and reached around him to keep him from falling. Crying, she lowered him gently back down onto his bed, looking him in the eyes the entire time, as the life in them faded away.

She placed him on his side, facing the wall, then slowly pulled the blanket up over him. She paused a moment, pretending to get the blanket just right, as she used it to wipe the handle of the knife, still stuck in Nathan's chest, clean of her finger prints.

"Is he dead?" General Bacca asked.

Jessica finished covering Nathan, kissing him on the cheek before answering. "He's gone."

"I'm killing the anti-surveillance field," Jessica announced, looking at each of them to ensure they were ready. She reached into the bag and deactivated the device, then placed it into the secret compartment and closed it up. Once complete, she looked at the general. "The procedure is finished, General," she said in Jung. "All nanites within the subject's body have been permanently disabled."

"Guard!" the general cried out. A moment later, the door lock deactivated, and the door swung open. "We have completed our task," the general announced to the guard who appeared in the door.

The guard looked at the prisoner, apparently unconscious on the bed. "He is unharmed?" the guard asked in Jung.

"He will be unconscious for several hours," the general explained.

"Why is he lying on his side like that?"

"His unconsciousness is deep," Jessica clarified. "We placed him on his left lateral side to prevent him from choking, in case his stomach contents should come up while he is out."

"See that he is not disturbed," the general reminded the guard.

"Yes, General."

"We are ready to depart," the general announced.

"Of course, General," the guard replied, turning to lead them out of the cell.

The general was the first to exit, followed by Jessica, who exchanged glances with the commander.

Commander Telles took one last look at the man he had once been programmed to protect. That task was not yet accomplished.

* * *

The shuttle smoothly touched down on the landing pad outside the general's residence, thanks to its automated flight systems. Before the engines could finish spinning down, the boarding hatch opened, and the commander stepped out, followed by General Bacca and Jessica. They headed quickly across the dimly lit courtyard, making their way to the patio doors, into the general's office.

Once inside, Jessica immediately removed the Nifelmian device from the Jung military-style bag, and placed it back into the civilian-style knapsack she had taken from the yacht.

General Bacca let out a sigh of relief, heading for his liquor cabinet behind his desk. "I have to admit, I did not think we would make it out of there alive," he said as he opened the cabinet and poured himself a drink. "You two were quite impressive." The general lifted his glass and poured the shot of red liquor down his throat in a single gulp. "Would either of you care for a drink?" he asked, helping himself to another serving.

"Our mission is not complete," the commander reminded him, as he closed the patio doors.

"Yes, quite right," the general agreed as he sat in his desk chair. "How are we going to get off of Nor-Patri?"

"*We*, are not," Jessica replied as she pulled off her Jung uniform jacket.

Commander Telles locked the patio doors and then moved to his right, taking off his own uniform jacket.

"What do you mean?" the general wondered nervously. He didn't notice that the commander was moving behind him.

Jessica grinned. "You didn't really think we were going to honor our agreement, did you?"

"You gave me your word," the general reminded her, as he slowly reached for the handgun under his desk.

"You butchered millions of my people," Jessica

said, seething. "And it was *you* who set Nathan up as a scapegoat, in the hopes of saving your *own* ass."

General Bacca pulled the weapon and took aim at Jessica, only to find the commander's strong right hand clutching his own. The general struggled to free himself from the commander's grip, but his opponent had his other arm around his neck, pinning him to the back of his desk chair.

The commander expertly slid his hand over the general's gun hand, and slowly forced the gun barrel up under the general's chin.

"You bitch!" the general growled through gritted teeth.

"Damn right," Jessica replied, nonchalantly.

The general used his last breath to scream out in rage as the commander pressed the general's trigger finger down. The weapon fired, sending a single red energy blast into the general's chin, instantly burning a tunnel through his brain and out the top of his head.

Commander Telles released the general's body, the dead man's head and hair still sizzling from the heat of the energy blast. The general's body went limp, his hand still clutching his weapon, as an acrid smoke rose from the smoldering wound.

"Damn, that stinks," Jessica commented, a smile on her face.

"Yes, quite unpleasant indeed," the commander agreed, as he stepped out from behind the general's body and continued changing out of his Jung uniform.

"Nicely done, by the way."

"Thank you," the commander replied. "We must move quickly, in case the general's concern of discovery was correct."

"I'm right behind you," Jessica said as she slipped on her civilian attire, a satisfied look on her face.

* * *

"Anything?" Josh begged.

"Not yet," Loki replied, his eyes glued to the sensor display.

Josh looked at the time display on the console. "We're smack in the middle of the rendezvous window," he said. "You'd think they'd be here by now." He looked at Loki in the seat to his right. "You don't think something went wrong, do you?"

"Josh."

"Sneaking in and out of prison on the Jung homeworld, carrying a Nifelmian brain scanner?" Marcus grumbled. "What could go wrong?"

"They should be here by now," Josh repeated.

"Dumbest plan I ever heard of," Marcus added. "Let alone participated in."

"At least we're out here, where it's safe," Josh commented.

"Safe?" Loki looked at Josh in disbelief. "You call cold-coasting in the outer reaches of the Jung home system *safe*?"

"I meant in comparison," Josh defended.

"We've been out here for two hours," Loki continued. "If there is a Jung ship patrolling anywhere near here..."

"We'd already have picked them up on passive," Josh interrupted, "and you know it."

"What if one happens to pop out of FTL nearby?" Loki asked. "Did you ever consider that?"

"Oh, come on, Lok..."

"You two argue like an old, married couple," Marcus said wearily. "Are you always like this?"

"Pretty much," Josh admitted.

"Somebody's got to force him to think things through," Loki added under his breath.

"Just because I don't analyze the life out of every decision before I act..."

"I think I got something," Loki said.

"...doesn't mean I'm not thinking... What?"

"Really small, but it was definitely an energy spike. It could be a jump flash."

"Is it them?"

Loki looked at Josh again, dumbfounded, then turned to Marcus. "See what I mean?"

"What?" Josh wondered.

"Who the hell else would be jumping in out here?" Loki pointed out.

"I meant, are you sure it's a jump flash!" Josh defended.

"I don't know, yet. Slow us down a bit so we can close the distance faster."

"Assuming there's something out there," Josh commented.

"Assuming there is, yes."

"But I thought we were cold-coasting?"

"Josh!"

"Just sayin'! If I'm firing thrusters, we're emitting an increased heat signature."

"Just do it!"

"I just don't want you to accuse me of not thinkin'."

Loki wasn't paying attention, his eyes still fixed on the sensor display. Josh applied reverse thrust to slow the ship down slightly.

"Anything?" Josh asked.

"Not yet," Loki replied. "But, if they're running cold like they're supposed to, we won't pick them up until we're almost on top of them, at least not with passive sensors."

"Mission plan says to flash them," Josh reminded him.

"Flash'em?" Marcus said, unsure what Josh meant.

"Light ourselves up. Do three jump field test bleeds, so they can spot us on their passive," Loki explained. "That way, they know it isn't a Jung ship, and they can hit us with their directional beacon so *we* know it's *them.*"

"It's like flashing our lights, but lights that only *we* can have," Josh added.

"You wanna light us up? Make us visible to everyone, including the Jung?" Marcus said. "Yet another stupid plan."

"My idea," Josh announced proudly.

"Like I said," Marcus commented.

"It's the only one we've got," Loki replied. "And I'm pretty sure that was a jump flash." He reached over to the jump drive control console and activated the first test bleed. "That's one," he reported as he initiated another. "That's two." Loki pressed the emitter test button one more time. "That's three."

"Now what?" Marcus wondered.

"Now, we either pick up their beacon, or we get painted by a Jung ship locking their weapons onto us."

"Jesus," Marcus mumbled. "I should've stayed on the Aurora."

The three of them continued watching the sensor display, holding their breath, until, finally, an icon appeared on the screen.

"Yes!" Josh declared.

"Is it them?" Marcus asked. "They're alive? They made it?"

"The response isn't automated, so yeah, they're alive!" Loki replied with excitement.

"I'll be damned!" Marcus said. "I would've bet a year's pay against them!"

"Good thing we're not getting paid," Josh replied.

"Okay, I've calculated their course and speed," Loki announced. "Line us up for intercept and recovery."

"You got it!" Josh replied.

"You'd better head aft and prepare to recover them, Marcus," Loki said. "We're less than five minutes out."

"On my way," Marcus replied, turning to exit the cockpit. He, suddenly, looked back. "Wait, we're not getting paid for this?"

Marcus entered the Mirai's empty cargo bay through the midship hatch, closing it behind him. He quickly climbed down the short ladder and made his way across the deck aft, pulling the face shield down on his suit helmet as he approached the door controls. "At the controls," he reported. "Depressurizing the bay."

Marcus activated the depressurization sequence for the cargo bay, then reached into the equipment locker next to the control panel and pulled out a safety tether. He hooked the tether to the overhead track, and deactivated the cargo bay's artificial gravity. "Killing the gravity," he announced. "Depress cycle fifty percent complete."

"*Jump sub is one minute out,*" Loki reported over the comms.

Loki checked his displays. "Be ready to fire forward thrusters to match their speed," he warned

Josh. "We don't want them ramming into the cargo bay's forward bulkhead, you know."

"I got this, Loki," Josh insisted. "Just give me the aft-facing cargo bay camera, will ya?"

"Coming up," Loki replied.

"*Depress cycle complete,*" Marcus reported over the comms. "*Opening ramp and inner doors.*"

The image on the center console display switched from the passive sensor data to the aft-facing camera located at the forward end of the Mirai's cargo bay. They could see Marcus standing off to the left side of the bay, peeking around the edge of the cargo doors as they finished retracting into the bulkheads.

"*I can see the jump sub,*" Marcus reported. "*They're closing fast.*"

"Copy that," Josh replied, adjusting himself in his seat to prepare for the recovery.

"One hundred meters," Loki reported. "Target is high and starboard, closing at one meter per second."

Josh manipulated the docking thruster controls, translating the Mirai upward and slightly to starboard.

"Ninety meters. A little more to starboard."

The port docking thrusters hissed again.

"Eighty meters."

Josh squinted, trying to make out the jump sub on the center display, but couldn't see anything. "You sure it's out there?" he mumbled.

"I've got them on passive," Loki assured him.

"*I can see them from here,*" Marcus insisted.

"Seventy meters," Loki reported. "They should turn on their lights at fifty."

Josh said nothing. He kept staring at the display, his hands ready on the docking thrusters.

"Sixty meters," Loki reported.

Four flashing red lights suddenly appeared on the display in the center of the console.

"I've got them," Josh announced.

"Fifty meters and closing," Loki reported. "Still a little low."

"I've got it now," Josh assured him as he fired more thrusters.

Marcus leaned out from the side of the cargo hatch, gazing at the large, ominous-looking silhouette of the jump sub as it floated toward them, its marker lights blinking in unison every other second.

"*Forty meters*," Loki reported over the comms.

"Are you sure this thing is going to fit?" he wondered.

"*It'll fit*," Josh replied.

"*Barely*," Loki added. "*Thirty meters.*"

Marcus felt the ship lurch slightly, the vessel accelerating slightly as Josh fired the forward thrusters to slow their rate of closure with the jump sub. The thrusters fired again, this time causing the ship to slide to starboard.

"I'm not so sure about this," Marcus warned as the jump sub grew nearer.

"*Twenty meters, half meter per second.*"

"Guys?"

"*It'll fit!*" Josh insisted.

"It's coming in awfully fast!" Marcus warned, pushing himself back behind the edge of the hatch frame.

"*Ten meters*," Loki reported.

The thrusters fired again, causing the ship to lurch once more. Two more squirts of thrust brought the approaching jump sub right through the middle of the cargo bay hatchway.

"*Five meters.*"

Marcus floated just inside the hatch frame, holding onto the overhead rail, wanting to stay out of the way.

"*End of ramp,*" Loki reported. "*Threshold.*"

Marcus's eyes widened as he watched the jump sub slide into the cargo bay. "Rotate thirty to port," he instructed, when he noticed the jump sub was not oriented correctly.

"*Rotating,*" Josh replied.

The jump sub began to rotate as it continued entering the cargo bay, only a meter above the deck. "Activating gravity," Marcus announced, reaching the cargo bay's artificial gravity controls. "Bringing it up slow."

The jump sub began to descend, ending its rotation. The Mirai lurched again as Josh fired the thrusters one last time to prevent the jump sub from making contact with the forward bulkhead.

Marcus's feet touched the deck as the slowly increasing gravity pulled him down. A moment later, he felt the reverberations of the jump sub contacting the deck as well. "She's down!" he reported happily.

"*Is she all the way in?*" Loki asked over the comms.

Marcus looked around the back of the jump sub, making sure that its aft end was inside the yellow warning lines on the deck. "She's clear of the inner doors," he replied. "Closing her up!"

"*Yes!*" Josh exclaimed over the comms.

"Nice going, kid!" Marcus congratulated him. "Starting the repress cycle," he added as the inner doors finished closing.

"*Told you I had this!*" Josh bragged.

Two minutes later, Marcus had his helmet off and was cracking open the hatch on top of the jump sub.

The hatch slid back, revealing the face of Commander Telles looking up at him. "Welcome back!" Marcus greeted, reaching down to help pull the commander up through the hatch.

Commander Telles climbed out, then turned around and pulled the knapsack containing the Nifelmian device out of the sub.

"Did you get it?" Marcus asked. "Is the captain's brain in there?"

"In a manner of speaking, yes," the commander replied, reaching back down into the sub to pull Jessica up.

"Amazing!" Marcus declared. "Welcome back, Jess!"

"Thanks," she replied, obviously relieved.

"*Are we good?*" Loki asked over the comms. "*Did they get him?*"

"They got him!" Marcus replied. "Let's get the hell outta here!"

CHAPTER NINE

Jessica stood next to her mother on the tarmac at the Porto Santo spaceport, holding baby Ania in her arms, watching as Jessica's father and brothers loaded the last of their belongings into the cargo bay of the Mirai. A distant screech from the sky caught her attention, causing her to turn and look skyward as a jump shuttle appeared on the horizon just offshore.

Jessica and her mother watched as the shuttle came in low over the base, turned, and descended smoothly onto the tarmac a hundred meters away, its engines spinning down as soon as its gear touched the pavement. The boarding hatch opened moments later, and Captain Taylor and Lieutenant Commander Kamenetskiy came down from the shuttle.

She watched as they approached, her focus jumping back and forth between her approaching friends and the infant in her arms.

"You know them?" her mother asked, noticing her divided attention.

"Yeah, I know them," Jessica replied. "Here, take her inside," she said, handing the child to her mother. "I'll join you shortly."

Jessica's mother took the child from her daughter and headed up the Mirai's cargo ramp, following one of her grandchildren who was pulling an oversized bag up the ramp.

Jessica turned to face her approaching friends, unsure of what to say.

"You were going to leave without saying goodbye?" Vladimir asked in an accusatory tone.

"Not much choice, really," Jessica replied. "Now

that I'm no longer in the Alliance, transportation to orbit is a bit more challenging."

"Are you sure about this, Jess?" Cameron asked with concern. "I mean, it's the *Ghatazhak*."

"Yes," Vladimir agreed. "They have no sense of humor."

"That's why they need me," Jessica replied. "To liven things up a bit. Besides, I think Telles is right. I *need* them. It's the only way I'll be able to move on."

"You could always date a handsome, Russian man, with a great sense of humor," Vladimir suggested helpfully.

"I think she's better off with the Ghatazhak," Cameron commented. "Are you sure you can handle it? The Ghatazhak training, raising Ania, living on an entirely different world, in an entirely different sector?"

Jessica laughed. "Funny, two years ago we were doing whatever we had to just to get back here. Now I can't wait to leave. It'll be fine. I'll have my parents, my brothers, and their families. I suspect my mom will be doing most of the work when it comes to Ania. She never lets her out of her sight. And, I'll have the galaxy's greatest soldiers to protect me."

"And put you in harm's way, I'm sure," Cameron reminded her.

"Not for some time, I imagine," Jessica assured her. "The Sherma system is at least a hundred light years from Takara, well outside the Pentaurus sector. The most dangerous thing there will probably be a bar fight, or some local pirates. It'll be a cakewalk compared to the last two years."

"The Ghatazhak? A cakewalk?" Cameron couldn't believe what she was hearing. "Did they reprogram you, as well?"

"Trust me, Cam," Jessica said. "This is what I want. This is what's *right* for me."

Cameron sighed. "I'm going to miss you," she finally said, stepping up and embracing her. "You sure you don't want to stay for the memorial service?" She asked as she pulled away. "It might bring you some closure."

Jessica smiled. "Trust me, I got all the closure I needed. Besides, I've got to get my family settled before the Ghatazhak move in. They've secured a pretty nice tract of land near the base site. They're going to become farmers and grow all the food for the base. Can you believe it?"

"So, I guess the next time we see you, you're going to be some kind of Ghatazhak, tough-girl?" Vladimir wondered, stepping forward to embrace her, as well.

"What do you mean, going to be?" Jessica said, hugging him tightly. "Keep them hands high, big guy," she joked as they embraced.

"Be safe, Jess," Vladimir said as he let her go.

"You, too," she replied. "Both of you," she added, as she turned and headed up the Mirai's boarding ramp.

When she reached the top of the cargo ramp, she turned and waved goodbye to them both as the ramp began to rise.

Cameron and Vladimir moved back a few steps as the Mirai spun up her engines and slowly rose from the tarmac, drifting quickly away from them. Once her gear was off the pavement, it retracted into her hull as she rotated to her departure heading and continued to climb away. A minute later, she disappeared behind a flash of blue-white light.

Cameron and Vladimir stood staring at the sky for several seconds.

"I can't believe she is gone," Vladimir said.

"Neither can I," Cameron said, patting him on the shoulder. "Neither can I."

* * *

Doctor Sato stood in the middle of the makeshift cloning lab that her newly formed team had slapped together in only ten days.

"What's wrong?" Doctor Megel asked, noticing her hesitation.

"Maybe we should wait until we have something resembling a true and proper lab?"

"Michi, that will take months, perhaps even a year. Half of the components needed are not available on this world, and have to be fabricated from designs. Designs that have to first be converted to Corinairan manufacturing standards."

"But what if you are not able to get the full-size bath ready in time for the transfer?"

"It will be ready," Doctor Megel assured her. "Frankly, I'm more concerned with building the consciousness transfer system. Their technologies may be more advanced, but their computer systems are vastly different from our own."

"Can't you just build one of our computers?"

"If I already had the components, possibly. But my expertise is not hardware. I am a programmer by training. All of my hardware knowledge is coincidental to that. It is better that I rewrite the code to work with the Corinairan operating systems and hardware. At least that I *know* how to do."

Michi nodded, stepping up to the makeshift control console for the primary cloning bath. "I cannot believe I'm going to grow a clone using baths. It's like doing surgery with knives, needles, and sutures." She activated the controls, and a moment later, the chemicals in the small primary cloning bath in front of her began to swirl and glow. "The process has started," she announced. She turned to look at Doctor Megel again. "I only hope their expectations do not exceed our abilities."

"All we can do is our best," Doctor Megel told her. "And if we fail, they could always go back and ask our leaders for help again."

"By that time, the captain's consciousness may no longer be viable," Doctor Sato reminded him.

* * *

Thousands gathered on the parade grounds of the still under-construction Earth Defense Force academy on the coast of the Florida peninsula. Tens of thousands more filled the streets outside, despite the heat and humidity. They could not see, but they could hear. More importantly, they could say that *they* were *there*, when Captain Nathan Scott was laid to rest.

Millions more watched via every broadcast medium that still functioned on planet Earth. In every country, and on every continent, and eventually, also on every Alliance world within the Sol sector.

There were no bands, no pipes, no roaring crowds. Only a deafening silence, broken only by the sounds of footsteps walking slowly along the pavement, and the brief snap of the snare drum rolls on every fourth step of the steady procession.

The line was led by President Dayton Scott, leader of the newly formed Earth Coalition of Nations, followed by a cadre of his youngest son's shipmates, headed by Captain Taylor, the new commander of the Aurora, and Lieutenant Commander Kamenetskiy, the ship's chief engineer—both of them close friends of the man they now carried to his final resting place.

With the suicide of Captain Scott leaving them no living body to torture to death, the Jung agreed to return the young captain's body to his family, and to the people whom he had died to protect. Some felt it a sign of goodwill by the Jung; others saw it as a bargaining chip to be used at the cease-fire negotiations that had only recently begun.

The procession made its way from the temporary spaceport on the far side of the academy grounds, across the vast campus, and finally to the eastern end of the parade grounds, where it butted up to the coastline.

Once at the presentation stage, the president and his aides stepped to one side, looking on as the bearers carried the casket up the side steps and to the front and center of the stage. They placed the casket carefully on its stand, then stepped back, lining up on either side directly behind the casket, and in front of the speaker's platform.

The flag bearers came next. Dozens of them, the first carrying the EDF flag, the rest bearing all the flags of the coalition, followed by those from the other Alliance worlds within the Sol sector. As they arrived, each flag bearer placed their flag into its holder along the top of the hillside bleachers on either side of the grounds, then took their positions alongside their respective charges, encircling the area.

Following the flags were the representatives from the different EDF academies from around the world, all of which were now overflowing with volunteers applying for entry. They lined up in front of the rows of flags, on either side of the parade grounds, directly behind and above the top rows of bleachers.

Finally, dignitaries, from both Earth and beyond,

entered the seating area, taking seats front and center, and filling outward from the stage one row at a time. After them, the rest of the public who had joined the procession began filling the bleachers.

President Scott stood motionless, his face devoid of expression, despite both the great sorrow, *and* the great pride that he felt. The manner in which every person conducted themselves, the respect that every person showed, and the incredible quiet, despite the almost coordinated movement of thousands of attendees, spoke volumes about the young man they had come to honor that day. His son.

The last of the attendees took their seats in the bleachers, as well as the open standing areas around the parade grounds. Once everyone was assembled, an EDF Marine sergeant stepped forward. His uniform was crisp, colorful, and fitted, with white hat and gloves, and a polished silver sword hanging at his side. He was young, with eyes of steel, square-jawed and shouldered, and a well-honed manner. He took a deep breath and barked...crisp and loud, "A-ten-SHUN!"

Every uniformed officer in attendance snapped to perfect attention at the exact, same time. The sound of their movement- the rustle of pant legs and the snap of their heels as they came together—like a cannon shot that would later be reported to have been heard for miles.

"Saaa-LUTE!" the sergeant barked next.

Again, in unison, a thousand uniformed officers raised their hands sharply, fingertips at hat brims for a full second, before lowering their hands to their sides.

The sergeant stepped back into the line, standing at attention, after which President Scott ascended the steps and took the speaker's platform, making his way to the podium to speak.

They lined the streets of Aitkenna on that cloudy morning. Hundreds of thousands. Men, women, children. People from all walks of life, all professions, all beliefs, and all political leanings... On that day, they all had something uniquely in common. They had all once been saved by the man they came to honor that day. The man they called Na-Tan.

They stood along the main roadway that led from the spaceport, through the center of the capital city, and to the Walk of Heroes located in the park at the city's center. At five point eight kilometers, the walk wrapped its way around the middle of the massive park. On either side of the broad walkway were the graves of those who had sacrificed themselves to protect their world. Their numbers had grown so much over the decades that there was scarcely room to accommodate them all. Even so, each and every grave was still marked with only a simple headstone that displayed a portrait and name laser-etched into the stone. At the foot of each grave was a display screen built into the stone that, when tapped with one's foot, projected a life-sized holographic image of the person buried there, allowing them to live on for as long as their world survived.

The people of Corinair watched as legions of pipers marched, blowing their lilting melody with practiced ease as they split in half, each taking their own route around the Walk of Heroes.

They finally came to rest, their haunting melody fading away, in front of the largest headstone installed. It was five times larger than the others, if not six, and had a life-size holographic display that was always on, and would remain that way, for as long as the world of Corinair survived.

Admiral Travon Dumar, retired, took the stage, pausing behind the podium before speaking. He looked out on the crowd that filled the park and spilled out onto the streets of Aitkenna, wondering if any words could befit such an occasion. Tens, if not hundreds, of thousands, were quiet at this moment.

"The man I knew was not Na-Tan. The man I knew was Captain Nathan Scott. He had no interest in being Na-Tan. He was only trying to do the right thing, for everyone. Everyone except for himself. Right up until the end of his young life."

"We have all lost someone," President Scott said, continuing his speech. "Sons, daughters, fathers, mothers, friends... All of us. I, myself, have lost two sons, a son-in-law, and..." The president paused, closing his eyes for a brief moment. "...and my wife. No one's pain is less, or more. Today, let us not grieve for one man. Let us grieve for all those who have been lost. Let us not honor the sacrifice of one man. Let us honor the sacrifices of all who have given so much."

Admiral Dumar looked to his right, at the life-size holographic image of Captain Scott, standing confidently, wearing his usual smile. "Captain Scott once told me that Na-Tan was not a man, but an idea. An idea that when the greater good of humanity is in need, there will always be someone who will step up to fill the role. Someone to lead us, to inspire us... Someone to make us *believe* that all hope is not lost. Na-Tans come and go every day. Teachers who inspire their students. Mothers who inspire their children. Philosophers who inspire thought. Artists who inspire emotion. And leaders, who inspire us all to do what we can to contribute to the greater good. *That* is what *Na-Tan* is. He is the good in all of us."

President Scott looked down at his data pad for a moment. "I'd like to share with you my son's last words, written on the eve of his death." The president looked down again, clearing his throat and struggling to keep from breaking down in tears.

> *"For the longest time, I wanted nothing more than to escape. To escape the expectations of my family, the expectations of the public, and especially the expectations of you. I thought that everyone wanted me to be something other than who I was. Who I am. Like I was supposed to become some great leader. Rich, powerful, charismatic. The man that you wanted me to be. And all I wanted to do was to be myself. Back then, I thought myself was the opposite of what everyone wanted me to be. But now, I realize that nothing could be further from the truth. Now, I realize that you only wanted me to find my own way. Well, it appears that I have done so. Unfortunately, it led me to this cell. But I do not regret the choices that brought me here. All men die. Rarely do we get to choose when, and even more rarely, do we get to die protecting something we truly cherish."*

President Scott's voice started to crack, tears streaming down his cheeks, as he continued reading.

> *"Do not for a moment believe that my death changes anything. There will always be those who prey upon the weak, just as there will always be those to defend them. I chose to be one who defended them. For the opportunity to do so, I am incredibly honored."*

"Captain Scott did not *give* us back our freedom," the admiral continued. "He *gave* us the ability to take it back ourselves. He gave us back our pride. He gave us back our dignity. He stood in harm's way on our behalf, and gave us the strength to fight back. Never again will Corinair allow itself to be subjugated. To do so would dishonor not only Captain Scott, but all those who died before him, and alongside him. To do so would dishonor the very *spirit* of Na-Tan."

Admiral Dumar looked out across the sea of faces, taking a deep breath. "Please, join me in a moment of silent respect for Captain Nathan Scott, as well as all those memorialized on this great walk."

Admiral Dumar closed his eyes and bowed his head. Tens of thousands gathered in the park bowed their heads as well, along with hundreds of thousands gathered in the streets nearby. An incredible quiet fell upon the entire city of Aitkenna, and perhaps over the entire planet of Corinair as well.

After two minutes had passed, a lone piper began playing the standard Corinari funeral tune, Ode to the Fallen. The pipes droned on, its haunting melody echoing off the tall buildings that surrounded the great park at the center of the planet's capital city. Finally, the song came to an end, and the silence returned.

There was no further ceremony. As was custom, the crowds began to slowly and quietly disperse, each of them reflecting on the man they had assembled to honor as they made their way back to their respective lives. Lives that Na-Tan had given them.

The EDF Marine sergeant stepped forward once again, barking out his commands. "Company, A-ten-SHUN!"

In unison, every person in uniform, military or civilian, snapped to attention in a brief rustle of clothing, clapping of hands at their sides, and the clicking of their heels as they came together.

Seven EDF Marines, each in full dress uniforms, raised their weapons toward the sky and fired in unison. One shot. Two shots. Three. Their last shots fired, they placed their weapons at their sides in unison, remaining at attention as a lone bugler began playing Taps from beside the gunmen. As he blew each phrase, another bugler located at the opposite side of the parade grounds repeated the phrase, as if it was an echo.

As the second bugler echoed the last note, a flight of six Super Eagles approached from low over the horizon. They streaked overhead, passing from the end of the parade grounds opposite the stage from which President Scott had spoken. As they passed, one Super Eagle pitched straight up, climbing like a rocket into the sky. A split second later, all six Super Eagles disappeared behind blue-white flashes of light, followed a second later by the screeching crackle of their jumps.

On Earth, just as on Corinair, those who had gathered to pay their last respects to the young man who had sacrificed himself to save them all, quietly dispersed, also returning to the lives Captain Scott had given them.

CHAPTER TEN

"Incredible." It was the only word Connor Tuplo could think to say. "You did all of that, for me... I mean, for him? For Captain Scott?"

"You... *He*, would have done the same for any one of us," Jessica replied.

Connor looked at Josh and Marcus. "You two, as well?"

"Yup," Marcus replied.

"You know me, Cap'n," Josh said. "I love a good adventure."

Connor shook his head, still in shock.

"Incredible," he muttered again. "But that still doesn't explain how *I* came to be. If I *am* a clone, how did I end up as Connor Tuplo?"

"Two years later, after your body had been grown to maturity, we attempted to restore your consciousness and memories."

"You *attempted*?" Connor did not like what they were implying.

"Both Michi and Turi warned us that it might not work," Jessica admitted.

"Michi and Turi?"

"Doctors Sato and Megel."

"I thought they were my medical doctors," Connor said.

"That's what we told you."

"I thought there was something different about them. So they're..."

"Clones, yes," General Telles confirmed. "Nifelmians have had their genetics skewed over the centuries, in order to facilitate the transfer process. In addition, there are risks associated with the

Portable Consciousness Capture Device. It is meant to be used only in emergencies."

"Which is exactly what we had at the time," Jessica added.

"When you regained consciousness, you had no memory of who you were, or of any of the events of your life. However, your personality had successfully been restored."

Connor looked confused. "Isn't your personality partly shaped by the events in your life?"

"Indeed, they are," the general agreed. "Also, by training and discipline, such as the techniques used by the Ghatazhak."

"Then I'm not really Nathan, am I," Connor concluded. "Not if part of me is missing."

"In a manner of speaking, you are correct. However, since *part* of your personality *is* genetic, *you* are the *only* person who has the *potential* to become Nathan Scott."

"And you want Nathan Scott back."

"We *need* Nathan Scott back," the general corrected. "The *want* is irrelevant."

"Maybe to you," Jessica objected.

"And here I just thought you needed my ship, or my piloting skills."

"They showed me the mission parameters, Cap'n," Josh said. "I'm pretty sure it ain't *your* piloting skills they're after."

Marcus slapped the side of Josh's head.

"What?" Josh said, flinching from the slap. "I didn't mean nothin' by it." He looked at Jessica. "Am I right?"

"Actually, yes." She looked at Connor. "No offense intended. I'm sure you're an excellent pilot. I mean,

Nathan was, so... It's just that Josh has done this kind of thing before, and *with* the Seiiki."

Connor looked at Josh. "You flew the Seiiki *before* I hired you?"

"Actually, it was called the Mirai, but, yeah."

Connor was still confused. "Wait." He looked at Marcus. "That guy in the bar in Forus, the one claiming that he'd seen my ship before, but it wasn't named the Seiiki. I remember he was threatening to tell the authorities that our registry was forged. He wanted money." He looked at Jessica and Telles again. "If everything you're saying is true, then that guy was right." Connor looked at Marcus again. "We never saw him again, and didn't hear anything else about it. And we've been back to Forus more than a few times." Connor noticed that Marcus was looking away. "Marcus?"

"Uh, yes, sir?"

"Did you..."

"I was just doin' my job, Cap'n, honest."

"Marcus and Josh were assigned to protect you," General Telles explained. "And, if unable to do so, to direct you back to us, so that the Ghatazhak could protect you."

"You *killed* him?" Connor shook his head, appalled. "Marcus, he was just trying to shake us down for a few credits..."

"I was doin' my job! That piece of shit was gonna bring us all kinds of trouble, Cap'n."

"He didn't deserve to die," Connor protested.

"Perhaps not," General Telles said, interrupting him. "But Marcus was smart to eliminate him. Once the thread of a lie is pulled, things begin to unravel at an accelerated rate. Your true identity could have been exposed."

"But I'm *not* Nathan Scott," Connor insisted, rising to his feet. "I may be a physical copy. Hell, I may even act a lot like him. But I am *not him*. I don't have his memories, or his experiences! For cryin' out loud, I don't even remember my parents, *or* my brother and sisters! Nothing! Nothing before I woke up in that hospital on Corinair!"

"Wait a minute," Jessica interrupted. "Did you say *brother and sisters*?"

"What?" Connor stopped, completely lost.

"The profile we created for you didn't say anything about a brother, just sisters."

"A slip of the tongue!" Connor said dismissively.

"Perhaps not," the general disagreed.

"Have you been having dreams?" Jessica asked.

"So what if I have," Connor argued. "Everyone has dreams!"

"About your brother, and your sisters?"

"In my dreams they are, but so what? Hell, I once dreamed some old guy was teaching me to fly this crazy-looking contraption with two cloth-covered wings and a propeller in front. A *propeller*! Can you believe that?"

Jessica looked at Telles. "They're still in there."

"There may yet be hope," the general replied, equally intrigued.

"What the hell are you two talking about?" Connor demanded to know.

"All of Nathan Scott's memories are stored in your head," Jessica explained. "They were put in there during the restoration attempt. Your brain just doesn't know where they are stored. It's like trying to find items in a massive warehouse, without any kind of map."

"You're making my head hurt," Connor said, getting frustrated.

"The Nifelmian device is designed to retrieve from, and restore to, a Nifelmian brain," General Telles explained. "One that has been altered through genetic manipulation. Imagine that your brain is a computer, and that the memory center of your brain is akin to a computer's data banks. The computer's operating system knows how to read the storage map, thus allowing it to retrieve data at will. Unfortunately, the Nifelmian device was unable to restore that map. The memories are there, but your brain does not know how to find them. They are, essentially, unmapped."

Connor stared at the general, dumbfounded.

"Now my brain is starting to hurt," Dalen mumbled.

"So those dreams...they're real?" Connor asked.

"Nathan Scott had an older brother, and five sisters," General Telles stated.

"And, his grandfather taught him how to fly in a replica of an ancient, propeller-driven biplane," Jessica added. "They're not dreams, Connor. They're memories. Nathan's memories. *Your* memories."

Connor sighed, shaking his head in disbelief again. "I can't believe this is happening." He looked at Jessica and General Telles. "What is it you people want from me?"

"We want you to become Nathan Scott again," Jessica replied.

Connor looked at General Telles, then back at Jessica. "What happens to me? What happens to Connor Tuplo?"

Jessica sighed. "I don't honestly know."

"Well, who does?"

"Michi and Turi," Jessica answered.

"Well, then, let's ask them," Connor said.

"That's the problem," Jessica replied. "They're trapped on Corinair, along with several others."

"We need your ship, and your copilot, in order to rescue them," General Telles added.

"Why not use one of your ships?" Connor wondered.

"There are more people than we can carry in a single jump," the general explained. "And a second jump would be too risky."

"Hell, a first jump is too damned risky," Marcus muttered.

"Then use one of your boxcars," Connor suggested. "You could probably fit a few hundred people in one of those things."

"Boxcars will not fit into the insertion environment," the general said.

"How many people are we talking about?" Connor asked. "And what do you mean by *insertion environment*?"

"Fifteen to twenty persons," the general replied. "And the insertion environment is a cave."

Connor's head snapped back in surprise. "You want me to let *Josh* jump *my* ship into a *cave*? Are you *nuts*?"

"He's done it before," Jessica said.

Connor looked at Josh.

"Piece of cake," Josh bragged.

Connor suddenly felt the need to sit back down. After a moment, he regained his composure. "Assume for a moment that I agree to all this, and we manage to pull it off and rescue all these people, *including* the two clone doctors. Then what?"

"*Then*," the general began, "we can better answer

your questions about what happens to Connor Tuplo, should you agree to become Nathan Scott."

"This isn't making any sense," Connor argued. "If my brain hasn't been, how did you put it...*genetically manipulated*? Then, how are they going to make *me* reconnect with those memories, and become Nathan Scott?"

Jessica sighed, looking at General Telles, who nodded his approval. She looked back at Connor. "By transferring everything in *your* head, into a new, genetically manipulated, cloned body."

Connor stared at her, unable to believe what he had just heard. "You're saying... You're saying there's a *third*, clone? That there's another one of me somewhere?"

"Yes," Jessica replied solemnly.

Connor was speechless for a moment. "Jesus," he finally said. "I can't believe you people. What gives you the right!?" he exclaimed, rising to his feet again. "This is my *life* you're fucking with!" Connor turned to look at his crew, then back at Jessica and General Telles, before throwing his hands up and storming out the hangar office door into the night.

Jessica moved to chase after him, but General Telles grabbed her arm to stop her. "Perhaps it is better if we give him some time," he suggested.

Jessica looked at the general, tears in her eyes. "But what if he never comes back?" she asked quietly.

"Main power is offline while they put in new power distribution lines to the nacelles," Dalen explained. "He couldn't take off if he wanted to."

"It's a big planet," Jessica insisted.

"He'll be all right," Marcus promised. "He always storms off this way when he's upset."

Jessica shook her head. "That's not like Nathan."

"That's the point," Josh said, getting up from his chair and heading for the door. "He ain't Nathan."

* * *

Josh poked his head up through the companionway hatch from the Seiiki's main foredeck into her cockpit. "Figured I'd find you here," he said, continuing up the companionway steps once he was sure the captain was there.

"Come to talk me into becoming *Na-Tan?*" Connor guessed.

"Actually, no," Josh replied, moving forward and slipping down into his usual position in the copilot's seat.

"I thought Nathan Scott was your friend."

"You're my friend, too. Probably even more so than Cap'n Scott was."

Connor looked at Josh, surprised.

"I was only with the Alliance for two years, and I was only around Cap'n Scott for the first few months. After that, Loki and I were usually off flyin' the Falcon. We hardly ever spoke. I've been flyin' with you for *five years*, Connor. Five years, sittin' right here next to you. I'd say that makes you a lot more my friend than Captain Scott ever was."

"But he was a great man, right?" Connor said. "Captain of the Aurora. Savior of the galaxy."

"He *was* a great man, *sure*," Josh agreed. "But his circumstances sort of demanded greatness of him. He didn't really have much choice in the matter. In fact, he didn't really want the job."

"He didn't?" Connor was genuinely surprised.

"Hell, no. Not at first, at least," Josh explained. "Sure, he grew into it later. Probably even came to love it. After all, he was a natural-born leader. That much was pretty obvious, even to a Havenite like me."

Connor thought for a moment, looking out the forward windows at the city lights beyond the spaceport. "Am I like him?" he wondered.

"Yeah, you're a lot like him."

Connor turned to look at Josh. "*Just* like him?"

"I'm not gonna lie to you, Connor. Sometimes, it's hard not to call you Nathan...although the beard helps."

"Is that why you usually call me Captain?" Connor wondered.

"Maybe, I don't know. I mean, you are the captain."

"Then I *am* him. Or at least a clone of him."

"Depends on your definition, I suppose. I mean, you *look* like him, minus the beard, of course. And, you sound like him. You even talk like him, mostly. I think the rest of us have sort of polluted your vocabulary a bit."

Connor smiled. "Marcus, for sure."

"But, there are things about you that are different from Nathan. If you were both in the same room, I'd be able to tell you apart, I'm sure of it."

Connor tugged at his beard.

"Even without the beard," Josh insisted.

"Thanks," Connor replied. "I needed to hear that."

"Of course, you do have that bump on your nose, from when it got broke in that bar fight on Kaladossa." This time, it was Josh who smiled.

"Do you think I should do it?" Connor asked, looking Josh in the eyes.

"I don't know that I can answer that for you, Connor," Josh admitted. "No one can. No one but you. I *do* think you need to learn more before you decide, though."

"What if I decide not to?" Connor asked. "What if I decide to take off as soon as they finish the repairs? Will you and Marcus come with me?"

Josh looked down, taking a deep breath and letting it out slowly. "Cap'n, Loki is my best friend, from *way* back. Long before you, long before Nathan. He and I have been through more than you can imagine. His wife and baby girl are among those who need to be rescued. I can't leave him in a lurch. This ship, or another, I'm gonna jump something into that cave, and get them outta there. So no, if you go, I'm staying. I'm sorry, but that's just how it is. Friends don't leave friends hangin'. Now, I can't speak for Marcus, but I'm pretty sure he'd say the same. Loki is like a son to him."

"Crew is family," Connor muttered, almost to himself.

"That's what you always say."

"I'm kind of wishing I didn't, at the moment." Connor sighed. "If your friends need our help, then that's what we're going to give them."

"You sure about this?" Josh asked.

"About the rescue, yes," Connor replied. "About becoming Na-Tan... Well, let's just say that I've got a few questions to ask those two clone doctors first."

* * *

Travon Dumar rejoined his guests, stepping out onto the dining deck that overlooked the lake.

"You have received word?" Doran Montrose asked, noticing the look on the retired admiral's face.

"I have just received a communiqué from General Telles. They are prepared to rescue us."

"When?" Yanni asked, sitting up straight in his seat and leaning forward with interest.

"Tomorrow at noon."

"At the caves?" Doran confirmed.

"They're going to jump into a *cave*?" Yanni asked doubtfully. He looked at Doran. "Is that even possible?"

"Apparently, it is," the admiral replied.

"I can think of only a few pilots crazy enough to try," Doran commented, exchanging a glance with Travon.

"Telles knows what he is doing," the admiral insisted. "He is not one to take foolish risks."

"How are we going to get there?" Yanni wondered.

"In Jerrot's truck," Dumar replied. "With the wine barrels removed, there should be enough room in the back for us all, including Jerrot's family."

"Now we have to take *his* family, as well?" Doran asked.

"In exchange for his help in smuggling you out of Aitkenna, yes," the admiral replied. "That was our arrangement."

Doran did the math in his head. "So, this ship must have room for eleven, in addition to her crew."

"It is eighteen people, not eleven. Including my extended family, and Jerrot's," Dumar corrected him.

"*And* it must be *jump capable*. It cannot be a shuttle or boxcar. What other ships does the general possess?"

"One called the Seiiki. I have not heard of it, but by the look on your face, it appears that *you* have," Dumar said, noticing the surprised look on Doran's face.

"You both know her as the Mirai. She was given to Captain Scott's clone, Connor Tuplo, after being retooled by acquaintances of Marcus's, with a new name and registry as the Seiiki," Doran explained.

"Marcus Taggart?" Dumar asked.

"Yes. He and Josh volunteered to act as protectors for Connor Tuplo. They signed on as his crew, without Captain Tuplo knowing their true mission."

"Then, it is young Mister Hayes who will be piloting the Seiiki into the crystal caves," the admiral realized.

"Either he, or Connor Tuplo," Doran said.

Travon sighed, shaking his head. "So, in a manner of speaking, Nathan Scott is coming back from the grave to save us yet again."

"I suppose so," Doran agreed, a slight grin on his face. "It *is* his destiny, after all."

Travon did not look amused. "We must pack only that which we can carry. Inform the others that we will depart at sunrise. I will contact Jerrot to secure our transportation."

* * *

Connor and Josh returned to the Ghatazhak hangar office, rejoining Jessica, General Telles, Dalen, Marcus, and Neli. Connor glanced at his crew, and then exchanged glances with Jessica and the general without saying a word. He took a deep breath and then spoke. "I need to talk to my crew," he told Jessica and General Telles. "Alone."

"Of course," General Telles replied, moving toward the exit.

Jessica followed, exchanging glances with both Connor and Josh, but saying nothing. She had already put enough pressure on Connor.

Once the door closed and they were alone, Connor spoke. "Okay, so now you two know as much as I know," he said to Dalen and Neli. "And, apparently, Josh and Marcus know more than all of us, but we'll get into that later."

"You gonna do it, Cap'n?" Dalen asked, unable to contain his excitement. "You gonna become Na-Tan?"

"One step at a time, Dalen," Connor replied. "First, there's the rescue mission."

"Then you're going to do it," Neli surmised.

"Yes, I'm going to do it," Connor admitted. "But only because it's the only way I'm going to get all my questions answered about who or what I am, and if I should become Nathan Scott."

"And, because it's the right thing to do," Josh reminded him.

"*And*, because it's the right thing to do," Connor agreed.

"The right thing to do?" Neli said skeptically. "For who? You don't even know those people, and now you want to risk all our lives to rescue them? How is that the *right thing*?"

"They're our friends, Nel," Marcus said. "Friends who would do the same for us. That's what makes it the *right thing* to do."

"I'm in," Dalen blurted out.

"Hold on," Connor urged, holding up his hands. "I already know that Josh and Marcus are in. Hell, they'd go with or without the rest of us."

"Damn straight," Josh agreed.

"But neither one of you has any obligation to these people," Connor added.

"And, neither do you," Neli pointed out. "You don't know them, either."

"But I *do* know that I wouldn't even exist, if it weren't for *these* people," Connor replied. "And that makes me feel awfully damned obligated to try to rescue them."

"And if we decide not to go?" Neli asked.

"Well," Connor said, thinking a moment. "I suppose you can wait here for us to return."

"And if you *don't*?"

"Nel," Marcus started.

Connor held up one hand, interrupting Marcus. "It's an honest question, Marcus." Connor sighed. "If we don't make it back, I'm sure the Ghatazhak can arrange transport for you to whatever world you wish to go to. I can probably make that a condition for my participation."

"What, so I can start all over again, with nothing?" Neli did not seem pleased with the idea.

"It's the best I can do, Neli. I'm sorry."

"You're sorry?"

"It's not like this is my fault, Neli," Connor defended. "It just is what it is."

"I'm in," Dalen said again.

"I got that," Connor replied. He looked at Neli. "I'd rather have my entire crew with me, Neli. A crew I can trust. I don't know these people."

"And, yet, you're still willing to risk all our lives to help them. And all because they told you some story about you being Nathan Scott's clone."

"It does answer a lot of questions," Connor admitted. "Put yourself in my shoes, Neli. If you didn't remember anything about yourself, about your past, your family, where you came from... Wouldn't you want to know?"

"I suppose, but..."

"That's all I want... To know *who* I am, not just who I've been for the past five years."

Neli looked at Connor with sympathy. "Connor, what if you don't *like* who you were? What if you'd *rather* stay Connor Tuplo?"

"I hadn't really thought of that," Connor admitted.

"Everyone always talks so highly of Nathan Scott, I guess I just assumed..." He paused and took another deep breath, letting it out in a long sigh. "Well, like I said, I haven't decided if I believe all of this, and I certainly haven't made a decision about whether or not I *should* become Nathan Scott. But rescuing those two clone doctors, along with the rest of their party, is the best way for me to get the answers I need in order to *make* that decision. I'm just asking you both to support me in this."

"I'm in," Dalen repeated, raising his hand.

"Shut up," Josh chided.

Neli stood up and gave her captain a hug. "I'm in, Connor," she whispered. She pulled back and looked him in the eyes. "Just don't get us killed. Understood?"

"Understood," Connor replied with a grin.

"But there's one condition," Neli added, turning to Marcus. "After this is all over, *you* are going to tell me *everything* that happened to you."

Marcus swallowed hard. "Everything?"

"From the time you left Haven, to the time we met. I want no more secrets. Understood?"

"Yes, ma'am," Marcus agreed.

Connor smiled, looking at Josh.

"Family," Josh said, smiling back.

* * *

Travon entered the living room of his residence on the far side of the main lodge. His wife and children, and his children's families, were all gathered, awaiting his news.

Travon went to the only empty chair and sat, the weight of what he had to say resting heavily on his mind. He looked into the eyes of his wife, and then his two adult children, all of whom were staring in his direction. There was no good way to break the news. "We must leave this world."

"What?"

The question came from all three of them in unison.

"This is our home," Travon's wife, Anise, replied. "This resort has been our dream. We worked our entire lives for this."

"I know," Travon replied.

"I start my internship in the fall," his son, Rorik, complained. "Do you know how hard *I've* worked for this?"

"I know."

"It's not fair," his daughter, Kyla, added.

"Maybe it isn't as bad as you think," Anise suggested. "So far, they have only attacked our defenses."

"That's not true," Kyla's husband corrected. "I heard that they have been rounding up many civilians, all over the world."

"You don't know if that's true," Rorik's wife argued.

"I know the Jung," Dumar said, raising his voice above the others. "They will come!" he yelled even louder, forcing them all to quiet down. "They will come. They will come because of me."

"But you're retired," his wife reminded him.

"It does not matter. I know things. And, even if I didn't, they will still want to interrogate me."

"So let them," Rorik argued. "Let them ask all the questions they want. What could you possibly reveal? You've been retired for seven years now."

"I know more than you realize," Travon said.

"Then let them come for you," Rorik shouted

angrily. “We are of no use to them, and we are certainly no threat.”

“They will use you, all of you, to get to me.”

“That’s ridiculous,” Rorik argued.

“Rorik,” Kyla scolded him.

“They will line you up in front of my eyes, and they will kill you, one by one, until I tell them what they want to know.”

“Then simply tell them!” Rorik insisted.

“I cannot!”

“You would let them kill us? Your own children and grandchildren? Just to protect the Terrans?”

“You’re talking about billions of lives, Rorik,” Travon pleaded.

“What could you possibly know that would...”

“I cannot tell you!” Travon shouted. “That would put you in even more danger! The fact that I have told you that I possess knowledge that the Jung would want is dangerous enough!”

“Rorik.” This time, it was his mother urging him to listen.

“None of you know the Jung as I do. They are more brutal than Caius could ever be! They will turn our world inside out, killing all who stand in their way. They will reshape this world into something none of us recognize.”

“Sounds pretty much like Caius to me,” Rorik said.

Travon sighed. “You are an adult, Rorik. I cannot force you to come with me. But, I beg of you, for the sake of your family, to do so.” He looked at his daughter, Kyla.

Kyla looked to her husband, Joffrey, who nodded. She turned to her father. “Yes, we will go with you.” She then turned to Rorik, with pleading eyes.

Rorik could feel everyone's eyes upon him, including those of his own wife, Fiora.

"They will need doctors, no matter where we are," Fiora told him, taking his hand.

Rorik sighed in resignation, then walked past his father on his way out. "This is all your doing," he said accusingly as he passed his father.

Travon bowed his head in shame, sighing. "Everyone prepare yourselves. We leave at sunrise. Pack only what you can carry on your back, or in your hands. No more. Space will be limited." He looked up again, his eyes meeting theirs once more. "I am truly sorry to have brought this upon all of you." Then he, too, turned and left the room.

* * *

Connor, followed by Marcus and the rest of the Seiiki's crew, stepped out of the Ghatazhak hangar office and back into the night air on Burgess. He spotted Jessica and General Telles standing by a combat jump shuttle in front of the hangar, presumably waiting for him to come out. They spotted him, as well, and started to walk toward him.

"You guys head back to the ship," Connor instructed his crew. "See how the repairs are going."

"You got it, Cap'n," Marcus replied.

Connor turned and walked toward Jessica and the general, his hands in his pockets.

"Captain," General Telles greeted, as they got within earshot of one another.

"So," Connor began as he came to a stop, "I'm still not sure about this whole Nathan thing, but I am willing to help you rescue those people. Mainly, because they are friends of Josh and Marcus."

"That's the only reason?" Jessica asked, surprised at his reasoning.

"No, it's not," Connor replied with a sigh. "It's more than just dreams. I've been having flashes of what I *think* are memories. People, faces, events. Some of them are good, but some of them are horrifying."

"Captain Scott had to make many difficult decisions in his lifetime," General Telles explained. "And he witnessed some terrible things, as well."

"It makes me wonder if I even *want* to remember who I really am."

Jessica and General Telles said nothing.

"But," Connor continued, "as I said, we will help you with the rescue."

"And after that?" Jessica wondered.

"After that, I'm taking it one step at a time. No promises. But I *am* going to have some questions for those two clone doctors, that's for damn sure."

"The extraction is scheduled for twelve hundred local time," General Telles said. "That is in approximately four hours, our time. How long will it take you to get to Corinair?"

"It's about thirty hops, so let's say forty minutes, just to be safe," Connor replied.

"Then, we should takeoff in three hours," Jessica suggested. "It's better if we get there ahead of them."

"Agreed," the general said.

"Yeah, and we might need a few extra minutes to plot that last jump," Connor added.

"Another reason to leave a few minutes early," Jessica said.

"You're sure about the size of that cave?"

"The opening is approximately the same size as this hangar," the general explained, gesturing at the open, well-lit space behind him.

Connor looked skeptically at the hangar. "I can't

believe I'm agreeing to this," he muttered, shaking his head in disbelief.

"Look at it this way," Jessica said, putting her arm around him and leading him back toward the Seiiki. "If you miss, you'll never know it."

Connor looked at her. "Thanks. I feel so much better."

* * *

Light was just beginning to fill the valley, as the Corinairan sun had not yet risen above the surrounding mountains.

Anise Dumar stood looking across the courtyard at the lake in the distance. She heard the crunch of her husband's footsteps from behind, followed by the gentle touch of his hand on her shoulder. "I love watching the mist on the water at this hour," she sighed.

"The mist will still be here when we return," Travon comforted her.

She turned to look at him. "Then, there is still hope?"

"There is always hope, my dear."

She put her arms around him in a tight embrace.

"I can never express how sorry I am that I lied to you all those years," Travon whispered. "But, I never lied when I told you I loved you, and still love you to this very day."

"I know," she whispered back.

"We must go," he said. "They are waiting." Travon let go, took her hand, and walked her back to Jerrot's truck, its engine running, and its bed loaded with their family and friends.

Travon helped his wife up onto the back of the truck, then climbed up himself. Jerrot raised the gate and latched it, then climbed into the cab and started turning the truck around toward the main gate.

Travon, Anise, Rorik, and Kyla all watched as the family's prized possession, their lovely resort, slowly disappeared into the forest.

"We'll reclaim it, someday," Travon promised them. "We'll reclaim it all."

* * *

Connor walked the perimeter of the Seiiki, carefully examining the work that had been completed only minutes ago by the Ghatazhak technicians. They had worked on his ship all through the night, starting shortly after first touching down at the Lawrence Spaceport on Burgess, even before he had agreed to help the Ghatazhak rescue their friends.

The Ghatazhak had kept their word. His ship was fully repaired, and in record time. In addition, it was fully fueled, and his stores were loaded. He could take off now, and leave the Ghatazhak behind, and have enough to get well away from the Pentaurus sector. But he had made a promise, to both Josh *and* to the Ghatazhak. And he wanted to know more about himself.

"Them techs did some nice work," Marcus said as he followed the captain around on his inspection. "And, they did it twice as fast as anyone I've seen. Ten times faster than the kid could've done."

Connor cast a sidelong glance at Marcus as he continued his inspection. He reached up and unlocked an inspection plate on the underside of the left engine nacelle, peeking inside. "There's no safety wire on the hydraulics reservoir fill cap," the captain said.

"I'll make sure that gets taken care of before we lift off," Marcus promised.

"Check it on the starboard engine as well," Connor added.

"Yes, sir."

"She passed all her diagnostics?"

"Yup. Twice."

"Fire up both engines, and run the tests with the engines hot."

"Cap'n, we only got twenty minutes before takeoff..."

"Both engines hot, Marcus," the captain insisted. "I don't want any surprises on this one. We *are* jumping into a *cave* after all."

"Good point," Marcus agreed. "I'll get it done."

Josh walked up to Connor as Marcus was walking away. "Cap'n, a word?"

"What is it, Josh?"

"Well, to be honest, I don't feel right asking you this..."

"Spit it out," Connor replied as he moved forward to inspect the leading edge of the Seiiki's port wing-body.

"Well, seeing as how we're jumping into a cave and all, and how you've never actually done that... I mean, you don't really do any jump calcs or nothin'. You always use the standard sets... Not that there's anything wrong with that. I mean..."

Connor turned to look at Josh. "What is it you're trying to say, Josh?"

"Well, I was thinking that maybe Loki should fly right seat on this one? I mean, he's done this kind of jump before. With me, in this ship, I might add."

"Loki flew the Seiiki?"

"Oh, yeah. Well, it was called the Mirai back then, but him and I did that jump down to Nifelm together. He's really good at doing jump calcs, too. Nothing against your piloting skills, Cap'n, but I just figured we should give ourselves the best chance possible, seeing as how we're jumping into a cave, and all..."

"Relax, Josh," Connor said, interrupting him. "I'm not insulted. But are you sure about this? You haven't flown with this guy in at least five years, and he hasn't flown this ship in just as long."

"Loki and I know each other," Josh said. "He knows how I fly, and to be honest, I fly better with him."

"Okay, if you think having Loki as your right seat improves our chances of success, then how can I argue? I want to survive this just as much as everyone else. But what do I do, then?"

"Uh... Be in charge? Like usual."

* * *

Jessica, General Telles, and three Ghatazhak sergeants walked up the Seiiki's cargo ramp. Everyone except the general was dressed in Ghatazhak battle armor.

"A new look?" Marcus commented, noticing the new armor.

"Auto-camo," Jessica said as she reached the top of the ramp. She tapped a button on her wrist controller, and her armor changed color to match the colors of the Seiiki's cargo bay interior. "Pretty spiff, right?"

"Whoa," Dalen exclaimed in awe.

"Marcus, these are Sergeants Todd, Anwar, and Willem."

"You guys expecting a firefight?" Marcus wondered.

"Insurance," Jessica replied. "Make yourselves comfy, boys," she instructed her men. "I'm headed forward."

"*The troops have arrived,*" Marcus announced over the comms.

"Close her up," Connor ordered, standing behind Josh and Loki on the Seiiki's flight deck.

"You gonna stand behind us the whole way, Cap'n?" Josh wondered from the pilot's seat.

"Probably."

Josh exchanged glances with Loki.

"Preflight is complete," Loki announced. "Ship is ready for liftoff, Captain."

"Very well," Connor replied. "Take us up."

Josh pushed the lift throttles forward, and the Seiiki began to slowly rise off the tarmac, beginning a lazy rotation to the right as it climbed.

Connor watched the Ghatazhak hangar come into view, disappearing below a moment later. It was an unusual feeling to watch someone else flying *his* ship, especially since he wasn't sitting in either seat. Yet, it somehow felt natural, as well.

"Gear is up and locked," Loki reported. "Gear doors are closed. One hundred meters up. You're clear to climb out."

"Climbing out," Josh reported, moving the main engine throttles forward and slowly pitching their nose up toward the sky.

Jessica climbed up the ladder into the cockpit, stopping behind Connor, who stepped aside to make room for her.

Connor looked her over, noticing her body armor. "Expecting trouble?"

"Nope. We just like to be prepared." Jessica looked out the window at the blue sky. "Everything working?"

"Better than ever, thanks," Connor replied.

She looked at Connor. "Are you going to stand there watching over their shoulders the entire way?"

"That's what I said," Josh protested. "Jess, tell him we've got this," he pleaded.

"They've got this," Jessica told Connor.

"My ship, my rules," Connor replied stubbornly.

"Twenty seconds to first jump," Loki reported. "Inertial dampeners at full power."

"Goin' vertical," Josh announced as he pitched the nose straight up.

"First jump in three......two......one......"

The Seiiki's windows turned opaque as the ship executed its jump from the atmosphere of Burgess into high orbit above it.

"Jump complete," Loki reported. "Go for acceleration burn."

"Throttling up," Josh replied, pushing the main throttles all the way forward.

"Jump series in three minutes," Loki announced.

"What's our ETA?" Jessica asked.

"Final jump point in thirty-eight minutes," Loki replied. "We'll take a few to triple-check our insertion jump calculations before we execute, though."

"Wake me up before you jump," Jessica replied, turning to head back down the ladder. "I'm going to take a catnap."

Connor looked surprised as he watched her climb down the ladder. "Who the hell could sleep at a time like this?"

"*She* could," Josh replied with a light chuckle.

After nearly six hours of travel on winding, mountain roads, some of them a bit worse for wear, Jerrot finally came to the turnoff to the crystal caves. After completing his turn, he came to a stop, then turned and slid open the back window of the cab. "This is the last stretch of road before we get to the caves," Jerrot explained to Dumar and the others riding in the open cargo bed of the truck. "It should take us about ten to fifteen more minutes from here. But I warn you, it will be quite bumpy."

"Why didn't you take the main road?" Rorik wondered.

"The main road is wide, and clear of trees that might hide us from satellites and aerial patrols," Travon explained to his son. "The back way goes through the forest, making us less visible."

"Hang on," Jerrot warned. He slid the window closed and put the truck back in gear, starting up the bumpy dirt road.

Immediately, the occupants in the back of the truck realized that their driver had not been exaggerating.

"Jesus!" Yanni exclaimed. "Fifteen minutes of this?"

"You will survive," Travon promised him. He looked over at the two Nifelmian doctors, both of them wide-eyed, as they clung to the rails for dear life.

The truck suddenly ran over a large rock, bouncing Travon several centimeters in the air. His eyes grew wide.

"That's it," Loki announced. "That's the last jump. We're just over one light year from Corinair. The next one will put us in the cave."

"We hope," Connor added. He tapped his comm-set. "Marcus, we're at the final jump point."

"*Copy that.*"

"Relax, Cap'n. We've got this," Josh insisted.

"You know, I never would have agreed to this if I didn't know you two had done this kind of thing before."

"You told him we've done this before?" Loki asked, casting a disapproving glance at Josh.

"Well, we sort of did," Josh argued.

"What?" Connor was not amused.

"We did this *exact* same maneuver to sneak onto Nifelm to extricate Sato and Megel," Josh replied. "Well, *almost* the same maneuver."

"Is it *exact*, or *almost*, Josh?" Connor demanded. "Because they're two entirely different things, you know."

"We jumped into a very tight valley, coming out only a few hundred meters from the cave entrance," Loki explained.

"Same thing," Josh insisted.

"It's not the same thing, Josh," Connor argued.

"Technically, it is," Loki agreed with Josh. "At least from a jump calculation standpoint."

"And I slid us in and parked us in that cave quite nicely, didn't I?" Josh added.

"Yes, you did," Loki admitted.

"You see, Cap'n, you've got nothin' to worry about."

"I don't believe this," Connor muttered to himself.

"Relax, Cap'n..."

"I swear, Josh, if you say *we've got this* one more time, I'm tossing you out the airlock."

"Well, what are we gonna do, turn back?" Josh asked.

"No, we're not going to turn back," Connor replied. "I'll tell you one thing, though. You're getting a cut in pay, that's for sure."

"I've gotten updated sensor scans," Loki

announced, trying to change the subject. "Our insertion jump calculations are good. Our jump point is coming up in one minute."

Both Josh and Loki looked at Connor.

"Well, you're the captain," Josh said.

Connor sighed. "Of course, we go," he said. "But you and I are going to have a talk after this mission is over," Connor warned Josh.

The old cargo truck continued to bounce and shake as it climbed the winding, dirt road leading up to the rendezvous point at the crystal caves. Its occupants, tired from their long, arduous journey, struggled to stay firmly seated, despite the vehicle's efforts to eject them into the surrounding wilderness.

A strange sound suddenly echoed through the canyons. A muffled eruption, much like a crack of thunder, only contained inside something.

"What the hell was that?" Rorik exclaimed, looking around frantically.

Travon looked at his son, annoyed. For all of his son's insistence that it would be safe for him and his wife to remain on Corinair, he appeared to be the most nervous. "A jump flash," Travon answered.

Rorik looked unconvinced. "I've heard jump flashes before, and they do not sound like that." He looked around some more, as if looking for a ship that might spot them. "It was like an explosion inside of something."

"Like a cave?" Travon replied, a knowing smile on his face.

Rorik looked at his father in disbelief. "A cave? You're saying they jumped inside a cave? That's impossible!"

"We shall see."

The Seiiki shook violently as the displaced air from their jump bounced off the surrounding cave walls, slamming back into them with incredible force.

"Fuck!" Loki exclaimed before talking quickly. "Lift at forty!"

"Decel at full!" Josh announced, speaking over Loki as he pushed the deceleration thruster throttles all the way forward.

"Jesus!" Connor exclaimed, holding onto the overhead rails for support.

"Negative clearance eight seconds!" Loki warned.

Connor stared out the forward windows in terror and disbelief. The cave entrance had been more than wide enough, but it narrowed quickly the deeper they went, and the concussion of their arrival had shattered most of the crystals hanging from the cave's ceiling, creating a sparkling rain. Almost immediately, the sound of broken crystal striking their hull filled the cockpit.

"Forward speed dropping," Loki reported, his voice calm, yet still talking quickly. "Five meters per second. Gear coming down."

The cave continued to narrow, as the Mirai slid low over the cave floor, brushing the pointed tips of the numerous crystal columns that grew upward from the floor of the cavern. Josh eased the deceleration throttles back to zero as he twisted the flight control stick to the left, causing the Mirai to yaw quickly to port.

"What are you doing?" Connor demanded, his eyes widening.

"Again?" Loki queried, not at all surprised.

Josh nodded. "Gear?"

"Down and locked," Loki replied, shaking his head. "The floor is not exactly level, though."

"Oh, well," Josh replied, unconcerned.

A moment later, the Seiiki's landing gear touched the cave floor.

"Contact on three!" Loki announced.

Josh eased the Seiiki's lift thrusters, allowing the ship to settle down gently on the uneven surface.

"Contact on one," Loki added. "Four...... We're down!"

Josh quickly pulled the thrust levers back to zero.

"Killing all engines," Loki reported. "Bringing the reactor down to one percent." He glanced across the console, checking the Seiiki's critical systems. He hadn't flown this ship in some time, and felt compelled to check everything twice. "We're good," he finally reported, then let out a long sigh of relief. "Leveling the gear," Loki added.

The cockpit began to move slowly, its low side rising upward as its landing gear adjusted to level off the ship. It stopped a few seconds later, however, still low on the starboard side.

"That's as level as we're going to get," Loki reported.

A big grin came over Josh's face. He turned to look back at Connor, whose color had not yet returned to his face. "So, Cap'n, you still wanna cut my pay?"

The Seiiki's cargo ramp made contact with the floor of the crystal cave on its starboard corner only, the ship still listing to one side because of the uneven landing surface.

Jessica was the first down the ramp, her weapon held high and ready. It was unlikely that anyone was inside the crystal cave when they had jumped in, as it had been closed to the public since Corinair was liberated from the Takaran Empire eight years ago. Even if someone *had* been there, they would not have survived the concussion of the Seiiki's jump insertion. Still, she and her team had been tasked with the security of the mission, and it was not one that she took lightly.

The four of them moved quickly and skillfully down the ramp, hopping down onto the floor of the cave. They constantly looked upward, to watch for crystals falling from the ceiling.

"No one exits without headgear," Jessica instructed over her helmet comms to the others still on the ship. "There are still a lot of cracked crystal formations hanging from the ceilings, waiting to fall."

"*Copy that,*" Connor replied from inside the Seiiki.

Jessica continued forward toward the mouth of the cave as two of her team fanned out to the right, and the other one to the left. The floor crunched under her feet as shards of crystal shattered under her armored boots. "Camo up," she ordered as she touched her wrist controller.

The Ghatazhak combat armor began to sparkle as its exterior changed color to blend in with its surroundings.

"Camo check," Jessica added, stopping dead in her tracks. She slowly rotated her head to her left, looking for Sergeant Todd. "Todd, move a little, I can't see you." It took her a moment, but she noticed a distortion moving up and down against the background. "Damn, this shit is good," she muttered. "Let's take up positions outside the cave entrance," she added, continuing her advance.

Connor, Josh, and Loki all stared out the forward

windows, trying to spot Jessica and the rest of the Ghatazhak, who they knew were walking ahead of the ship toward the cave entrance.

"I can't see them, can you?" Josh asked.

"I've got nothing," Loki admitted.

"There," Connor said, pointing to the left. "Look for the distortion moving slowly forward across the wall."

"I've still got nothing," Loki said.

"*We're almost at the mouth of the cave,*" Jessica reported. "*It's clear inside, and there don't appear to be any more crystals falling, but I'd wear headgear just in case.*"

"Understood," Connor replied over the comms. "Everyone assemble in the cargo bay. We need to inspect the exterior of the ship for damage."

"*Once we get outside, we'll set up a sensor range extender, to monitor the immediate area,*" Jessica added.

"Understood," Connor replied as he started down the ladder, with Josh and Loki climbing out of their seats to follow.

Four tiny flashes of light, almost imperceptible against the bright noontime skies, appeared low on the horizon. A moment later, the sound of distant thunder filled the canyons that led up to the crystal cave.

From behind the flashes of light, four tiny, metallic objects appeared just above the ridgeline, their surfaces glistening in the midday sun. The dots seemed motionless at first, but quickly grew in size as they approached.

"Oh, no, no, no," Dalen cursed as his pace across the top of the Seiiki's starboard wing-body quickened.

"*What is it?*" Connor called over the comms, noticing his engineer's alarm.

Dalen knelt down over the object of his concern. A large shard of crystal had landed point-first into the middle of one of the jump emitters.

"Oh, fuck!" Marcus exclaimed as he came to look over Dalen's shoulder at the damaged emitter.

Dalen looked up at Marcus. "We don't have any spares."

"Cap'n," Marcus called over the comms, "we've got a problem here."

Jessica kept her eyes focused on the tactical display inside of her helmet's visor, as the tactical logic computer in her system identified the four targets that had just appeared in the distance.

"Shit," she cursed under her breath. "Todd, you seeing the same?"

"Yup," the Ghatazhak sergeant next to her confirmed.

"Seiiki, Nash. We've got incoming."

"Stop the truck! Stop the truck!" Travon ordered from the back.

Jerrot slammed on the brakes, bringing the vehicle to a skidding stop in the middle of the dirt road.

"Everyone out of the truck!" the admiral ordered.

"What is it?" Rorik asked. He had also heard the distant thunder, but thought little of it since it seemed so far away.

"Those were jump ships arriving," Doran explained as he helped his wife and daughter down out of the truck. "Head for those rocks, over there," he instructed his family.

"Shouldn't we keep going?" Rorik asked. "If it's only one ship, maybe the trees will provide us cover?"

"It was multiple ships," Travon told him, helping Doctor Sato down. "Probably fighters, which means they have sensors that will see through the trees. We must get behind cover, quickly!"

"Can we jump without it?" Connor asked, standing next to Marcus and looking down at the damaged emitter.

"No way, Cap," Dalen replied. "It's right in the middle, between the central topside emitter and the emitter on the top of the starboard nacelle. There will be a gap about two meters wide without it."

Connor sighed. "Which means we'll end up with a two-meter hole in the top of the ship, right over the starboard cabins."

"I've got a truck about half a click down the road, stopped, with a bunch of people spreading out from it," Jessica reported over the comms. *"Different sizes, most of them moving in uncoordinated fashion. It's got to be them. We're going to move closer. They're going to need help if those shuttles land."*

"Understood," Connor replied after tapping his comm-set. "Josh, Loki, Neli; take up defensive positions at the mouth of the cave."

"On our way," Josh replied.

"We could seal off either end of the aft starboard corridor," Marcus suggested. "At least it would keep the entire ship from depressurizing."

"No good," Connor disagreed. "Half the control lines for the starboard nacelle run under the hull here. We'd lose them all, and probably the main power trunk below it, as well."

"We wouldn't be able to land," Dalen realized.

"I don't suppose you could fix all of that in space, could you?" Connor asked.

Dalen looked up at his captain. "I...I don't know, Cap. Maybe?"

"We could move one of the bow emitters a bit further back, then remove the one behind it and relocate it here," Marcus suggested. "They're closer together than they need to be, anyway."

"But will their fields still connect if we remove it?" Connor wondered.

"They should," Dalen replied.

"May have to boost the power to them, though," Marcus added. "Gonna make for an inaccurate jump, that's for sure."

Connor sighed. "Better an inaccurate jump than a gaping hole in the top of my ship. How are you going to route the power if you move that emitter back?" Connor asked, pointing toward the bow.

"The conduit runs along that center channel all the way aft," Dalen explained. "It was added when they fitted the ship with her jump systems. Shouldn't be a problem."

Two more claps of thunder, each only a split second apart, echoed through the cave from outside, causing them all to turn toward the mouth of the cave.

"*Two more inbound,*" Jessica reported over the comms. "*Troop shuttles.*"

"Fuck," Connor cursed. He turned to Marcus and Dalen. "Work fast. No points for pretty."

Four Jung jump fighters streaked low over the treetops, heading straight for the mouth of the cave.

"I don't like this," Jessica muttered. A warning alarm flashed on her visor, and an alert tone sounded in her helmet comms. "We're being painted! They know we're here! Move! Move! Move!" she ordered, rising and running for better cover just as the approaching fighters opened fire with their energy cannons.

Debris surrounded them as the impacts exploded dirt and rock, and cut through massive tree trunks. Jessica heard an ear-splitting crack. She glanced back as she ran, only to see one of the towering, centuries-old trees crashing through the surrounding canopy, falling toward her and Sergeant Todd. "To the right! To the right!" she ordered, pushing the fleeing sergeant in that direction. They jumped toward cover, their enhancement undergarments accentuating the strength of their legs, allowing them both to leap forward several meters, clearing a large cluster of rocks before they tumbled to a landing on the other side.

Both Jessica and Sergeant Todd came up shooting at the fighters as they streaked over their heads, skimming the tops of the massive trees near the mouth of the cave. "This just became a firefight!" Jessica announced over the comms. She glanced at her tactical display again, noticing that both shuttles were preparing to land on the roadway between the cave and the stopped truck, in an attempt to block their advancement.

"*I don't understand!*" Connor cried out over the comms. "*How did they know we're here?*"

"They may not know about the Seiiki," Jessica replied, as she and Sergeant Todd ducked down behind the rocks to avoid being struck by fire from the next two approaching fighters. "But they definitely know about the four of us, as well as Dumar and the others! They're putting troop shuttles down between us and Dumar!"

"Oh, my God!" Loki cried out, rising from his covered position on the left side of the cave opening.

"Loki!" Josh yelled. "Whattaya doin'?"

"I'm going after them!"

"The hell you are!" Josh insisted, running over and grabbing his friend to hold him back. "You heard the captain! We've gotta cover the entrance while the Ghatazhak go after them!"

"But that's my wife down there!" Loki argued, panicked. "My child!"

"I know!" Josh replied, grabbing his old friend with both hands. "Jess will get them! You gotta trust her! Besides, if the Jung get the Seiiki, then we're all fucked! Your wife and daughter included!"

Loki stared at Josh, absolutely terrified.

"*Anwar! Willem! Split up and engage the troop shuttles,*" Jessica ordered over the comms. "*High-low, on the go, fire and move! Try to pull them away from the package. We'll cut down the middle to make contact!*"

"*Understood, moving right,*" Sergeant Anwar replied.

"*Moving left,*" Sergeant Willem added.

"Jess?" Loki pleaded over the comms, his voice trembling.

"*We'll get them, Loki!*" Jessica promised. "*Just hold the cave mouth so we've got someplace to go!*"

Jessica moved quickly down the rocky mountainside, leaping over rocks, dodging trees and brush as she made her way toward the roadway. Four red icons appeared on her visor, and she suddenly stopped, allowing her auto-camo system to blend her in with the scenery and remain invisible.

Four Jung soldiers moved quickly up the road toward her. She fired two quick shots, dropping the first two. As the remaining two opened fire, she stepped to the side allowing their shots to streak past to her left.

The targeting alert suddenly sounded in her comms. "Oh, shit," she cursed, diving and rolling to her right as she opened fire again. Her first shot struck the road, blowing dirt and rocks into the air. Her second and third shots struck one of the two remaining attackers, and her fourth shot struck the front of the troop shuttle directly behind them. Once she stopped rolling, she fired again, dropping the fourth man. A quick spray of fire into all four writhing bodies ensured that they would not fire on her again, but that would not be enough.

Her targeting alarm sounded again.

The shuttle!

Jessica jumped up and ran toward the side of the road as the troop shuttle one hundred meters down the road began to lift off. Within seconds, it opened fire with its automated belly turret, easily carving through trees and rocks, chasing Jessica as she ran for cover.

One, two, three shots struck the ground around her as she ran, the fourth one impacting the armor plating on her left thigh as she dove for cover behind a cluster of large boulders on the side of the road. Despite her armor's dissipative properties, she could feel the intense heat, even as her protective enhancement undergarment fought to cool the affected area.

"Fuck!" she cursed as she leaned against the rocks, energy bolts slamming into the other side. "Somebody pull this fucker off of me!"

The shuttle began to climb, and the angle of its fire increased, causing Jessica's safe area to diminish as the shuttle gained altitude and grew nearer to her hiding place. Knowing she would be cut down if she tried to run, she prepared to do the only thing she could. To stand and fire, head on, and hope that her chest armor and helmet would protect her. She took a deep breath and tensed up to leap upward, realizing that it might very well be the last thing she ever did.

"*Nash! Stay down!*" Sergeant Todd warned over the comms.

Jessica did as instructed, as several rounds of friendly fire erupted from her left.

The turret on the underside of the approaching troop shuttle came apart, sparks flying in all directions. The shuttle immediately turned away and took evasive action. Jessica rose quickly and turned toward the fleeing shuttle, just as the troop shuttle disappeared behind a blue-white flash of light, followed a split second later by the whoosh of air and the subdued ripping sound of the enemy shuttle's departure jump.

"*Four more coming up the middle,*" Todd warned over the comms.

"Head back up toward the cave," Jessica ordered. "I'll head right, you go left. They'll split up to chase us. After you take yours out, skirt down along the sides and get behind the troops from the second shuttle. If we flank them, we can cut them down before they reach the package."

"*Understood,*" Sergeant Todd replied.

"And watch out," Jessica added as she started to run. "They can track us, even with our auto-camo."

"*Copy that.*"

"Josh, go help Dalen!" Connor ordered as he ran toward the mouth of the cave. "Loki! Get us ready to take off!"

"Jess told us to guard the cave entrance!" Josh argued.

"You don't work for her, you work for me! Get moving!" he reminded him as he and Marcus ran past them, headed outside. "If we don't get that emitter fixed, we're screwed no matter what!"

Josh and Loki looked at each other.

"Oh, fuck," Josh muttered, turning to head back to the ship.

Neli turned and watched in dismay as Josh and Loki both left their posts to return to the ship. "Wait!" she cried out. "How am I going to hold the entrance all by myself?"

"Here," Josh said, tossing his energy rifle to her as he passed. "You can shoot for both of us!"

Neli caught the rifle clumsily, her eyes wide with fear.

"For all three of us," Loki added, tossing his rifle to her, as well, then followed Josh back to the Seiiki.

Neli caught the second rifle, dropping the first two and nearly falling over. "Oh, this is just great!"

Jessica flew through the air, landing in the middle of six Jung soldiers, catching them by surprise. She fired once, dropping the soldier directly in front of her, then dropped and rolled to her right, coming up to fire again, and dropped two more.

A soldier to her left lowered his rifle to take aim at her head, but she shot her left hand up and knocked the rifle barrel upward, causing the shot to graze the Jung soldier to her right in the arm. She rolled onto her back, pulling on the muzzle of the soldier's rifle as she curled up and placed her left foot into the falling soldier's belly, using his own momentum to pull him over her and into the soldier to her right as he charged forward.

The two soldiers collided, one knocking the other over, allowing Jessica a moment to deal with the two others charging from behind. She spun around just in time to see the butt of the fifth soldier's rifle coming toward her visor. She leaned to her right, twisting her head and allowing the rifle butt to graze off her visor. She pulled her combat knife from her right hip, and drove it into the soldier's side as he followed through with his own body weight to strengthen his blow.

She continued to spin around, elevating her knife hand just enough as she rotated to plant her blade into the left eye socket of the sixth soldier. The additional force added to her blow by her undergarment's enhancement systems was enough to clothesline the sixth man, knocking his feet from under him, landing squarely on his back.

One of the two soldiers who collided had, by now, managed to scramble back to his feet, and was charging toward Jessica. She turned toward him, took one powerful stride, and leapt upwards, rotating in the air, placing her right foot into the side of the soldier's helmeted head. The blow knocked the soldier down again, blood and teeth spraying out from his open mouth.

The other fallen guard was also recovering, but found a knife suddenly lodged firmly in his throat. He grabbed at his spurting neck wound, gasping for breath as he dropped back down to his knees.

Jessica, now lying on the ground after landing, rolled to her left side, pulling her energy pistol from her right thigh holster. She fired two shots into the soldier she had just kicked in the face, ending his involvement in the engagement, once and for all. She rose to her feet, turned, and fired once into the face of the soldier on his knees as she pulled her knife from his neck and allowed him to topple backward, blood still gushing from his neck and mouth.

Jessica quickly surveyed the men lying around her, firing several more shots to ensure that none of them would dare challenge her again. Noticing that the tactical display on the inside of her visor had gone out, she beat against the side of her helmet several times. The display lit up again, showing red dots on either side of her.

A crossfire!

Energy weapons fire streaked over their heads, slamming into the rock faces where they hid, cringing in fear for their very lives. In the background, they could hear the sound of weapons not of their enemies, but of the friends who had come to rescue them.

Doran and Travon returned fire as best they could, popping up every few seconds in an attempt to slow the enemy's advance on their position.

Jerrot also returned fire, although only on occasion, as several of the enemy soldiers were closer to him, and were constantly bombarding the old man.

"Give me a weapon!" Rorik begged his father. "Allow me to defend myself!"

Travon hesitated.

"Father! Please!"

Travon reluctantly pulled his sidearm, tossing it to his son behind the next boulder over, firing across the top of his boulder at the same time, as enemy fire continued to pound their hiding place.

"Travon!" Doran called out. "They mean to circle us! If they flank us..."

"I know!" Travon thought for a moment. He did not want to make the call, but he had little choice. "Rorik," he finally called out. "Fall back to the trees! Then circle to the right, to prevent them from flanking us on that side!"

"No!" Travon's wife cried out, fearing for her son's life.

"Go! Now!" Travon yelled, as he fired back at the enemy, giving his son a chance to move back as instructed.

Rorik quickly fell back, scrambling on his hands and knees in the dirt, his wife reaching after him in futility.

"Doran!" Travon called out. "The same to the left! We must force them to go wide! To buy us time until help arrives!"

"I'm ready!" Doran replied.

"Now!" Travon ordered, opening fire again.

Doran quickly kissed his wife, then crawled backward, away from their position, keeping low to avoid being seen by the enemy.

"When are they coming?" Yanni wondered as he crouched down low next to the admiral and his wife, his arms around Lael and her baby girl, to protect them from flying bits of rock and dust as the enemy continued to fire.

"Soon, I am sure of it," the admiral replied.

His wife exchanged looks with him. She knew he had no idea.

Jessica fell to the ground, face down, as flat as she could be, taking cover behind the bodies of the soldiers she had just killed. Jung weapons fire came from both sides, slamming into the bodies around her with sickening thuds. Smoke from the energy weapons's burns on the corpses that protected her swirled amidst the dust, its acrid odor filling her nose and burning her eyes. She caught the strap of her energy rifle lying near her with her foot and dragged it toward her.

Two shots struck the combat pack attached to her backplate, blowing it apart. Her visor went dead, as did her comms. She could feel the heat from the unit as sparks flew from it in all directions. Still lying flat on her belly, she reached under her chest and hit the eject button, shaking her body just enough so that the pack fell away to one side, just as it took two more direct hits from incoming fire.

She reached down and pulled her rifle to her side, then rolled over onto her back, firing the weapon toward her feet in the direction of the incoming fire.

She had only seconds. Soon, more Jung would show up, having circled ninety degrees to either side in order to stay out of the crossfire that kept her pinned down. She would have to be ready.

But it would not come.

Shots rang out. Not energy weapons, but projectile. Repetitive zings and crackles, the familiar sound of slugs being propelled down launch rails. She could hear the sounds of slugs ricocheting off of Jung armor, slamming into exposed flesh, then followed by cries of pain. The sounds repeated, over and over, coming from the opposite side this time.

Jessica turned to look in the direction from which the sound of projectile weapons had come. Two men, running toward her. She swung her weapon around to take aim, but relaxed as two familiar faces came into view.

Marcus and Connor ran toward Jessica, their projectile rifles still crackling and zinging as slugs left their barrels.

Connor continued forward, jumping over her, rifle still firing.

Jessica couldn't believe what she was seeing.

"Are you all right?" Marcus asked as he paused momentarily to help her up.

"Yeah! But my comms are down!" Jessica said. She turned her head to see Connor charging down the road, cutting back and forth to make for a more difficult target. "Jesus!" she exclaimed, watching him charge down the road. "Don't just stand there!" she yelled, turning back toward Marcus. "Stay with Nathan!" she added, scrambling back to her feet to follow them.

"Have you got that thing moved, yet?" Dalen asked as he installed the relocated emitter in place of the damaged one.

"We're disconnecting it now!" Loki replied as he helped Josh.

"Well, hurry the fuck up!" Dalen urged.

"When did you learn how to work on jump systems?" Loki wondered.

"About two minutes ago," Josh replied, working frantically. "Same as you."

Connor charged up on the Jung position from behind, spraying the unsuspecting soldiers with projectiles from his rifle. From such close range, the slugs tore through the Jung body armor, sending pieces of armor, flesh, and blood flying out in all directions.

Connor's mouth dropped open, his eyes widening at the death he had just caused. The others had been further away. All he had seen were bodies falling. But this...this was personal.

Suddenly, a memory hit him. Bodies being unloaded in a massive hangar. Bodies, disfigured and burned so badly that they hardly seemed human.

Connor froze, the memory nearly making him sick. He heard a familiar voice cry out a warning, but did not move. He looked away from the carnage before him, turning toward those they had come to rescue, even though he only saw the burned bodies in the hangar.

Travon Dumar took advantage of the sudden cessation in weapons fire to look at the enemy position. But he nearly dropped his weapon when he saw a familiar figure, standing next to the enemy position not twenty meters distant, looking directly at him.

Nathan!

Movement to his left caught the admiral's eye. Two Jung soldiers, likely having moved from their position to the right of their now-dead comrades, were coming to close the gap that had just been created by the very man who Travon had believed dead all these years.

Travon rose from his position, yelling a warning to the man he believed to be Nathan Scott. He fired his weapon as he charged out from behind the rocks, turning toward the charging Jung soldiers to his left. He fired again and again, yelling Nathan's name the entire time, warning him to get down, unable to bear seeing the young man die again.

Two energy bolts slammed into Travon's right side, causing his legs to collapse under him. More energy weapons fire sounded, along with projectile weapons fire from further out. Travon hit the ground hard, his weapon flying out in front of him.

Seconds later, he found himself surrounded by Ghatazhak soldiers who were still firing sporadically. His wife was huddled over him, sobbing, begging him to hold on. His daughter and the rest of his extended family were also nearby, crouched low for safety.

His son, Rorik, came running up, his handgun still glowing from constant firing. The young man dropped to his knees beside his mother.

Then he appeared. Standing behind the others.

"Nathan," Travon gasped, barely able to speak.

Connor looked confused, hesitant. Jessica stepped up behind him. Connor turned to her, a lost look on his face as the dying man called him Nathan again. "He thinks I'm..." Connor couldn't even say the name.

"Go to him," Jessica said. "Let him die happy."

Connor stepped forward, coming around to kneel next to Travon, opposite the dying man's wife.

"Nathan," Travon whispered.

Connor leaned closer.

"You must become Nathan," Travon whispered to

Connor. "You are the only one who can lead them... The only one who can help them take it all back, just as before."

"I, I'm not sure how," Connor admitted.

"You will find a way," Travon said, a smile finding its way forward through the pain. "You are Na-Tan."

Connor looked at Travon's wife, unable to find words. He looked back down at Travon as his breathing stopped, and the life slowly left his eyes.

Two more claps of thunder sounded in the distance.

"More troop shuttles," Sergeant Anwar reported.

"We have to move," Jessica told Connor and the others. "Willem, carry Dumar. We're not leaving him behind."

"I'll carry him," Connor offered.

"Thanks, but it's better if..."

"I said, I'll carry him!" Connor repeated more forcefully, cutting Jessica off.

"Do it," Jessica told Sergeant Willem, grabbing Connor by the collar and pulling him aside.

"Damn it, Jess!" Connor protested.

"Look, I appreciate you wanting to carry him and all, especially since you don't even remember who he is," Jessica said. "But about twenty more troops are about to drop in on us, and Willem can move more quickly while carrying Dumar than you or I can. So Willem is carrying him...end of discussion. Got it?"

Connor paused for a moment, staring at her angrily. "Got it," he finally agreed.

"Now, help me get all these people back to the cave so we can get the hell out of here, so he doesn't die in vain."

"Okay, apply a test load," Dalen instructed Loki over his comm-set.

"*Applying test load, now.*"

Sparks shot out from the sides of the emitter, causing Josh to fall back on the topside of the Seiiki's hull.

"Kill the power!" Dalen ordered, reaching into the sparks with his gloved hand, to try to pull one of the wires free.

The sparking stopped, and Dalen leaned in, blowing away the smoke in order to see clearer. "What the fuck, Josh?" he cursed. "Did you forget something?"

"What?"

"Like the ground?"

"There's a ground?"

"Jesus, you're worse than Marcus!"

"They're coming!" Neli yelled from the mouth of the cave.

"Great," Dalen muttered as he worked.

"Please tell me the emitter isn't damaged," Josh groaned.

"The emitter isn't damaged," Dalen replied as he tightened the screw on the ground wire. "I hope."

"Oh, man..."

"Just go, get us ready for liftoff," Dalen told him. "I've got this."

"Are you sure?"

"Go!"

Josh stepped over Dalen, running across the top of the Seiiki's hull to the starboard nacelle, toward the access ladder. "I'm on my way up, Lok!" he called over the comms as he headed down the ladder.

Josh ascended the short ladder up into the Seiiki's

cockpit, and quickly made his way down into the pilot's seat on the left. Loki was straining to look out the windows toward the mouth of the cave, hoping to catch a glimpse of his wife and daughter.

"We spooled up?" Josh asked as he scanned his side of the console.

"Everything except for the forward lift fans," Loki replied as he kept a vigilant watch. "Mains are in pre-ignition and standing by. We can liftoff within a minute of order."

Josh glanced down at the sensor display, noticing icons for the shuttles outside, as well as the four Jung fighters flying cover over them. "How the hell did you get that to..."

"I patched it into the Ghatazhak tactical system's sensor stakes outside."

"Nice."

Loki suddenly stood up, pointing. "There she is!" he cried out with unbridled excitement and relief. "Both of them!" Loki waved his hands frantically at his wife, hoping to catch her attention, but she was too busy watching her steps on the uneven cave floor to notice him waving from above. "Oh, my God," Loki exclaimed, his voice cracking as if he were about to cry. He fell back down in his seat, tears of joy streaming down his cheeks. He looked at Josh. "They're alive," he sobbed. "They're alive."

Josh leaned over and put his hand on his friend's shoulder in comfort. "Yeah, buddy, they are," he said, his own eyes welling up. "I told you she'd get them."

Two more Jung shuttles swooped in and landed not more than fifty meters from the mouth of the cave, their belly turrets firing. They hovered a meter above the ground as troops leapt to the ground from either side, also opening fire as they landed and ran toward either side of the road for cover.

"Keep them back!" Jessica yelled as she fired on the approaching troops. All four of them attacked relentlessly. Within seconds, half of the men who had jumped out of the two hovering shuttles were lying on the ground, either dead or dying, as the two shuttles turned away and disappeared behind flashes of light.

"Keep them to the sides to slow them down," she instructed the other men.

"Try it again!" Dalen yelled over his comms, barely able to hear over the sounds of Ghatazhak weapons fire echoing throughout the cave.

"*Applying power now!*" Loki replied.

Dalen watched hesitantly, afraid to get excited.

"*It's holding,*" Loki reported.

"Yes!" Dalen exclaimed, jumping up in the air. A stray energy blast from a Jung weapon outside streaked past his head, slamming into the ceiling a few meters away, sending shards of hot, melted crystal spraying in all directions.

"Jesus!" Dalen yelled, nearly falling over. He dropped to his belly and began replacing the cover plate around the emitter assembly.

"*Get inside!*" Loki ordered. "*They're falling back now.*"

"Just a second!" Dalen replied. "I'm closing the cover plate now!"

Jessica and the Ghatazhak came running back toward the ship, leaping across the uneven surface of the cave as Jung energy weapons fire streaked by all around them. Each Ghatazhak sergeant would systematically take turns pausing to return fire, all in practiced fashion, in order to keep their pursuers from advancing too quickly.

Connor and Marcus stood on either side of the Seiiki's cargo ramp, facing forward toward the cave entrance, firing carefully to either side of the returning Ghatazhak to provide additional cover for their withdrawal to the ship.

"Spin up the mains and get ready to depart!" Connor ordered over his comm-set as he continued to fire.

Jessica was the last of the Ghatazhak to reach the ramp, and turned to join Connor in holding off the enemy. "Get inside!" she instructed Connor.

"The captain is the last one aboard!" Connor argued.

"Bullshit!" Jessica insisted. "Get moving!" She turned to Marcus as she continued firing. "Get him inside!"

"Come on, Cap'n!" Marcus yelled, grabbing Connor and shoving him up the ramp as Sergeant Todd stepped to the side and fired back.

Jessica glanced back to check that Connor and Marcus were on their way up the ramp, just as Dalen jumped down from the back end of the ship and headed up behind them. "Tell them to takeoff!" Jessica yelled at the sergeant.

"Seiiki! Todd! Nash says to takeoff! Now!" the sergeant instructed over comms.

The Seiiki's engines began to spin up, and her forward lift fan kicked up the smaller shards of broken crystal lying on the cave floor, scattering them in all directions.

Jessica and Sergeant Todd ceased fire and jumped up onto the end of the cargo ramp as it lifted off the ground along with the ship, running up the ramp as it began to rise.

"Let's get out of here," Josh said, as Jung weapons fire slammed into their underside and streaked past the cockpit windows.

"Nice and easy, Josh," Loki reminded him. "We only need a few meters per minute to jump."

"Coming up."

"One......two......three meters. Initiating escape jump," Loki announced.

Josh released the controls, expecting the auto-flight systems to take over while they were in the jump sequence. The ship dipped slightly left, and the windows did not turn opaque. "What the..." Josh grabbed the flight controls again. "We're not jumping, Loki!"

"I know we're not jumping, Josh! I can see that!"

Josh glanced forward, noticing that the mouth of the cave was coming up. "Fuck this," he declared, slamming the throttles forward.

Loki was pushed back in his seat. "What the hell are you doing?"

"I'm not being a sittin' duck, that's what I'm doing!"

"A what?"

"Why aren't we jumping?" Connor asked, climbing up into the Seiiki's cockpit.

"I don't know!" Loki replied as the ship dipped to the right and started a quick turn to avoid striking a rock face half a kilometer beyond the mouth of the cave.

Connor grabbed the overhead rail to steady himself. "I thought you guys fixed the emitter!"

"We did!" Josh assured him. "At least, I think we did!"

"Why aren't the inertial dampeners on?"

"We didn't have time to spin them up before departure," Loki replied.

"You could've warned us!" Connor tapped his comm-set. "Neli! Marcus! Make sure everyone is strapped in until we get the inertial dampeners online! Dalen! Figure out why we can't jump!"

"Hang on!" Josh warned as he pitched up to clear the ridgeline in front of them.

Connor felt his feet coming off the deck as Josh passed over the ridge and then pitched back down sharply. "What the hell are you doing, Josh? Trying to kill us?"

"Actually, I'm trying to keep those fighters from killing us!" Josh replied, maneuvering wildly as the bright red bolts of energy fired from the pursuing Jung fighters streaked past the ship.

"Jesus!" Connor cried out, trying to hold on. "Get the fucking inertial dampeners up, will you?"

"Online in ten seconds, Captain," Loki replied.

"*There's nothing wrong with the jump drives or the emitters!*" Dalen reported over the comms. "*Not that I can see, anyway!*"

"Then why couldn't we jump?" Connor wondered, frustration in his voice.

The ship lurched suddenly, knocking him against the port bulkhead.

"Inertial dampeners in three......two......one......"

Connor suddenly felt the ship become more stable, despite the fact that the horizon outside was dancing.

"You're free to maneuver at will," Loki told Josh.

Josh immediately rolled the ship over several times in rapid succession, as more red bolts of energy streaked past them. Another bolt struck the ship, rocking it again.

"*Maybe the crystals in the caves had something to do with it!*" Dalen suggested. "*Try it again!*"

"What?"

"*Try it again, Cap'n! It should work!*"

"Anything's better than this," Josh declared as he continued to dodge the enemy's attacks.

"We'll never outrun those fighters, Captain," Loki pointed out.

"What the hell," Connor declared. "Jump us again!"

"Point us to the sky," Loki instructed. "Jumping in three..."

Josh pulled the Seiiki's nose up, again pushing her main engines up to full power.

"Two..."

Two more energy bolts slammed into the ship, causing her port side to lurch.

"If those energy bolts hit our jump fields..." Connor began.

"One......jumping."

The windows turned opaque as the Seiiki slipped into a jump, clearing a moment later to reveal a field of stars against the blackness of outer space.

"Whoo-hoo!" Josh cried out.

"Jump complete!" Loki declared.

"Thank God!" Connor added.

"Contacts!" Loki reported. "Jump flashes! Four of them, directly astern and two million kilometers and closing. They'll detect us in seconds."

"Snap jump!" Josh ordered.

Loki didn't even reply, already executing the

emergency snap jump algorithm he had programmed into the Seiiki's jump computers prior to leaving the Lawrence Spaceport.

"What the hell?" Connor said as they jumped.

Josh immediately changed direction, bring the ship hard to port. "Make them longer as we go," he reminded Loki.

"I remember," Loki assured him, as his fingers danced across the jump interface.

"Snap us again," Josh ordered.

The windows cycled opaque and clear again, after which Josh turned to starboard and then pitched down. Seconds later, Loki snap-jumped the ship again.

Finally, after six snap jumps, Josh turned to Loki and said, "That ought to buy us a few minutes."

"What the hell was that?" Connor asked.

"We call it, *shakin' a tail,*" Josh replied proudly. "It was originally Loki's idea."

"I didn't know we could snap jump like that," Connor admitted.

"Normally, you can't," Loki explained. "I programmed it into your jump systems before we left. I hope you don't mind."

"No, not at all, believe me," Connor replied.

"Let's head home," Josh suggested, "before they figure out where we went."

"Good idea," Connor agreed.

"Captain," Loki asked. "If you don't mind, I'd like to go check on my wife and daughter."

"Of course, Loki," Connor replied. "I think I can handle it from here."

Loki looked at Josh and smiled, as he climbed out of his seat.

"Give them both a kiss for me," Josh told Loki as he headed aft.

Connor slid down into Loki's seat to take his place. He paused a moment to look around and get his bearings. "Huh. I don't think I've ever sat on this side," he realized.

"You wanna switch places?" Josh offered.

"No, that's all right, Josh," Connor replied, as he called up the jump series to return to Lawrence. "I think you've earned the right to sit in that chair for a while."

* * *

Connor walked solemnly down the cargo ramp, pausing at the foot to look out across the group of people they had just rescued. It had been a tense, two-hour journey back to Burgess, due to the convoluted route required to ensure that they could not be followed.

Once they had landed, and the passengers stepped onto solid ground and felt safe, their rejoicing could begin. They had escaped their captive world, frightened by the ordeal, but unscathed, nonetheless. All except for the Dumar family, who had suffered the loss of their patriarch.

Connor felt guilty that he had no memory of the man. Jessica had spoken of him during her tales about the rescue of Nathan Scott's consciousness, but she had never told Connor of Nathan's relationship to the man. He felt as if he should be devastated by the admiral's death, yet he felt...indifferent.

Jessica and the three Ghatazhak sergeants came down the ramp behind him. Jessica stopped beside Connor, placing her hand on his shoulder as the rest of the Ghatazhak continued down the ramp toward the gathered evacuees, who were now being greeted by med-techs and others sympathetic to their plight. "This is the good part," Jessica told him.

Connor looked at her, puzzled. "How so?"

"Follow me," she told him, continuing down the ramp.

Connor hesitated a moment before following her. As they followed the other Ghatazhak through the crowd, those who had just been rescued parted to make way, offering thanks and grateful handshakes as their rescuers passed.

Connor felt odd accepting such thanks, as he felt he had done very little, despite his fleeting moments of bravery on the surface of Corinair. But it also felt good, as if he had done something noble...something that few men would have done.

As Connor passed through the crowd, his eyes caught those of Rorik, Anise, and Kyla Dumar. He nodded politely, doing his best to express his sorrow and respect for their loss. His mind flashed back to that moment on Corinair only a few hours ago, where he had stood there, frozen, and the retired admiral had risen up to save him, sacrificing himself. The guilt was overwhelming.

On the far side of the crowd stood General Telles, leader of the last of the fabled Ghatazhak, along with his trusted second, Commander Jahal. Neither man smiled, which, as Connor understood it, was customary for the Ghatazhak.

The general shook the hands of the three returning sergeants. Jessica paused a moment to talk to the general before joining her team for their debriefing with the commander.

Connor turned and looked back at the crowd of people. His own crew was among them, enjoying the well wishes of the thankful evacuees. The sight made him smile. His crew had also gone above and beyond for these people, and he had never been more proud of them.

"Congratulations, Captain," the general greeted.

Connor turned and shook the general's hand. "General."

"Lieutenant Nash tells me you were instrumental in the completion of the mission. She even tells me that you joined in on the firefight, quite possibly saving the lieutenant's life. I wish I could say I was surprised."

"I am," Connor admitted.

"I, for one, am not. You are the clone of Nathan Scott, after all. And he was, *you* are, one of the bravest, most honorable men I have ever known."

"Thank you, I think," Connor replied.

Two med-techs wheeled the covered body of Travon Dumar on a gurney, the admiral's family following close behind.

"We didn't save everyone, though," Connor admitted.

"The lieutenant tells me that the admiral sacrificed himself to save you," the general said. "That also does not surprise me. It is the nature of brave men, which Travon Dumar most certainly was."

Connor scratched the side of his head. "I still can't figure that one out," he admitted. "Why he did that. Stood up and charged forth into the gunfire that way."

"To save someone he felt all humanity would be better served, if kept alive," the general explained. "Think about that, while you decide what to do next."

Connor watched as General Telles turned and headed back across the tarmac toward the Ghatazhak hangar, Admiral Dumar's last words still echoing in his mind.

You are Na-Tan.

Thank you for reading this story.
(*A review would be greatly appreciated!*)

COMING SOON

"RESURRECTION"
Episode 3
of
The Frontiers Saga:
Rogue Castes

Visit us online at
www.frontierssaga.com
or on Facebook

Want to be notified when
new episodes are published?
Join our mailing list!
http://www.frontierssaga.com/mailinglist/